SOMEWHERE WITHOUT YOU

DAPHNE PARKER

Copyright © 2025 by Daphne Parker

All rights reserved.

No part of this publication may be reproduced, distributed, or transmitted in any form or by any means, including photocopying, recording, or other electronic or mechanical methods, without the prior written permission of the publisher, except as permitted by U.S. copyright law. For permission requests, contact Otter House Publishing.

The story, all names, characters, and incidents portrayed in this production are fictitious. No identification with actual persons (living or deceased), places, buildings, and products is intended or should be inferred.

Book Cover by Getpremades.com

Title by Danielle Moore

First edition 2025

For Denver—my greatest love, in every life.

Content Warning

This story contains content that might be disturbing to some readers—including, but not limited to, depictions of and references to death, suicide, sexual assault, and domestic abuse. Reader discretion is advised.

For a more comprehensive list, please visit my website at:
www.daphneparkerbooks.com

"Whatever our souls are made of, his and mine are the same. If all else perished, and he remained, I should still continue to be; and if all else remained, and he were annihilated, the universe would turn to a mighty stranger."

—*Emily Bronte, Wuthering Heights.*

One

Now

Be brave. It was my mother's mantra—the one she wove into the fabric of my childhood like armor, pressing it into my bones each time fear threatened to take root. She whispered it before every scraped knee, every first day of school, every monster I swore was hiding beneath my bed. It was her lullaby, her battle cry, and a promise that I could face whatever came next.

Now, standing at the mouth of my long, winding driveway bathed in pale moonlight, I was anything *but* brave.

Two brick pillars flanked the entrance, each topped with a brass lamp meant to cast a welcoming light over the dull iron gate stretched between them. But tonight, both lamps sat cold and hollow, surrendering the entire scene to darkness.

No light meant Jackson was home. Which meant my hope of slipping in unnoticed had just gone up in smoke.

Normally, I was back before he arrived. But tonight, I was two hours late. Not because I was being reckless or testing my curfew, but because a wreck on the Five had frozen traffic for miles, turning the freeway into a parking lot. By the time I hit downtown, not far from the Coronado Bridge, I already knew I was fucked.

Actually, let's be real. . . I was fucked the moment our security system failed to register my arrival at exactly 8:00 p.m.

My hands trembled as I typed the code into the keypad.

Zero. . . five. . . three. . .

Shit. Wrong number. I tried again.

Zero. . . five. . . two. . . six.

The keypad chirped. A heavy click followed, and the gate groaned as it creaked open, vanishing slowly into the shadows.

I crept forward, steadying myself against the wheel and drawing in a deep breath. Jackson hadn't called all night, and that was never a good sign. Most nights, I had more time. If everything had gone to plan, I'd have been curled beneath the covers before he stumbled through the door—reeking of whiskey and drugstore perfume. And if I was lucky, he'd be too hungover by morning to remember I even existed.

But luck wasn't on my side tonight.

I parked my crimson Lexus in the driveway. The last thing I needed was the mechanical shriek of the garage door giving me away. I slipped out quietly, the soles of my sandals whispering against the pavement.

Our home towered in the moonlight, all 6,000 square feet of glass and stone—a fortress on the island of Coronado. But to me, it looked hollow and empty. Like something long dead. Its darkened windows glared down at me like accusing eyes.

I should have called. I should have told him I'd be late.

Forcing down the lump in my throat, I kept my eyes forward. The grand oak door swallowed me whole as I stepped inside, the silence collapsing around me as I exhaled. Slipping off my sandals in the foyer, I moved like a thief in my own home, stealing a few quiet seconds before the inevitable storm.

I tiptoed into the kitchen, where a flood of light spilled onto the black Catalina tile and into the butler's pantry at the far end of the room.

Maybe he was asleep. Maybe by some miracle, I'd managed to pull it off.

My shoulders lowered a fraction as I hugged my purse tight and crept upstairs, careful not to let the stairs creak beneath me. The landing was dark. No light under the bedroom door.

Just a few more steps. . .

Jackson always kept his office door shut and locked. No one was allowed in—not even the maid. So I should've noticed the sliver of space between the frame as I crept past. I should've registered that something was off. But I'd been so focused on reaching the bedroom, so desperate to disappear, I missed it entirely.

"Emily. . ." The low growl of his voice cut through the silence like a blade.

He was awake.

There was no use pretending I hadn't heard him. I turned slowly and leaned my head around the doorframe.

"Yes?" My voice came out thin and weak.

The room was cloaked in shadow. Jackson sat behind his enormous mahogany desk, an open decanter of whiskey resting in front of him.

"You're late," he said, taking a slow, deliberate sip from the crystal glass between his fingers. He was drunk, but not in the careless, forgetful way I sometimes prayed for.

This was the kind of drunk I feared.

My pulse stuttered. The air around me thickened, heavy with dread.

"Sit," he ordered.

I obeyed, lowering myself into the leather chair like a prisoner before the judge.

"Where have you been?"

I swallowed hard. "I—I'm sorry. There was an accident on the Five. Traffic was backed up for miles." The words were tumbling out faster than I could catch them, and I knew better than to offer him excuses.

"Don't insult my intelligence, Emily." He took another sip, the ice in his glass rattling like bone. "Where have you been?" he asked again.

I forced myself to meet his eyes. "I told you. I swear I wasn't—"

"DON'T LIE TO ME!" His voice exploded across the room, followed by the crack of glass smashing against wood. I jumped as it shattered into a dozen tiny pieces, whiskey bleeding between them like an open wound. Jackson rose, his towering figure casting a long, ominous shadow as he came to stand over me. "You know the rules," he said, his voice a sharp knife against my throat.

The rules. The unspoken, suffocating rules embedded into every corner of our marriage.

Curfew. Obedience. Silence.

They wrapped around me like a noose, binding me to a man whose love shifted like the tides.

"I didn't. . . I wasn't. . . I'm sorry," I stammered, the words breaking apart in fragments.

My knees pressed together instinctively, hands clenched tight in my lap to stop them from shaking.

Jackson circled like a predator. The broken glass crunched faintly beneath his shoes, and I flinched at the sound. Even in the dark, I could see the blaze in his bloodshot eyes. I used to think they were the most beautiful shade of blue—bright and coastal, and inviting. But now? Now they were a raging storm, full of destruction and malevolent intent.

"Sorry?" he laughed. The rasping sound of it scraped down my spine. "Sorry doesn't buy back my time, Emily. It doesn't undo what's already been done."

I kept my gaze fixed on the shattered glass scattered across the desk, its jagged edges catching the light like tiny warning signs.

"I won't ask again," he said, his voice deadly calm.

I blinked hard, forcing the tears to retreat. "I did tell you," I whispered. "It was the truth."

There was a long pause—too long. I knew what came next. I braced for it. But the strike still hit like lightning.

His knuckles cracked across my cheek with brutal force. The world reeled, spinning as my head snapped back and I barely caught myself before slipping from the chair. Stars swam across my vision, and for a moment, everything blurred. Jackson towered over me, rage carved into every line of his face.

"Clean this shit up," he snapped.

I nodded, the ringing in my ears drowning out everything but the thud of my own heartbeat.

When he was gone, I let out a shaky breath. Silent tears slipped down my face, tracing the raw, throbbing ache blooming across my cheek.

Across the room, the window creaked open, the wind slipping through like a whisper. And for just a moment, I swore I heard my mother's voice riding the breeze.

Be brave.

Two

A THIN SLIVER OF LIGHT cut through the closed curtains, slicing across the bed in a sharp, golden line. But the pounding in my temples had dragged me from sleep long before the sun had a chance.

With a groan, I rolled onto my back, wincing at the stiffness in my jaw. My fingers brushed over the swollen skin, and a quiet, breathless whimper escaped my lips.

Fuck.

The space beside me was cold and empty. Jackson had slipped out of bed hours ago, but his scent still clung to the sheets. Propping myself up on my elbows, I caught a glimpse of myself in the dresser mirror and was greeted by an all too familiar reflection. My face was swollen, and a purple bruise painted itself over my left eye.

As I kicked off the tangled sheets, I searched my mind for excuses. But how many times could I blame the bathroom door? The stairs? My own clumsy feet?

Outside the bedroom door, I heard movement, followed by muffled voices. I stood, the chill of the white oak floor biting at my heels as I pulled on my robe and opened the door.

"Mrs. Bishop!" Rita gasped, pressing a hand to her chest. "I didn't know you were here."

She did. Of course she did. Where else would I be?

Her warm, caramel eyes flicked to my face, then darted away. "I'm sorry. We didn't mean to wake you."

I offered a small smile as a young girl rushed past her, eyes averted.

"New girl?" I asked, my voice hoarse.

Rita nodded. "My niece. She just moved here from Mérida with her mother and two brothers. Mr. Bishop was kind enough to offer her a job."

Kind.

The word stuck to the roof of my mouth like peanut butter.

"Oh. Well, that's good," I managed tightly.

If anyone feared Jackson more than I did, it was the staff. Unlike the rest of the world, they didn't buy into the charm. They knew *exactly* what kind of man he was—and kind wasn't it.

Rita had seen the marks before. They all had. The staff watched in silence, an unwilling audience to a show no one wanted to see. Still, I often wondered what they truly thought of me.

Did they pity me? Think I was weak? Or maybe, to them, I was just another spoiled wife—draped in designer clothes, floating in wealth, too blind or too foolish to leave.

On the outside, I had it all. A picturesque life, a handsome husband, the illusion of happiness. But beneath the gloss, I was a prisoner—trapped inside a gilded cage of privilege.

She knew Jackson wasn't kind. They all did. But like any good housekeeper, she kept her mouth shut. After all, there was a reason her green card had never expired.

"Have you seen my husband?" I asked, not expecting an answer—just hoping to gauge how long I'd been alone, or if I'd simply gotten lucky and missed him.

Rita shook her head. "Mr. Bishop left before I arrived this morning. He did, however, leave something for you downstairs."

I nodded. I didn't have to ask what it was. I already knew.

"Is there anything else you need, Mrs. Bishop?"

I shook my head, fighting back the urge to remind her that it was ok to call me Emily. Bishop was *his* identity, and my first name was the only thing I had left to claim.

"That'll be all. Thank you."

She hesitated for half a second, then turned sharply and walked away.

I didn't rush heading downstairs. If there was one thing I had in abundance, it was time. And with no one to entertain but the staff, there was no reason to hurry.

In the living room, a soft breeze drifted through the floor-to-ceiling windows, carrying the sweet, heady scent of hydrangeas and oleanders.

Outside, José, our gardener, moved methodically through the flower beds, his back bowed under the weight of the morning sun. I gave a small wave. He glanced up, the brim of his wide hat shadowing his dark, unreadable eyes. He nodded once before turning back to his work.

I closed my eyes and inhaled the luscious scent of daylilies and azaleas, letting it carry me back to childhood summers with Gran. We'd spend long afternoons in her garden, her sun-spotted hands guiding mine, until my knees were stained and my fingernails came away caked in dirt. I loved how the earth smelled after a fresh rain, echoing the perfume off each peony and coneflower wafting into the open windows of her old farmhouse.

But here, in this manicured paradise, it felt different. I rarely stepped into the garden—no matter how beautiful. It had been a gift from Jackson, an elaborate apology planted in the aftermath of violence.

Just as Rita had said, a grand bouquet of dark pink roses sat perfectly centered on the dining room table. His signature gesture. The one he made after every painful night.

They were always flawless. But even if the petals hadn't begun to wilt, the sentiment behind them had long since withered. Once the fallout from last night settled, the cycle would start all over again.

I *was* surprised to find a slim white box, wrapped in a velvet ribbon waiting beside the vase. I hesitated before lifting the lid.

Inside, nestled on a bed of crisp, white tissue paper, lay an elegant nightshade gown. The sequins caught the morning light, glittering like fallen stars. I held it up, letting the silk cascade over my hands. The dress was breathtaking. But it felt. . . wrong.

"Wow," a soft voice breathed behind me.

I whirled around to face Rita's niece. She looked no more than fifteen, her dark hair falling loosely around her olive-toned face. Her wide, curious eyes blinked at the dress, full of quiet awe.

I swallowed and clutched the gown to my chest as she stared, the envy in her gaze as clear as day.

"What's your name?" I asked.

She blinked, hesitated, then said, "Mia."

"Pretty," I offered, though I wasn't sure if it came out genuine or hollow. I tried to smile, but it felt tight on my face. "How old are you, Mia?"

"Sixteen." Her voice was small but steady.

I nodded, folding the dress back into its box with careful hands, the sequins catching one last glimmer of light before disappearing.

"Do you like it?" I asked, though I wasn't sure why. Maybe I just wanted to hear someone say yes to something Jackson touched.

She nodded, doe eyes wide. "It looks like something a queen would wear."

I let out a dry laugh. "Maybe. But crowns can be heavy."

Mia tilted her head, not quite understanding, and I instantly regretted saying it. I didn't want to ruin her illusions, not yet. She had time for reality to catch up.

"Is the rest of your family working here?" I asked instead.

She nodded again. "Mr. Bishop said if we finish early, my brothers and I can swim in the pool."

Of course he did. Always the savior, always the hand extended—just long enough to remind you who it belonged to.

I gently closed the box, tying the ribbon back into a neat bow.

"Well," I said, straightening, "I hope you like it here. If you need anything, come to me, not him."

She looked at me, startled. "Okay."

An awkward silence settled between us.

"You should go now. Rita's probably looking for you."

She gave a quick nod and slipped away without another word.

When she was gone, I let my shoulders drop. My fingers lingered on the velvet ribbon. The dress, the flowers, the fragile illusions. It was all so practiced now—a performance.

And I was so very tired of playing the part.

Three

Before

THE FIRST THING THAT STRUCK me was how bright everything was. Beyond the towering glass windows overlooking the bay, an endless stretch of cerulean sea melted into a brilliant horizon.

The airport hummed with the clatter of rolling suitcases and the rhythm of hurried footsteps. I was still jittery from the flight, my nerves a tumbled mess in my stomach as I rolled my pink suitcase alongside me.

It was early afternoon as I scanned the crowd, watching travelers come and go. My eyes flicked from face to face in search of my sister, panic pricking at my spine when I couldn't find her.

I glanced up at the digital clock above the baggage carousel—thinking I had arrived too early, only to discover I was running late. I freed my phone from my pocket.

Just landed, the message I'd sent twenty minutes ago, stared back with no reply.

With a sigh, I tapped on her name, pacing as the phone rang and rang before kicking me to voicemail.

Shit.

"Kat, it's Emily. I'm at the airport. Where are you? Call me."

Turning around, I started retracing my steps, remembering a Starbucks I'd passed earlier, when a voice behind me called my name.

"Emily?"

I spun around and saw a man I didn't recognize walking briskly in my direction.

I hesitated, but he didn't seem to need confirmation as he stopped directly in front of me.

"Emily Hart?" he asked again.

I gave a cautious nod. "Yes. . . do I know you?"

He shook his head. "I'm Jackson Bishop. I'm a friend of Grant's."

A knot of panic tightened in my stomach. Grant was my sister's husband. Oh god. Had something happened?

"Where's Katherine?" I asked sharply.

"They had something come up last minute," he reassured me.

"So they sent you instead," I guessed, the tension easing in my chest.

"I offered," Jackson smiled. "Didn't seem right making you Uber all the way to La Jolla."

He was distractingly good-looking—the kind of handsome that made you look twice. A classic Californian with sun-kissed blonde hair falling into his eyes, a piercing blue gaze, and a grin that could thaw glaciers. He looked like he belonged on a surfboard, not in an airport terminal.

Jackson bent down, gently coaxing the suitcase from my hand, and I caught the faint scent of fresh aftershave curling around the sharp lines of his jaw.

"How was the flight?" he asked, guiding me through the automatic doors to where a sleek black SUV waited at the curb.

"Exhausting," I yawned. "Is it just me, or does the legroom shrink every year?"

He laughed, and the sound sent goosebumps skittering across my arms.

"That's why I fly private," he said, settling into the cool, buttery leather seat beside me.

I blinked. "You have a private jet?"

The surprise must've been all over my face. Who the hell *was* this guy?

"Technically, it belongs to the company," Jackson shrugged. "But yes. And a helicopter."

Ah. Suddenly, the luxury SUV and the waiting driver made sense. I hadn't even been in California an hour and was already neck-deep in its gold-tinted world.

"How do you know Grant?" I asked, suddenly hyperaware of my thrifted sundress and the crinkled Walmart bag cradled in my lap.

"We grew up together," he said with a nostalgic grin. "Our parents attend the same country club."

Of course they did. I knew Grant had money. He was a senior software engineer for Bishop Enterprises, a multibillion-dollar tech giant known for it's cutting-edge AI and clean design.

Bishop.

I twisted in my seat to look at him, realization striking like a flashbulb.

"Wait. . . are you *the* Jackson Bishop?" I asked, my soft brown eyes going wide.

His lips curled into an amused grin. "I don't know about *the* Jackson Bishop—but I am *a* Jackson Bishop."

How had I not recognized him? His face had been splashed across the covers of *Time, Forbes,* even *People.* The tech world's golden boy turned media darling. And yet, somehow, I'd mistaken him for a casual family friend.

I sank a little lower into my seat, feeling small.

"Oh," I managed, scrambling for something—anything, that wouldn't sound painfully stupid. "You look. . . different in person."

It's funny how a title alone can change the way you see someone. Five minutes ago, he was just a friendly guy picking me up. Now, I suddenly felt like I didn't belong in the same car.

Jackson tilted his head, amused. "Different as in better? Or worse?"

My cheeks flushed. "Better. I mean—not that you looked worse before. Obviously. You never looked bad. That's not what I meant. . ." The words kept tumbling out, clumsy and fast, as if sheer momentum could rescue me from total humiliation.

Jackson chuckled, clearly enjoying my flustered state. "So. . . better," he repeated, leaning back casually, one arm draped along the back of the seat. "That's a relief."

I gave him a sidelong glance. "Don't let it go to your head."

"Too late," he grinned. "I'm very fragile, you know. Compliments only inflate my ego by dangerous amounts."

"Oh, you poor thing," I teased, shaking my head. "Must be so hard being wildly rich, famous, and attractive."

He laughed. "You think I'm attractive?"

I opened my mouth, then closed it again. Dammit. I'd walked right into that one.

"I think *you* think you're attractive," I said, trying to salvage my pride.

"Mm," he mused, feigning deep thought. "I *am* known for being devastatingly humble."

I rolled my eyes, but couldn't hide my smile. "You're ridiculous."

"And you're cute when you're flustered."

That stopped me.

My breath caught, his eyes lingering on mine a little longer than necessary. I looked away first, pretending to focus on the view outside the window. Palm trees whipped past, sunshine gilding everything it touched.

When we finally pulled up to Katherine's house, I blinked in surprise. It wasn't the extravagant, gated estate I'd expected from someone married to a senior engineer. And definitely not what I imagined for a close friend of a billionaire. Instead, it was charmingly understated. A classic American Craftsman with a wide, welcoming porch, tapered columns, and a steep, sloping roof.

The driver, who remained silent the entire trip, stepped out and began unloading my luggage, but Jackson was already there, waving him off.

"I've got it," he said, effortlessly lifting my bag like it weighed nothing.

From the doorway, Katherine's warm voice rang out. "The sun looks good on you."

I glanced up to see her leaning against the frame, arms folded, eyes crinkling with amusement. "Sorry for the mix-up," she added. "But apparently, it comes with VIP perks."

"Apparently," I echoed as Jackson stepped beside me, his shoulder brushing mine.

Kat's gaze flicked between us. "Thanks for picking her up, Jackson."

"Happy to," he said, handing me my suitcase. Our fingers touched—just barely, but the spark that followed shot straight through me.

Katherine arched an eyebrow. "I hope he behaved himself."

"He was a perfect gentleman," I smiled, though my pulse was still racing.

"A gentleman, huh?" She gave Jackson a pointed look. "That's a new one. I've heard him called a lot of things, but 'gentleman' usually doesn't make the list."

"That's because you've never acted like a lady," he shot back smoothly.

Katherine smirked, but I caught the flicker of something unreadable in her eyes as she stepped aside and motioned me inside. "Come on. Let's get you settled."

As Jackson turned to go, something tugged at me.

"Hey," I shouted, and he paused, half-turned toward me. "Will I see you again?" I asked, trying to sound casual, not like my heart was stupidly hoping for a yes.

His gaze lingered on mine as he slid his hands into his pockets. "I hope so."

Four

Now

THE GOWN JACKSON BOUGHT CLUNG to me in all the wrong places. I was a size 16, and this dress was meant for someone with half my waistline.

Still, with a bit of wriggling and careful maneuvering, I managed to slip into it—strategically concealing the safety pins and the inch-wide gap where the zipper refused to close. One wrong move, and it would split. Embarrassing for the dress, but even more humiliating for me.

My honey-brown hair was swept into an elaborate updo. Jackson had brought in a makeup artist named Anya to mask the bruises. She didn't flinch as she dabbed at the violet stains blooming over my eye and across my cheekbone, her brush moving with a quiet efficiency that made me wonder how many wives like me she'd painted over before.

You didn't get hired for gigs like this unless you knew how to keep secrets.

I kept my face still, afraid that if I cracked the illusion Jackson had orchestrated, he wouldn't hesitate to punish me later.

When Anya was done, I barely recognized myself. The foundation was thick, the eyeshadow garish. I couldn't remember what I looked like anymore—barefaced or made up. Over time, my amber eyes had dimmed, and the freckles that once danced across my nose and cheeks had faded like stars at dawn.

Jackson used to love those freckles. Back when we were new, he'd name them like constellations, mapping them out with his fingers as we'd lie together in bed, our skin still hot from the fire we'd kindled out of passion and lust.

Now, he thought they made me look childish, and he no longer traced them like a galaxy he was once so eager to explore.

Outside, the driver laid on the horn as I made my way down the steps. I opened the car door, but the hem of my dress snagged on my heel. I stumbled, catching myself with a graceless sprawl against the pavement.

"Jesus Christ, Emily. We're already late. Can you hurry the fuck up?" Jackson didn't even look at me as I gathered myself and slid into the seat beside him.

"Sorry," I murmured, keeping my eyes forward while he sipped whatever dark poison swirled in his glass.

"I see you found my gift," he said, tilting his head, letting the ice clink against his teeth.

"It's beautiful." I ran my fingers along the sequined fabric. "Thank you."

He gave a tight nod. "And is it... comfortable?"

What he really meant was, *Does it fit?* Jackson was careful to never comment on my weight outright. He preferred veiled criticisms.

"Like a glove," I said, forcing a polite smile and willing my makeup not to crack. But the truth was far from comfortable.

Since my mothers death, I couldn't seem to keep my weight steady, but this was the heaviest I had ever been. When Jackson and I first met, I'd weighed around 160. These days, I hovered near 200, and he found a new way to remind me of it every day.

I'd tried everything to lose it—pills, workouts, starvation diets, kale for every meal. Even a desperate detox at a sketchy sauna that landed me in the hospital with severe dehydration. But nothing worked.

"Listen, about last night..." Jackson began.

I cut him off gently. "Nothing happened. I walked into the bathroom door."

He nodded, slow and approving. "Yes. You did. Honestly, Em, you really should be more careful."

My eyes flicked to the driver's in the mirror as I turned to face Jackson. "It was an accident," I said with a bright, brittle smile. "I'll be more careful next time."

His hand found mine in my lap, giving it a soft squeeze. "You know I love you, right?"

I nodded, though the gesture felt hollow. "I love you too."

The words were automatic now—reflexive. Like locking a door or checking the oven. I said them because I was supposed to. Because not saying them was dangerous.

The first time he hit me, I told myself it was a mistake. A flash of anger, a moment he couldn't control. A misunderstanding.

The second time, I decided it was my fault. I'd pushed too hard, said the wrong thing, chosen the wrong moment.

By the third and fourth, my excuses began to fray. Each new bruise came wrapped in an apology and a vow to change—always tender, always temporary.

By the twentieth time, I'd stopped counting. I gave up the excuses and traded them in for acceptance instead. This was my life now. I just had to do better.

The rest of the drive passed in silence, broken only by the occasional clink of ice in Jackson's glass and the low hum of the engine. I kept my gaze on the road ahead, watching the streetlights blur past the tinted windows like ghosts. My dress itched. The safety pins dug into my skin. I was sweating, but I didn't dare move too much. Not now. Not with our carefully crafted illusion still intact.

The car eased to a stop, and Jackson reached over to tuck a curl behind my ear—one Anya had carefully arranged only hours ago.

Sometimes, I didn't know which was worse—that I fell in love with someone who hurt me, or that I hated myself for it.

Five

THE CORPORATE PARTIES I USUALLY attended were held at the convention center downtown. But tonight was different.

We pulled up to a private estate near Sunset Cliffs, string lights hanging from the trees. From the balcony, I could see the naval air base stretched along the palm-fringed coast of Coronado, clinging to the Pacific. Most guests would be awestruck by the house's pristine Mediterranean Revival, its Spanish influences woven into every archway and tile.

But I wasn't impressed.

Once you've seen one mansion, you've seen them all.

The driver opened Jackson's door first, of course. Then mine. I stepped out carefully this time, clutching my purse to hide the gaping zipper that still refused to close all the way.

Jackson adjusted his tie and offered me his arm. "Smile," he said through his teeth, the corner of his mouth twitching. "You're the luckiest woman here tonight."

I slipped my hand into the crook of his elbow, painting on the smile he wanted.

With my arm draped around his, we made our way inside, greeted by a flurry of familiar faces and forced smiles.

"There he is!" a voice boomed above the chatter.

Stanley Greer—an oil executive with more hair on his face than his head, pushed his way through the crowd, a statuesque blonde draped over his arm like a designer handbag.

"Stan the Man," Jackson drawled, flashing a polished grin. "You remember my lovely wife, Emily."

"Of course!" Stanley barked, his mustache twitching with amusement. "How could I forget?"

Jackson's eyes drifted to the woman at Stanley's side. "And who's this vision you've brought tonight?"

Stanley puffed up. "Allow me to introduce my wife, Natasha."

Natasha offered a dazzling smile, her hand extending toward Jackson in a perfectly rehearsed gesture. Her nails were French-tipped and flawless, her ring so large it looked like it belonged in a museum, not on a finger.

"A pleasure," she said in a syrupy accent I couldn't quite place—somewhere between Moscow and Malibu.

"The pleasure's mine," he insisted, his grip loosening slightly at my waist.

She was Stanley's fourth wife since I'd known him—each one following the same tired pattern. Young. Foreign. And short-lived.

Jackson smiled, but it wasn't for Stanley. His gaze drifted lazily down Natasha's frame, lingering a moment too long. Stanley didn't notice. But I did.

"It's lovely to meet you," I lied, my voice cutting in sharply.

Jackson cleared his throat. "Looks like quite the event," he said, glancing past Stanley toward the crowd.

"Mostly the regulars," Stanley grunted. "A few high-end investors and senior consultants thrown in for flair. I imagine you've met most of them, but a couple flew in from New York last night. I'm sure they'll want a word before your trip."

"You're going to New York?" I asked, surprised. Jackson's business trips were common, but rarely this unannounced.

"It came together last minute," he said, not quite meeting my eye. "Wasn't sure it would pan out."

"Oh, it's happening," Stanley cut in with a grin. "The board's chomping at the bit to hear your projections for next quarter. Formalities, really, but you know how they get when they feel ignored. High-maintenance bastards."

Natasha laughed politely, the kind of laugh meant to fill space, not respond to humor. Jackson offered her another charming smile.

"How long will you be gone?" I asked, trying to sound casual but already mentally planning my freedom—no matter how temporary.

"About a month," he said, glancing at me. "Maybe less."

It would be the longest stretch he'd been gone since our wedding. A month where I could breathe a little easier. A month where I could sleep a little deeper.

"Sounds like a big opportunity," I said.

"For the company," Jackson replied, his tone smooth, and rehearsed. "Nothing's set in stone, of course. Just a series of meetings."

"High-stakes ones," Stanley added, clapping him on the back. "Don't let him downplay it. Jackson's the golden boy right now. The board practically wets themselves when he walks in the room."

Jackson laughed, humble but pleased. I'd heard that laugh before. I knew it well. It was the one he used when charm was currency.

"Do you travel often?" Natasha asked, her bright blue eyes locked on Jackson with unwavering interest.

"Often enough," he said, letting his arm slide from my waist without a second thought. "Most of my work keeps me local, but I travel when the occasion calls for it."

"How exciting!" she said, her smile wide and practiced. "This is my first time leaving Russia. I keep telling Stanley I want to see the world, but so far he only brings me here."

Jackson turned to Stanley with mock disapproval. "You mean to tell me you haven't taken your stunning wife on a proper honeymoon? Shame on you old man."

"She's free to travel as she pleases," Stanley waved off as if the matter were beneath him.

"Well then, it's settled," Jackson announced with a grin. "Emily and I would be delighted to have you both join us on our next getaway."

"We would?" The words slipping out before I could stop them.

Natasha turned to me, her expression perfectly blank. "I would love to accompany you and your. . . wife." She let the word hang in the air like a challenge. "What was your name again?"

"Emily," I said flatly.

"Emily," she repeated slowly, like it didn't sit well on her tongue.

If it didn't hurt, I would have rolled my eyes. Whatever "vacation" Jackson had in mind, I knew damn well I wasn't invited. At least not in any meaningful sense. And judging by the way the two of them were mentally undressing each other, Natasha didn't seem too interested in quality time with her husband either.

"Excuse me," I mumbled, swiping a flute of champagne off a passing servers tray as I stepped away.

Stanley might've been clueless, but I knew better. I'd been with Jackson long enough to recognize the signs. Suspecting what he did behind my back was one thing—seeing it unfold in front of me was something else entirely.

As I slipped out onto the stone patio, the sound of the party dulled behind me. The ocean stretched beyond the cliffs, dark and endless. The breeze tugged at the hem of my dress, teasing the pins holding it in place.

For a moment, I let myself pretend I was someone else. A woman with choices—with a future.

I stood there, staring out at the horizon as it faded into dusk, the sky swallowing the last traces of light.

"It's breathtaking, isn't it?" A man with a beer in his hand crept up behind me, his voice smooth. "Beautiful, and danger-ous."

"Dangerous?" I asked, tilting my head.

He took a small step closer. "Absolutely. There's an entire world beneath those waves, and we've barely explored half of it."

I turned back to the ocean, watching as the water folded over itself in soft, rhythmic whispers.

"I'm Max, by the way. Max Meyers," he said, extending a hand.

The name didn't ring a bell, but I accepted the handshake carefully. "Emily. Emily Bishop."

"Ah," he grinned, "the big man's wife."

"You know my husband." Of course he did. Everyone knew Jackson, and more importantly, what he was worth.

"Considering he's looking to merge with my company, I'd say I've had the pleasure." Max took a sip from his bottle, his dark hair stirring slightly in the breeze.

"You must be from New York then," I mused, piecing things together.

"I'm from everywhere," he smirked. "But yeah, our main offices are in Manhattan. That's where I spend most of my time."

I nodded, turning my gaze back to the waves. "Must be a nice change of pace, then. . . San Diego this time of year."

"It has its charms," he mused.

When I didn't respond, he added, "Your husband and I were supposed to meet earlier this evening, but he canceled last minute. Something about entertaining potential investors."

"Sounds about right," I said, lifting the champagne to my lips. It was flat now, but I didn't mind.

Max studied me for a moment, his eyes searching. Not in the way Jackson looked at people, as if deciding whether they were valuable, but like he was trying to see past the surface.

"He doesn't strike me as the type to let things slip. Which makes me wonder what could be more important than a deal that size."

I gave a dry laugh. "Probably someone younger. Or louder."

He raised an eyebrow, but didn't push. "You don't seem particularly surprised."

"I'm not," I said simply, watching a wave crash hard against the rocks, then retreating into itself. "You get used to disappointment when you know where to look for it."

Max was quiet for a moment. Then, gently asked, "And what are you looking for, Emily?"

I hesitated. No one had asked me that in a long time. Not without expecting something in return.

"Air," I said finally. "Just a little space to breathe."

He nodded like he understood, then took another pull from his beer. "Well, you picked the right spot for it."

He was attractive in a quiet, understated way—with eyes like a shadowed moon and a boyish face.

Behind us, the party continued through the French doors in a swirl of laughter and music, the energy clashing against the calm of the ocean breeze.

"What about you? Are you married?" I baited, softly.

Max shook his head, and a few strands of raven hair fell across his long lashes. "No wife. No kids, either," he said. "And your infamous husband—where's he hiding?"

"He's. . . occupied at the moment," I replied, the words tasting artificial. "Enjoying himself, I suppose."

"I've never been one for these kinds of parties," Max said, glancing toward the glow of the estate. "But I'll admit, I am enjoying the view tonight."

My cheeks flushed as I suddenly realized the precariousness of the situation. I shouldn't be out here alone with this man—especially one Jackson intended to do business with. But there was something about the ease of it that sent a quiet thrill through me.

"Yes, well," I said, raising the champagne to my lips. "It is a lovely night."

I focused on the horizon—trying to ignore the sharp awareness prickling across my skin. Max's attention was obvious, but what surprised me most was how much I didn't mind it. A small voice in my head reminded me this was wrong, but it was drowned out by the ache of being noticed.

It was a rare thing, to be seen. To be more than Jackson's wife, more than a well-dressed fixture meant to smile on cue. And besides, Max wasn't just some stranger. He was part of Jackson's world. A potential business partner. Wasn't it wise to get to know the people my husband surrounded himself with?

Max must've sensed my hesitation. "I'm sorry," he said, his voice gentler now. "I didn't mean to come on too strong. Most people at these things are too busy admiring themselves to hold a real conversation. But when I saw you out here, I figured you might be different."

"You're not being rude," I said quickly. "I'm just not used to someone being so. . . direct."

"You mean shameless," he teased, flashing a grin, his white teeth stark against the shadows of his face.

I laughed, surprising even myself. It had been so long since something genuine slipped past my guard.

"Maybe a little shameless," I admitted, lowering my glass. "But not in a bad way."

Max leaned against the stone railing, the bottle dangling loosely from his fingers. "I figured if I only had time for one real conversation tonight, I'd rather it be with someone who looks like they don't want to be here either."

"That obvious, huh?"

Max shrugged. "Only a little."

A salt-laced breeze swept over the ridgeline, sending a shiver up my spine.

"Here, take my jacket," he said, already slipping out of his gray sports coat before I could protest. He draped it gently over my bare shoulders.

"Thanks," I whispered, offering a small, uneven smile. The jacket was still warm from his body, and a familiar scent clung to the fabric—a cologne similar to Jackson's.

I should've stepped away, should've said something to break the moment. But I didn't.

Our conversation had been harmless, but I knew better than to believe Jackson would see it that way. Being seen alone with Max, even in passing, was a risk.

"We should probably head back in," I said, shifting uncomfortably under the weight of his coat.

Max gave me a slow, thoughtful smile. "Probably," he agreed. "But I can't say I've enjoyed anyone's company this much all night."

I hesitated. "That's. . ." I searched for something neutral, something that wouldn't lead us any further down this road. "Kind of you to say." I slipped out of the coat and handed it back to him. "It was nice meeting you, Max."

His smile fell as he took the jacket. "Likewise."

The heat and hum of the party swallowed me the moment I stepped back inside. Laughter and music crashed over me like a wave as I scanned the room, my eyes darting through the blur of bodies and noise.

Jackson was sprawled comfortably on a velvet sofa, his arm draped around Natasha's shoulders like it belonged there. She leaned in close, laughing at something he'd said. Across the room, Stanley was deep in conversation with two men in tailored suits, completely unaware—or unwilling to notice, his wife's proximity to my husband.

Jackson stood abruptly when he saw me. "Emily," he said, feigning concern, "where have you been? Are you alright?"

"Not really," I confessed, my voice rigid. "I'm not feeling well. If it's okay with you, I think I'd like to go home."

His jaw flexed, and I could see it in his eyes—that familiar, distant glaze. Leaving early wasn't an option. Not without a fight.

"There are plenty of beds upstairs. Why don't you find one and lie down for a bit?"

"No, it's fine," I said, forcing a smile, my gaze flicking past him to Natasha. She offered me a sympathetic tilt of the head, but her eyes narrowed a second later—like she'd already written me off.

"You stay," I added, each word laced with restraint. "I don't want to ruin your evening."

The lie stung as it left my mouth. But I knew better than to cause a scene, not here, not now.

"If you're sure," Jackson said, relief softening his features. He liked when I didn't make things difficult. "I'll have the car brought around."

He leaned in and brushed a kiss across my cheek. I turned just enough for it to miss my skin, pretending I hadn't.

The ride home passed in silence and shadows. The lights of the city blurred through the windows as tears slid down my face—quiet and unchecked. Not because of Natasha, or Jackson's obvious wandering interest.

But because I no longer recognized the woman I'd become.

I used to have dreams, edge, fire. Now, all I had was silence.

And as the car wound through the hills toward the house I called home, I realized something far more painful than anger or heartbreak.

I hadn't just lost myself. I'd surrendered.

Piece by piece. Smile by smile. Until there was nothing left but a name.

And even that was starting to feel like a stranger.

Six

THE NEXT MORNING, I FOUND Jackson sitting at the kitchen table, absorbed in the newspaper, a cup of black coffee beside him.

"Good morning," I said, taking a seat across from him. Jackson didn't bother looking up.

I rubbed my eyes, still fighting sleep, as memories of the previous night drifted through my mind. A plate of freshly baked banana muffins sat in the center of the table.

"Quite the party last night," I remarked, reaching for a muffin.

"How would you know? You left early," he said, shifting the newspaper. I braced for the usual tension but was taken aback when he added, "How are you feeling?"

"Great," I lied, stealing a bite. "Never better."

"Hmm," he hummed over a sip of coffee. The steam curled upward, lingering between us like an unspoken question. Was he waiting for something? A confession, maybe?

"Natasha seems. . . lovely," I ventured, knowing I was walking a fine line.

Jackson lowered the paper, his gaze locking onto mine. His eyes were like stained glass, catching the first light of morning filtering through the dining room window.

"I give it six months," he said, picking up his paper again. "Stanley's already bored of her. Poor girl—dragged away from everything she knew, only to end up with someone like him."

I bit back a retort, feeling the sting of his jealousy.

"About New York. . . when are you leaving?" I asked, pulling my robe tighter around me.

"Two weeks. Maybe sooner, if necessary," he replied flatly.

Relief flooded through me. At least a month, maybe more, of freedom.

"Do you think you'll visit often?" I asked, watching him carefully.

He exhaled through his nose. "I don't know. Depends on work, I guess."

I nodded. It wasn't the answer I was hoping for, but then again, I wasn't sure what I was expecting. I helped myself to another muffin.

Jackson set the newspaper down, his eyes lingering on the muffin in my hand. "Don't you think you've had enough?"

My stomach growled. "Yes, of course." I put the muffin back down and forced a smile.

Two more weeks. I could already see myself, carefree, at a seaside cabana with a margarita in hand, the salt from the ocean clinging to the rim of the glass. Maybe I'd even wander into SeaPort Village, drifting in and out of shops like a tourist.

When I first arrived in California, Kat and I ventured out a few times. But between her and Grant's busy schedule, I quickly found myself spending more time with Jackson than with my sister.

I couldn't get enough of him. He was handsome, charming, and he wanted me. What started as easy beach days with Katherine quickly morphed into quiet afternoons with Jackson, our time together becoming more and more precious. I was craving something new, something more, something that only Jackson could promise me. And in my desperation for belonging, I ignored all the subtle signs, the warning bells that slowly turned into glaring red flags.

"Your sister stopped by earlier," Jackson said casually.

"Kat was here?" I asked, struggling to keep my composure.

"Said she needed to speak to you. . . in person," he added, arching an eyebrow. "Any idea why?"

I shook my head, though the knot in my chest was growing. We hadn't spoken in over a month. It wasn't the longest stretch, but with our history, I expected more distance.

"I'm sure it's nothing," I shrugged, attempting to ease his suspicion. "You know how she is about little things."

But they weren't *little* things.

Katherine knew what Jackson was capable of. She tried to warn me, but even she didn't fully grasp the depth of his cruelty. He hadn't struck me then, only scarred me with his words when his anger got the best of him. Or when he had too much to drink.

"He was just drunk," I'd argue, defending him as if calling me a whore could ever be justified. I'd say things like, "He didn't mean it," or, "It won't happen again," even though deep down, I knew it would.

In the morning, those words would blister, scabbing over into lavish gifts and passionate sex aboard a yacht anchored somewhere off the coast. And like a fool, I believed him.

As our relationship progressed, so did the abuse. Bruises became more difficult to explain. And despite my best efforts to conceal them, Katherine knew. She always knew.

"Please don't do this," she begged the night before our wedding. "He's only going to get worse." But I ignored her.

Katherine had always been protective, stepping in to shield me from the world when Mom died. She knew a monster when she saw one. And to her, Jackson was the boogeyman.

"You're just jealous!" I snapped, even though I knew how absurd it sounded. There was nothing to be jealous of. Jackson might've been rich and attractive, but she and Grant had something real.

Jackson and I didn't share that kind of love. We had passion, lust—a dangerous fire that burned between us. But eventually, fires die out. And sooner or later, you're left with nothing but ashes and dust.

Katherine wasn't jealous of me. I knew that because *I* was jealous of *her*.

After that, our relationship began to fade. We talked until we didn't, and eventually, she and Grant moved up to the Bay Area. And that was that.

"Did she say how long she'd be in town?" I asked Jackson.

"No, she didn't," he replied.

I didn't believe him. Kat wouldn't have come all this way without wanting to see me.

Jackson never outright stopped me from seeing my sister, but the unspoken rule was clear, and it was easier to avoid the tension.

Still, curiosity gnawed at me. What could have brought Kat all the way from San Francisco? It had to be something important enough for her to knowingly cause unrest in my household. She wouldn't risk angering Jackson over something insignificant.

She wouldn't risk me.

"Either way, she's probably long gone by now," I said, my eyes fixed on the plate of muffins. Another low growl rumbled through my stomach.

Jackson checked his watch. "I've got a meeting downtown in half an hour," he said as he stood. "There's some green Bali Juice in the fridge. Maybe you should drink that." His lips brushed the top of my head. "I love you. I'll see you later."

I waited, listening for the faint groan of the garage door as it closed behind him. Once the sound of his car faded, I took out my phone. Jackson kept track of my calls, but with him gone for the next month, I'd deal with the fallout later.

"Emily?" My sister's voice cracked through the phone—soft, wet, and broken. She'd been crying. I could tell.

"What's wrong?" I asked, my heart tightening. Images of my niece and nephew flashed through my mind. "Is everything okay?" A quiet sob slipped through the phone. "Kat, you're scaring me." Anxiety was rising in my throat. I could hear the distant call of seagulls, the rhythmic crash of waves against the shore. "Where are you? What's going on?"

Kat cleared her throat, drawing in a shaky breath. "It's Gran..." My chest clenched. I knew what was coming. "She's gone."

Seven

CALIFORNIA DOES THINGS TO YOU. It gets inside your head. It changes the way you think, what you look like—who you are.

Katherine's dark brown eyes clashed violently against her bottle blonde hair, her fake lashes framing them like some kind of mask.

I barely recognized her anymore.

I dabbed at my mascara, trying to conceal the marks of Jackson's rage, but Katherine wasn't fooled. She saw right through it.

I guess we were both guilty of hiding something.

"So," she said, her voice slicing through the low buzz of the restaurant, "does Jackson know you're here?"

"Of course," I lied.

Sometimes, when the light hit them just right—Katherine's eyes looked like they were on fire. They were smoldering embers now.

"Bullshit," she hissed. Her leering gaze was enough to burn a hole through my skull—the way a magnifying glass does to an ant in the sun.

Except I was the ant.

"I thought we were here to talk about Gran, not my marriage," I shot back. I didn't risk a visit with my sister only to be condemned by her.

"We are," she countered, studying my face. "But if you're going to start off by lying to me, I suggest we get the elephant out of the room now."

When did we get here?

Katherine and I had been inseparable once—bound by blood, and misfortune. Now that bond had become frayed at the edges, barely holding us together.

"I don't have much time," I said. "Can we just get on with it?"

But before Katherine could respond, a young waiter appeared at my side. "Ready to order?" he asked, his gaze shifting between us.

"I'll have a California burrito, guac on the side, and a Bloody Mary—extra spicy," Katherine ordered, her eyes locking onto mine. "You should try the carne asada. I know how much you like—"

"—A chef salad for me, and water. Thank you." I could feel the weight of Katherine's stare as the waiter took our menus and walked away.

"You love carne asada," she pressed, like she was trying to convince me.

"Yeah, well. . . maybe I don't feel like it today," I replied, the words tight.

"You don't *feel* like it today?" she repeated, her brow furrowing. "Just like you don't *feel* like returning my calls?"

"I'm here, aren't I?" I said evenly.

"Are you?" she snapped. "Jesus Christ, Em. You ordered a salad for fuck's sake. And not because you *felt* like it. Jackson's onto you about your weight again, isn't he?"

"Jackson only wants what's best for me," I said, the defense coming too easily. "There's nothing wrong with having expectations."

I might as well have slapped her.

Katherine stiffened, her face tightening with anger. "And what about your expectations? Or do you not have any for him?"

"That's none of your business," I bit out.

"It *is* my fucking business," Kat argued, gesturing at the bruise creeping over my tawny eyes.

I winced, my stomach sinking.

"You know what?" I said, standing abruptly. "This was a mistake."

"Emily, wait," she urged, rolling her eyes. She sounded so much like our mother. "I'm sorry, I'll drop it."

She wouldn't, but I sat back down anyway.

Noise from the street filtered through the open windows, a blur of snippets from random conversations as strangers passed by.

"I need that file on my desk by Tuesday," a sharp-suited woman demanded into her phone.

"Can we go to the beach?" a child's voice piped up, small and hopeful, followed by a heavy sigh from her mother.

Sometimes I liked to tuck myself into other people's lives, just for a moment. I wondered how many had done the same to me, watched me walk by and, for a brief second, envied what they saw.

The server returned, setting our meals in front of us. "Anything else?" he asked, hands clasped behind his back.

"No, thank you," Katherine answered, already lifting her cocktail glass to her lips.

He nodded and walked away.

"Gran's things will probably go to auction," Kat said, breaking into the guacamole with a casual dip. Bits of steak and Pico de Gallo clung to the edge of her plate. "Most of it was junk anyway, and I don't have the time, or the space, to sift through it all." She didn't look at me as she spoke. "Then there's the house. She left it to both of us."

I stared at her, still trying to come to terms with the fact that Gran was gone. "What happened?"

Katherine sighed, her fingers tracing the rim of her glass absentmindedly. "What do you think happened? She was old, Emily. She got sick. And then, she was just. . . gone."

A wave of nausea washed over me. "What do you mean she was sick? And why didn't you call me when you found out?" Raw guilt clawed at my throat. I couldn't even recall the last time I'd spoken to her.

"What do you want from me?" Katherine's voice was sharp. "You weren't returning my calls, my messages. Hell, I even emailed you. You were a fucking ghost."

I thought about the endless phone calls, the voicemails I'd deleted without ever listening to. Not because I didn't want to, but because I couldn't.

"I did what I could," she mumbled, tipping her glass back to finish what was left. "Distance played a role, too."

"When's the funeral?" I asked.

"What funeral?" Katherine laughed. "Gran didn't want one. And even if she did, who would come?"

I shrugged. "I would."

"Would you? Or would your husband find some excuse to keep you home?" she asked, bitterly.

I shot her a glare.

Katherine's shoulders sagged as she let out a long breath. "I'm sorry. It's been a rough few days and I'm just tired."

I watched her, the anger draining out of me, replaced by a heavy sense of understanding. Katherine, always the one to carry the weight alone, was struggling.

"So, what?" I lingered. "We're just going to bury her and be done with it?"

Katherine shook her head. "Gran was very specific about what she wanted done. I had her cremated. I'll be heading back next week to pick up the ashes."

"What about Mom?" I asked.

Her face hardened, the way it always did whenever our mother was mentioned. "What about her?"

I poked at my salad, pushing the lettuce around more than actually eating it. "Don't you think we should. . . I don't know, maybe bury them together?"

Katherine's brow furrowed. "Why would we do that?"

Gran and Mom hadn't been close for years before Mom died. After we moved in with Gran, it was as if our mother had never existed. We never spoke her name, never acknowledged her memory. I didn't even know where she was buried.

I shrugged. "It just feels like the right thing to do, I guess."

Kat snorted. "The right thing to do would have been not to abandon us in the first place."

My fork clattered onto my plate, the noise startling a couple sitting nearby. "What did you say?"

I knew Katherine carried trauma over Mom's death, but it wasn't like our mother had a choice in the matter.

Katherine continued eating, unfazed. "Look, I'm not trying to speak ill of the dead. What's done is done. But come on, Emily, even you can't deny that what Mom did was cowardly and selfish. As a mother myself, I can't—"

"Mom was *not* a coward," I snapped, my patience fraying. "Seriously, Kat, are you so caught up in your own demons that you can't let it go? Mom didn't abandon us—she's fucking dead!"

Katherine stared at me, her eyes wide. "How do you think Mom died?"

"A heart attack. Or an aneurysm. . . I don't know," I murmured.

Katherine blinked, pushing her plate aside as she settled back in her seat.

Lunch was over.

"Em. . ." she began, her voice thick with something I couldn't quite place. Pity, maybe? "Mom didn't die from an aneurysm or a heart attack," she said, her eyes glistening. "She committed suicide."

I stared at her as though she'd sprouted another head. "You're lying."

My sister lowered her gaze. "No, Emily. I'm not."

I shook my head in disbelief. "Mom would never do that. She was happy."

"Was she?" Katherine challenged. "Because happy people don't pop pills."

"Just because she needed help doesn't mean she killed herself," I shot back, still reeling from the accusation.

Kat leaned back in her chair, her eyes narrowing. "Unfuckingbelievable," she breathed, crossing her arms over her chest. "You're just like her, you know that? Hell, you might as well be one slap away from joining her."

The words slammed into me, and I flinched.

Katherine seemed to realize what she'd said, her face falling. "I'm sorry, I didn't mean that. . ."

I tossed my napkin onto my plate and stood. "Except you did."

The waiter, oblivious to the tension, hurried over. "Would you like to take a look at the dessert menu?"

I pulled a twenty from my purse, slapping it down on the table in front of Katherine. "I hear the cheesecake is delicious."

"Emily, stop. I'm. . ." But my sisters voice trailed off as I turned and walked out the door.

Eight

Before

THE CHAIN ON MY BIKE snapped halfway up the hill. It was an old bike, one Mom had picked up from the local Goodwill about a year ago. The pink spokes between the tires had faded over time, and the rubber grips—once white, were now torn and worn down. My hands slipped over them as I huffed up the hill toward our neighborhood.

We didn't live far from the school, a few blocks at most. Normally, Kat and I would ride home together, but today she stayed behind to audition for the lead role of Dorothy in *The Wizard of Oz*.

At six years old, I wasn't allowed to walk home alone. Mom was going to be so upset when I showed up without Kat.

It was fall in southern Michigan, and the rain was coming down in sheets from angry gray clouds. Bare trees lined the sidewalk, their fallen leaves scattered across the wet pavement, leaving a trail of colorful autumn confetti behind them.

I pocketed a few. Mom's birthday was coming up, and I figured I could use them to make her a card. Maybe Kat could bake a chocolate cake to go with it.

Our house sat at the bottom of the hill, squeezed between two other homes near the end of the road. It wasn't really *ours*—we rented, but Mom promised it was only temporary. She said that every time we moved.

Before I was born, Mom and Kat had lived somewhere in Florida. Even though my sister was still little when Dad left, some of her earliest memories were of the three of them. Dad would take her fishing off the dock, and Mom always smelled like sunshine.

Then I came along and ruined everything.

She never said it, but I knew Katherine blamed me for dad leaving. At night, when she thought I was sleeping, I'd hear her whispering wishes on stars for him to come home, and to take me instead.

I never met him, but I saw his face in mine every day. Our eyes were the same flecked copper, our noses both sharply curved. I couldn't blame Katherine for resenting me.

I turned onto Wildwood Loop, out of breath as I pushed my bike down the sloping hill and into our cracked driveway.

Mom's gold Taurus gleamed in the rain, its rust barely hidden by a coat of wax.

"Mom?" I yelled over the blare of the TV. Montel Williams' voice crackled through the speakers. I dumped my backpack by the recliner and grabbed the remote, shutting it off as Sylvia Brown walked onto the stage.

"Mom?" I tried again. Silence. Mom worked the night shift at Pete's Coney, so it wasn't unusual for her to be asleep at this time of day. I called her name once more as I shuffled into her room—only to find it empty. "Mom, I'm home! Kat said I didn't have to wait for her."

Still no answer. Maybe she'd gone out looking for me.

A soft meow drifted down the hallway, followed by the faint sound of scratching. I stopped in front of the bathroom door as Sushi, our cat, slid her white paw through the crack.

"Mom?" I called out, pushing the door open. Sushi bolted between my legs as I peeked inside.

There, lying in the tub with her auburn hair spread out around her like a halo, was my mother.

"Where's Mom?" Katherine asked when she got home an hour later.

I took the last Dunkaroo, scraping it along the edges of the container, licking up the sugary white icing at the bottom. "Taking a bath," I said, wiping my fingers clean.

Kat twisted her head, glancing down the silent hallway.

"Don't bother her," I whined, turning in my seat as Katherine started toward the hall. "She's sleeping."

My sister narrowed her eyes. "I thought you said she was taking a bath?"

"She is," I replied. "She's taking a nap in the tub."

If you asked me to remember the taste of that Dunkaroo, I couldn't tell you. I couldn't tell you the name of the neighbor who sat with us after Kat called the police, or how long it took for them to arrive.

But I could tell you exactly what Katherine's scream sounded like. How it scratched at the back of her throat, full of choked terror, as she fought to pull our mother from the water.

I could tell you the shapes of the distorted shadows thrown by the police lights flooding through the living room windows, staining the walls in an eerie glow of red and blue.

I could even tell you what I had for dinner that night as we waited for Gran to arrive. A four-piece chicken nugget Happy Meal with chocolate milk and a small fry. I remember because Mom could never afford fast food, and I was excited about the toy inside.

Katherine's hand was heavy in mine as we were led out of the house, the flashing lights reflecting in her wide, vacant eyes.

"What's going to happen to us?" I asked as we settled into the back of a waiting police car.

By now, the neighborhood had gathered to gawk. Katherine's lower lip trembled as she sucked in a shaky breath. In that moment, the weight of my future fell onto the shoulders of a ten-year-old girl.

"Kat?" I pressed, my head finding its way into her lap.

My sister's fingers brushed through my hair, and I felt the tremor in her touch as she swallowed a sob. "Everything's going to be okay," she whispered, her voice breaking. "Everything's going to be okay."

Nine

Now

I WANTED TO SCREAM, BUT instead, I drove home in silence, my grip so tight on the steering wheel my knuckles turned bone white.

Katherine was lying. She had to be. If she wasn't, then my entire life had been a lie.

Jackson wasn't home when I pulled into the driveway, and honestly, I wouldn't have cared if he had been. No slap to the face could hurt worse than the betrayal I felt right then.

I sat there in the car, engine idling, staring at the gaudy white columns of the front porch. Useless and expensive. Each one had raised the value of the house by thousands, yet I would've traded it all in a heartbeat to be back in that tiny, two-bedroom rental on Wildwood Loop. I'd give anything for the janky AC, or the water that sometimes turned orange, or even to fight over the bathroom one more time.

The bathroom.

I blinked, shaking off the grainy images of my mother's lifeless body floating in the tub.

Pulling into the garage, I watched the door close with a soft thud behind me. But I didn't turn off the car.

Still wearing my seatbelt, I leaned back and closed my eyes. How long until darkness took me? Was that what it had been like for my mother? Minutes, seconds, before she ended it all? And what about us? Were we even a second thought?

I wondered what Jackson would do when he found me—my body cold and unmoving, like a shattered statue in the driver's seat.

Would he call out my name, desperate for some sign of life, or would he just walk away? Maybe he wouldn't care at all. Maybe he'd be relieved, even grateful, that I'd finally stopped making everything so complicated. I imagined him standing there, looking at me—stone still and lifeless, while feeling nothing at all. But it wouldn't matter. Because by then, I would be beyond caring.

"... Mrs. Bishop?"

Rita's voice broke through the hum of the idling engine. I opened my eyes to see her standing near the side entry, her russet eyes flicking from me to the closed garage door, then back again.

"Is everything okay?" she asked.

I nodded, shutting off the ignition.

Hesitation pulled at Rita's face, but it felt more like pity than concern. She stepped aside, silently waiting for me to follow.

We'd done this before.

A rush of cool air hit me as I stepped inside, and Rita quietly closed the door behind us. "Is there anything else I can do for you, Mrs. Bishop?" she asked cautiously.

I shook my head, waving her off. I needed to be alone.

Sinking into a nearby chair, I buried my face in my hands. I thought of those nights when Katherine would stay up late, begging for Dad to come home. He never did of course, but maybe the rest of her wish could still come true.

I was my mother's daughter, after all.

Jackson returned two hours later, but he wasn't alone. Laughter echoed up the stairs as Rita and her niece rushed down the hallway. I froze on the landing, a tight knot forming in my stomach. Jackson's voice was unmistakable, but the other. . . it sounded familiar, yet I couldn't place it.

"Emily!" Jackson called, spotting me leaning over the banister. He motioned toward the man standing beside him, still with his back to me. "I'd like you to meet my wife, Emily."

I made my way down the stairs, a tentative smile on my lips, but it quickly vanished when I reached the bottom.

Max grinned at me, his perfect smile even more dazzling in the daylight.

Jackson placed his hand on the small of my back. "Max, this is my wife, Emily. Emily, this is Max Meyers, owner and founder of Meyers and Associates."

I expected him to act like this was our first meeting. But instead, Max's hand extended toward me, "It's nice to see you again."

My blood ran cold.

I quickly pulled my hand back. "It's nice to see you too. Welcome to our home."

"You two know each other?" Jackson's gaze locked on mine.

I opened my mouth to explain, but Max cut me off. "We met briefly at Don's party the other night. I'm afraid I found myself without good company, and your wife was kind enough to engage me."

"And were you?" Jackson's voice was flat, but there was an undeniable edge to it.

"Was I what?" I asked.

Jackson tilted his head slightly, eyes narrowing just enough. "Good company?"

I glanced at Max, who seemed unbothered, still smiling like everything was perfectly normal. "Nothing more than friendly conversation," he said with a wink. "At least, I thought so."

I chewed on my lip, trying to gauge the situation. Jackson's face was composed, but his eyes held the gathering darkness of a storm.

"You mentioned a bottle of Pappy's earlier. . ." Max interjected smoothly. "I'd love a glass."

Jackson's mood shifted as he slapped Max on the back. "Of course!" he boomed, suddenly all smiles. "Upstairs in my office. Come on, lets toast to a fruitful partnership."

I stepped aside, noticing the pointed look Max threw over his shoulder before Jackson steered him out of sight.

An hour later, I found myself tucked into a wicker chair, the warmth of the sun resting on my face as it filtered through the windows of the sunroom. I'd hoped to slip into the background, to disappear while Jackson and Max worked out their deal. The laughter I'd heard earlier suggested the negotiations were going well.

I'd gotten lost in the pages of a book. That was, until a shadow fell across the pages. I looked up. Max stood in the doorway, his outline sharp against the light.

"What are you reading?" he asked, voice low and careful, as though not wanting to startle me.

"*The Tenth Circle,*" I replied, marking my place with a finger. "By Jodi Picoult."

Max stepped inside, hands tucked into the pockets of his jeans. "Heavy stuff," he said. "She's the one who writes about the hard things, right? Loss, trauma, stuff people don't like to talk about."

I nodded slowly, surprised he knew that.

"Where's Jackson?" I asked, acutely aware we were alone.

"Took a call," he said, glancing toward the hallway. "Said it might take a while." He paused, his gaze drifting back to me. "You okay?"

I blinked. "Of course. Why?"

He hesitated. "The bruise," he said carefully, tipping his chin toward the faint shadow still lingering below my eye. "Saw it the other night, too. I didn't want to assume, but. . . I've seen things like that before."

I stiffened, the instinct to deflect rising fast. "It was an accident."

Max didn't push. He just studied me, his expression blank. "Doesn't really matter how it happened," he said. "But if something's wrong, you don't have to pretend it's not."

I looked away, throat tightening.

He knelt beside my chair—not close enough to crowd me, just enough to meet my eye level. "Look, I know I'm not your friend, but I'm not blind. You've been on edge since I walked in. And the way you keep looking over your shoulder. . . that's not nothing."

I exhaled shakily. "You don't understand—"

"I might not," he interrupted gently, "but I know what fear looks like. And I don't want to stand by if something's happening and say nothing."

Silence stretched between us, heavy but not hostile.

"If you ever need someone—someone who doesn't owe him anything, I'm around," Max added. "No pressure. Just. . . think about it."

I nodded faintly, unsure what else to say.

Max stood, giving me a small nod before backing toward the door. He paused just before leaving. "By the way. . . I've read all her books." He managed a faint grin. "But if you tell anyone, I'll deny it."

I almost smiled. Almost.

Then he was gone, the door clicking softly shut behind him. I sat in the sunroom, the book still open in my lap, my pulse unsteady.

It had been so long since someone looked at me and actually *saw* me. Not as a wife, or an accessory to a deal—but as a person.

And maybe that shouldn't have meant so much.

But it did.

Ten

DINNER PASSED IN SILENCE. Jackson had retreated into his office, lost in whatever task kept him occupied, while I sat at the table, aimlessly pushing my food around.

Max had left shortly after our conversation, but his words lingered like smoke—subtle but impossible to ignore.

I know what fear looks like.

I hadn't expected that.

He saw more than I wanted him to. More than I meant to show.

I should've been afraid—but instead, all I felt was. . . exposed. As if someone had gently peeled back the mask I wore so tightly, just to see if I was still breathing underneath.

A wave of nausea rolled through me, and I shoved my plate away.

Maybe Jackson's absence was a good thing. Maybe his refusal to leave his office meant he was simply focused—dotting every *i*, and crossing every *t*.

Or maybe he knew something.

I sank back into my chair, the quiet pressing in around me. And for the first time in weeks, I couldn't tell if I was more afraid of what came next. . . or the possibility that nothing would happen at all.

After dinner, I followed my usual routine. Brushing my teeth, washing my face, slipping into a pair of white floral pajamas. Jackson's office door remained shut, but I could hear the rustle of papers and soft footsteps from inside.

I climbed into bed shortly after 9 p.m. when my phone buzzed with a text from Katherine. I didn't respond. She followed up with another call, but I let it go to voicemail, a familiar cycle of avoidance she must've expected by now.

I powered off my phone and tucked it in the drawer, deciding it was time to go to bed. I wasn't tired. I just wanted the day to be over.

Sleep didn't come easily. I spent what felt like hours tossing and turning, until exhaustion finally took over and I drifted off—only to be jolted awake a few hours later by the thumping sound of music.

I blinked through bleary eyes, squinting at the clock on the nightstand. 3:02 a.m. Slowly, I climbed out of bed, the deep bass vibrating through the floorboards with each soft *thud, thud, thud.*

The house was dark as I crept down the hallway, the only light a thin sliver seeping under Jackson's office door. I hesitated, pressing my ear against the wood, but all I could make out were jumbled lyrics from a song I didn't recognize.

I should've ignored it. I should've turned around and crawled back into bed. But curiosity got the best of me.

The doorknob was cold against my trembling fingers. I steadied my breath, trying to quiet the rush of my heartbeat, and turned the handle.

Inside, Jackson sat slumped over his desk, his usually neat blonde hair in disarray, his navy blue shirt wrinkled and stained. The pungent stench of bourbon filled the room, and a sharp pang of regret hit me.

I had made a mistake.

I started to retreat, hoping to slip back into the shadows without him noticing.

But just as I began to turn, the music stopped—the sudden silence shattered by the creak of the door. Jackson's head jerked up, his bloodshot eyes locking onto mine.

"Emily?" His voice was raw.

"I'm sorry," I mumbled. "I saw your light was on. I just wanted to make sure you were okay."

A cold, unsettling grin spread across his face. "Everything's great," he said, leaning back in his chair. "Just having a little... celebration."

I looked around the room. Books lay scattered across the floor, a shattered decanter tipped on its side, its amber liquid spilling onto the floor like a pool of blood. This didn't look like a celebration to me.

"Jackson. . ." I started.

"Come in. Have a drink with me," he said.

I shifted my weight from one foot to the other. "I'm not sure I—"

"It's not an option, Emily." A flash of something dark, flickered in his bloodshot eyes.

I waited in silence as he pulled out a bottle of Pappy's from somewhere in his desk. The label was faded, worn from use. The way he handled it so casually told me it was already more than half empty.

He took a long swig, the poison disappearing down his throat before passing the bottle to me. I reached for it tentatively, but he yanked it away.

"Ah, ah, ah," he teased. "Not until you say please."

"Please," I managed, my pulse racing like a warning drum.

He grinned, finally handing me the bottle. The smell hit me immediately, thick and overpowering, making my stomach churn. I raised it to my lips, forcing myself to drink. The burn was immediate, searing through me, and I fought not to cough, the bitter aftertaste clinging to my tongue like a curse.

"Thata girl," he praised, watching me closely. "It's good, isn't it?"

I nodded, dragging the back of my hand across my mouth, trying to erase the shame.

"Yeah, you can't do much better than this," he remarked, finishing off the rest of the bottle in one last gulp.

In the background, the music shifted to something slower. "These Days" by The Black Keys filled the room.

"Oh man, I love this song," Jackson said, rising from his chair and extending his hand toward me. "Dance with me, Emily."

I glanced at the mess—at the scattered books, and shards of broken glass, before placing my hand in his. Together, we moved to the far side of the room. Jackson pulled me in close, and I held my breath against the familiar scent of his cologne battling against the sharp tang of alcohol.

Maybe the meeting with Max had gone well. Maybe this *was* a celebration, after all. I tried to relax, letting the tension in my shoulders melt away. Jackson's arm wrapped around my waist, pulling me in tighter as I rested my head against his chest.

This was the man I'd fallen for—the one who could be gentle, the one who danced with me in the stillness of the night, long after the rest of the world had gone to sleep.

I closed my eyes, trying to lose myself in the warmth of the moment. Jackson lifted my face to his, his mouth brushing softly against mine. His lips were tender, and he held me close as we rocked gently back and forth.

I couldn't remember the last time he'd kissed me like that, let alone touched me at all. I fell into him, allowing myself to be pulled back into old memories of passion, of love that once felt like it could last forever. Maybe this was a fresh start. Maybe this was a new beginning.

But then, the kiss deepened. Jackson's need grew, his touch becoming insistent, almost brutal. His hand tightened on the back of my neck, the pressure sharp and painful. When I tried to pull away, his grip only tightened further.

"Watch what you say, the devil is listening." His words were hot and suffocating against my lips as he twisted the lyrics of the song into something more sinister. "He's got ears you wouldn't believe."

A cold shiver ran down my spine, and the room seemed to tilt.

One of my favorite movies growing up was *The Pagemaster*, but there was one scene that always terrified me—when Dr. Jekyll transformed into Mr. Hyde. I would cover my eyes or leave the room until it was over. The way Hyde's face contorted into that sinister grin haunted my nightmares. I would always try to convince myself it wasn't real.

Except *this* was real.

Jackson's eyes were black with fury, his face twisted in a mask of rage. "Did you honestly think I wouldn't find out?" he snarled.

For a moment, I forgot how to breathe. My mouth opened, but nothing came out. The words were there—somewhere, but my voice had vanished. I could only shake my head, a silent, trembling plea.

"You cozied up to Max behind my back," he spat, his voice venomous. "Parading around like I wouldn't notice. Like I'm some kind of idiot."

My heart pounded. "That's not what happened."

He let out a cold, humorless laugh. "Don't lie to me. You think I didn't see the way he looked at you? The way you *let* him?"

"I didn't let him do anything," I said, my voice cracking. "Max was just concerned. That's all. He asked me if I was okay, and that's it."

"Oh, so now he's your therapist?" Jackson sneered. "What, you think flashing a sad little bruise is going to get you a sympathy pass?"

My stomach sank. "You're twisting this."

"I *trusted* you," he hissed. "And you humiliated me."

He stepped closer. I could smell the bitterness on his breath—rage and control simmering beneath the surface.

"I didn't do anything wrong," I whispered, backing away.

But that only made him angrier.

"You cost me a deal because you couldn't keep your mouth shut—or your eyes to yourself." His voice dropped lower. "Do you have any idea what that deal meant for us? For *me*?"

The song playing on his speaker ended, and in that split second of silence, adrenaline surged through me. I shoved him backward with everything I had and darted toward the door.

I could hear him laughing behind me, a sick, twisted sound, like he thought this was some kind of game.

I didn't look back as I ran, but my foot caught on the corner of his desk, and I crashed to the floor. Jackson's hand clamped around my ankle, a vice-like grip, pulling me across the rug.

"Where do you think you're going?" he taunted, his voice dripping with malice. He flipped me onto my back, his face looming above me. "If you want to act like a fucking whore. . ." He grunted, his hand moving swiftly toward his belt. "I'll treat you like a fucking whore."

An unsettling realization washed over me.

He was going to rape me.

"I fucked her you know," Jackson said, struggling with his belt. "Stanley's wife. That crazy bitch had my cock so far down her throat she was choking." His breath was hot on my face as he knelt over me, the stench of Pappy's filling my nostrils. Jackson took my face in his hands, forcing me to meet his gaze. "Would you like me to show you?"

"Please, don't do this," I pleaded, my voice trembling as I tried to pull away. His grip was relentless, his fingers digging into my cheeks like iron clamps. "I swear, Jackson, I didn't do anything wrong. You have to believe me."

A strangled breath escaped me, swallowed by the terror that was tightening around my chest. He was bigger, stronger, and I was helpless.

Jackson shifted, sitting back on his knees, his hands fumbling with the belt, struggling to free it from its prongs. It was stuck.

This was my chance.

I yanked my leg back, bracing myself, and kicked—hard, hitting him square in the chest. It didn't knock him over, but it staggered him, giving me just enough space to break free.

He gasped, a breath of pain and surprise escaping his mouth. I didn't hesitate. I pushed myself up, ignoring the agony as shards of glass tore into the bottoms of my feet. I had to get out, had to reach the front door, scream for help, find someone—*anyone.*

But I didn't make it that far.

Jackson was too fast. Before I could even get halfway to the stairs, a sudden jolt of pain shot through my scalp. His fingers tangled in my hair, yanking me backward.

My head slammed against the wall with a sickening thud, and the world spun. His shadow loomed over me, his grip still firm, the belt now hanging loose in his hand.

I gazed up at him, blood soaking through my pajamas as tears carved streaks down my face. But it wasn't the blood or the tears that consumed me—it was the sickening crack of his belt against my skin. My body tensed, and a scream ripped through me, followed by another as the leather dug into my chest, then my arms as I desperately tried to shield myself.

Each strike was a brutal reminder of my helplessness, the sound of the buckle slamming into my skin echoing down the empty hallway. The coppery taste of blood filled my mouth as my lip split open. I curled in on myself, but it didn't matter. The pain kept coming.

"LOOK AT ME!" His voice shattered the air, and I arched involuntarily as another blow landed, this time across my spine. "You fucking bitch, look at me!" he shouted. "I've given you everything! A house, a car, a perfect life. And this is how you repay me?"

Thwack. Thwack. Thwack.

The blows came so fast, they blurred together. After a while, I didn't even feel them anymore. Just a searing, blinding white pain, flooding every inch of me, drowning everything else out.

Jackson hovered over me, his face so close I could smell the sour, rancid heat of his breath. He was yelling, but his words were lost beneath the roar in my head. It was as if he were speaking through water, muffled and distant.

I felt his fingers close around my throat, squeezing the life from me. My lungs burned, gasping for air that wouldn't come. Blood thundered in my ears, drowning out everything—my fear, my pain, the world itself.

This was it. He was going to kill me.

I clawed at his hands, but it was like fighting against stone. My efforts were useless.

His eyes were wild, desperation turning his grip to iron. "Look what you made me do, Emily. Why? Why would you make me do this? I love you, don't you understand?"

"I. . . love. . . you too," I coughed, voice rasping. "Please. . . don't. . ."

Jackson was crying now, his tears falling onto my face, mingling with the blood. His sobs were a bitter mix of rage and sorrow. But his grip didn't loosen.

"I'm sorry," he choked out.

And just like that, the world around me plunged into darkness.

Eleven

People think leaving is easy. They believe that after the first insult, the first blow, there's no room for second chances.

But those people are wrong.

I used to think the same way. I didn't know anyone who had been in a violent relationship, but I'd read books, watched movies, and seen plenty of true crime documentaries. They always ended in tragedy—fatalities, not just bruises or broken bones.

I used to roll my eyes, thinking those women were weak, cowardly.

Now, I knew better.

I knew how easy it was to justify bad behavior—to pull excuses from thin air, letting them slip off your tongue in sweet, comforting lies.

I knew how easy it was to turn a blind eye, to believe every word they said—that they loved you, that they'd never do it again. I knew how easy it was to convince yourself that it wasn't their fault.

You made them do it.

The monitor next to me beeped steadily. My eyes flickered open, struggling to focus on the blinding white walls of the hospital room. The world swam around me, the sharp scent of antiseptic cutting through the haze.

Every muscle in my body screamed. My arms were covered in angry welts, a map of hurt etched in red.

They were marks of anger. Marks of rage. Marks of hate.

"Emily," my sister's voice, thick with emotion, broke through the stillness. She leaned forward, her hands enveloping mine. There was so much she wanted to say, but instead, a strangled sob stole the words from her throat.

I tried to speak. "It's—" My voice came out raspy and unrecognizable. Flashes of Jackson's hands around my neck danced before my eyes—the crushing pressure, the frantic battle for air. The fact that I could even utter a word was a miracle.

"It's okay," I managed, forcing the words through the pain. "I'm okay."

"It's not okay," Katherine insisted, her voice shaking. "None of this is okay." She pressed her face into my hair, her breath hitching. "This is my fault. This is all my fault."

"None of this. . . was your fault," I gasped, each word a monumental effort. "Where's Jackson?"

Katherine's grief instantly morphed into hatred. "Hiding," she hissed, her face flushing with anger. "And if that piece of shit knows what's good for him, he'll stay hidden."

My mind flickered to New York. "I'm so sor—"

"Don't you dare," Katherine cut me off, her brown eyes blazing. "Don't you dare fucking say you're sorry." Her fingers gently cupped my face, and I flinched, the reflex uncontrollable. The fierceness in her eyes softened. "You have nothing to be sorry for. Do you hear me? You did nothing wrong."

I shook my head, tears blurring my vision. I knew she was right, but the years of conditioned self-blame were hard to shake. I'd grown used to Jackson's rage, accepting it as a punishment I deserved.

I sat up, trying to focus on Katherine's face—raw grief clashing with a protective anger. Even now, a small weight of guilt pressed heavily against my chest. By tolerating Jackson's violence, I had dragged her into its suffocating grip. Seeing her like this twisted something deep inside me. I might have been the victim, but she was the collateral damage.

"How did you know I was here?" I asked, still trying to piece together what had happened. "Did Rita call you?"

Katherine shook her head, her normally vibrant bleached hair looking dull and lifeless against her sun-kissed skin.

"I was angry," she confessed. "Angry with how we left things. Angry at you for walking out on me at lunch. But mostly, I was angry at myself." Her chest rose and fell with a heavy sigh, broken and defeated. "I tried calling you to apologize. I wanted to fix things, to try again, but you didn't answer. I wasn't surprised. I figured you wouldn't want to speak to me, even if you could. But something told me to try again, and it went straight to voicemail." She looked away, the shame and guilt evident on her face. "I've spent my whole life trying to protect you, and when you needed me most, I wasn't there."

"Kat—" I started, reaching for her hand, but she pulled away.

"No," she insisted, her voice firm but shaking, "let me finish. I knew what kind of man Jackson was, and I introduced him to you anyway. If I'd never sent him to the airport that day, you wouldn't be here."

"You don't know that," I countered.

"I do," she shot back. "It was Grant's idea to send him, but I didn't argue. I should have argued. I should've picked you up myself. Instead, I rationalized it, told myself I was being over-protective. But when I saw the way he looked at you that day, I knew I fucked up."

Above, a woman's voice crackled over the speakers. *"Paging Dr. Daniels. Dr. Daniels, please report to the third floor nurses' station."*

Katherine's voice softened again, the heartache bleeding through. "I couldn't sleep. I just had this awful, gnawing feeling that something was wrong. So I drove over to your house. The gate was open, and that's when I knew something wasn't right. I found you. . . lying on the floor, and I. . ." She trailed off, her voice breaking. A raw, anguished cry escaped her lips. "The house was empty, Emily. He just left you there, like you were trash. What kind of person does that to someone they supposedly love?"

A bitter irony twisted in my chest. The man who had claimed to love me had left me to die.

"What about the staff?" I asked, my mind racing. Rita would be there first. Would she recognize something was wrong—or just sweep up the glass, ignore the blood, and carry on?

"I dismissed them this morning with a month's pay, until we figure things out," Katherine replied flatly.

I arched a brow. "We?"

"Yes, *we*," she said firmly. "If you think for one second I'm going to let you go back to that house alone, you're out of your mind."

"Where am I supposed to go?" I asked, desperation creeping in.

"Is that a serious question?" Katherine leaned back in her chair, crossing her arms. "You'll stay with me."

I shook my head. "What about Grant?" I asked. "He's Jackson's best friend, don't you think. . ." I trailed off, watching as my sister's face drained of color. "Wait, does he know?"

Katherine bit her lower lip. "No," she replied, her gaze falling to the floor. She looked like she hadn't slept in days.

"Are you sure?" I pressed, noticing the flicker of regret passing over her face. She was caught between her loyalty to me and her marriage to Grant. "This is my mess to clean up," I insisted. "I won't bring my trash to your doorstep."

Her jaw clenched. "You're not going back to that house, Emily. I won't let you."

"Jackson isn't even there," I argued.

"Exactly," she countered. "Who knows where he is and when he'll be back. And you know he *will* be back."

She was right. God, I hated when she was right.

"I have a little bit of cash saved up for emergencies," I said, thinking of the small, rose-painted tea tin stashed in the back of my closet. "I'll stay at a hotel until I figure things out."

"And what if you don't?" Katherine sat up straighter, eyes hardening. "What if you run out of money before then? What if Jackson finds you?"

"What do you want from me, Kat?" Anger bubbled up in my chest as the weight of everything came crashing down. "Jackson isn't stupid. Your house will be the first place he'll look. And I'll be honest with you, I don't know if I'm strong enough to leave him. You don't understand how charming he is, how convincing he can be." My voice cracked, and hot tears spilled down my cheeks. "Mom's gone, Gran's dead, and—"

"Gran!" Katherine shouted, her voice frantic. "Oh my God, Emily. . . that's it."

I tilted my head. "Did you not hear me? Gran's dead. She's gone."

"Yes, but her house isn't," Katherines eyes gleamed with manic excitement. "She left it to both of us. It's perfect."

Perfect. Perfect for her, maybe. But for me? I thought of the old farmhouse on the outskirts of Windhaven, tucked away in the Appalachian hills. The one I'd been dragged to after Mom's death. The one I'd sworn I'd leave and never return to.

"Kat, I can't. . ." I murmured, sinking further into the bed.

"Why not?" she asked, eyes narrowed.

I sighed, trying to find the right words, but there wasn't a good enough reason. At least not one I could share with her. Crawling back there felt like admitting defeat. It wasn't just the stifling small-town atmosphere, or the way people avoided us because Gran had always been different. There were other things. Things I'd buried so deep I thought they were gone for good. Things I wanted to run from and never look back. Going home would mean reopening wounds I had spent years stitching shut.

"I don't want to be alone," I said, the words a half-truth.

Katherine's small hands wrapped around mine, her grip tight as she searched my face. "As long as we have each other, you'll never be alone."

Twelve

Before

Rows of yellowing magnolia trees stood like silent sentinels along the long, dirt driveway. Their branches hung heavy with petals drifting to the ground, shedding themselves for fall.

Ahead, the farmhouse rose up, small and weathered against the towering mountains behind it. Gran's Crown Vic rumbled to a stop near an old red barn, a few paces from the house. The eight-hour drive from Michigan to West Virginia had been mostly quiet, save for the occasional hum of the radio. Katherine had spent most of the journey staring out the window, while I hummed along to whatever came on the radio.

When Gran finally killed the engine, I was quick to jump out, flinging the back door open with a loud creak. Rust peeled off in flakes as I stretched my legs.

"Aren't you coming?" I called to Katherine, still buckled in her seat.

She nodded slowly. "You go ahead, I'll be right there."

I shrugged. Gran stood waiting on the porch, as I bounded toward her.

"Careful where you step," she pointed to a small circle of painted stones near the porch. "Your papa took his last breath right there. Bad luck to stand on it."

My eyes widened as I sidestepped the memorial.

As Gran fumbled with the keys to unlock the door, I turned to take in the view of the backyard. A small, tidy garden sat neatly behind the house, framed by a white picket fence. Beyond it, endless fields of tall grass danced in the breeze, leading up to the mountains, their trees already dressed in the deep reds and golds of autumn. It was unlike anything I had ever seen—like something straight out of a rich oil painting.

"You comin'?" Gran's voice pulled me back. "Or you gonna stand out here all day, waitin' to catch your death?"

I glanced back at the car. "What about Kat?"

Gran shot a quick look at Katherine and shrugged. "She'll come when she's ready."

The inside of Gran's house looked nothing like the outside. For one, it was crowded. Shelves sagged under the weight of several books and various colored rocks lined the windowsills.

A massive stone fireplace dominated the living room, its hearth filled with fresh ashes. The faint scent of smoke lingered in the air, evidence that it had been used recently.

I sank into the worn floral sofa as my eyes scanned the cluttered coffee table. A broken remote. A burned out candle. Several mismatched crocheted coasters, alongside a stack of old magazines.

I fidgeted, crossing and uncrossing my legs, clearly uncomfortable in my new home. Gran joined me a few minutes later, settling into a matching armchair opposite me. She set the two large mugs down, each on its own coaster. I picked one up, eyeing the dark, murky liquid inside.

"It smells weird in here," I blurted out, setting the mug down without taking a sip.

Gran glanced at a smoldering stick on a shelf across the room, a thin wisp of smoke trailing from the end. "Pachouli," she murmured, "and a touch of sage. Keeps the spirits away."

"Spirits?" A chill ran down my spine. "Like. . . ghosts?"

Gran took a slow sip from her mug, then set it down with a soft thud. "The mountains are alive with things," she said, her voice lowering. "Some natural, others. . . not so much. Best to be prepared." She winked at me.

I thought of the sprawling field stretching into the mountains and a shiver crept over me. We were alone out here, three miles from town, in this little white house—just Gran, Katherine, and me. I stared at the mug in front of me, unsure of what to say next.

Gran sat back, studying me. "You don't have to be afraid of it, you know," she said, breaking the quiet. "Whatever's out there, whatever's in here. . . it's been here long before us. And it'll be here long after we're gone."

I took a deep breath, looking around the room, at the faded furniture, the cluttered shelves, the smoky air. This was our home now, for better or worse.

Katherine didn't come in until an hour later, her eyes red and swollen from crying. Dinner was quiet. No one spoke—there wasn't much to say. Gran made hamburger helper. It was ok, but I wasn't hungry. Katherine didn't eat at all.

Afterwards, I helped Gran clean up. The kitchen was small and old, the two of us barely fit. Through the window, the setting sun bathed the mountains in a soft, golden light. Gran told me that in the summer, hummingbirds would come flitting through the garden, drinking the nectar from wild zinnias and columbines that grew along the fence.

The TV was ancient and Gran only got two channels—QVC and the local news. Around eight, Katherine and I carried our few belongings upstairs and down the hall to what was now our shared bedroom.

Two twin beds with iron frames flanked a small white nightstand. I chose the bed by the window, hoping to catch a glimpse of a hummingbird when summer came around.

Neither of us spoke as we unpacked. I hated it—this heavy weight of grief between us. We'd lost the only parent we had and now we tiptoed around her death as if it never happened at all.

Buried beneath the sheets, in a bed that felt wrong, I tried not to breathe in the unfamiliar scent of this strange place. Before all this, we'd only seen Gran on a handful of holidays. Now, she was all we had left.

The soft glow of the lamp on the nightstand cast long shadows across the room. I watched in silence as Katherine reached over and flicked the switch, plunging the room into darkness. Moonlight flooded through the window, painting eerie shadows across the pale pink quilts.

None of this felt right.

"Kat?" I squeaked into the darkness. "Kat, I want to go home."

Katherine's voice was flat. "This is home now."

"No, it's not," I shook my head, my body trembling. This bed, this room—it was all wrong. "I want to go home. I want Mom." I couldn't get comfortable. Not here, in this bed that wasn't really mine in this room I didn't like. Hot tears finally spilled over. "I want to go home. I want to go home," I chanted, inconsolable. "I want to go home. I want to go home. I want to go home."

"Emily, stop it!" Katherine shouted. She was out of bed now, standing beside me. "Whether you like it or not, this is home now. Crying and screaming isn't going to change that."

Snot bubbled beneath my nose, and I wiped it away with the back of my hand. "I want to go home," I repeated, quieter this time.

Then her arms were around me, pulling me close as the weight of her body settled in next to mine. "It's just a house Emily," she whispered, her voice soothing as she brushed her fingers through my hair, mimicking Mom's familiar touch. "As long as we're together, you'll always be home."

Thirteen

Now

The sliding glass doors parted with a soft whoosh, and the glaring California sunlight hit me all at once. I breathed in the warm air, feeling it press against my skin. It had been four days since that terrifying night. Four days with Katherine's constant presence—sometimes comforting, other times grating. Four days of silence from Jackson.

Miraculously, nothing was broken. Dark bruises circled my throat, and angry welts marked my arms and legs. Some would scar—a permanent reminder, but at least I was alive to carry them.

Katherine stood next to me, her expression blank. We'd argued before leaving the hospital. I'd wanted to go home—*his* home now, to gather some of my things, but Katherine had insisted she go instead. So here we were, standing at the edge of an uncertain future.

The hospital staff had been discreet, offering the number for a battered women's shelter in a quiet, almost unnoticeable way. Katherine had immediately dismissed it. We had a plan, a place to go. It might feel more like a prison than a refuge, but at least we'd have each other.

We walked in silence past rows of parked cars, finally stopping in front of a beat-up red Ford Focus.

I glanced at my sister, confused, but her face remained a hard line. "Katherine?" I asked. "What's going on?"

"I'm sorry, Emily," she said, unable to meet my eyes.

She wasn't coming with me.

"I know it's not the Lexus, but driving your car is too risky." Katherine unlocked the back door, revealing my dusty pink suitcase. My heart sank. "I only took what was absolutely necessary."

I stared at her, a cold knot forming in my stomach. "So that's it?" I croaked, my throat raw. "After everything, you're just going to leave me?"

"It's not like that," Katherine started, but I didn't let her finish.

"What isn't? You're leaving me here, after everything that's happened?" The tears I'd fought so hard to hold back finally spilled down my cheeks. "I should have known better. I should've known you were going to abandon me. . . again."

Katherine flinched. "Grant's already asking questions," she mumbled. "And I can't just leave my kids without any explanation."

I wanted to scream, to tell her that wasn't good enough, but the words stuck in my throat. In the end, I knew it wasn't fair to blame her. She had a life here, a good one, and it wasn't her responsibility to care for me anymore. But that hollow ache in my chest felt like a betrayal all the same.

"What about Gran?" I asked.

Katherine fidgeted with the keys to the Focus. "Her ashes are waiting at Wyger's funeral home in Charleston. Everything's been paid for. Just give them your name."

I swallowed hard. "You're not even going to say goodbye?"

"I said goodbye the day I left," she replied, her eyes finally meeting mine. "I've made peace with it. Please don't make this any harder than it already is."

I thought of the last few days—of the doting sister who refused to leave my side. I stood there for a moment, my eyes fixed on the car. I was drowning in a sea of unmet expectations and lost promises.

"Where did you even get this thing?" I asked, motioning to the car.

Katherine's lips twitched upward in a half-smile. "Craigslist," she confessed. She dug around in her bag and pulled out a small phone, its screen spiderwebbed with cracks.

"Seriously?" I said, taking the phone from her.

"The guy at the pawn shop sold it to me for ten bucks," she shrugged. "There's no way to trace it, and you'll need something in case of an emergency. It's prepaid, and already loaded with minutes."

I opened the driver's side door, wincing at the musty smell of cigarette smoke and stale fast food. I rolled down the windows, desperate for fresh air.

"Before I forget. . ." Katherine said, handing me an envelope. I hesitated before opening it, and when I looked inside, my stomach dropped at the sight of dozens of bills stuffed into the small pocket. "There's ten thousand dollars in there. It's not much, and it won't last forever, but it should get you by for a while."

I crossed my arms tightly over my chest. "I don't want your money."

"You might not want it, but you're going to need it," Katherine said, rolling her eyes. "Even if Jackson doesn't cut you off, he'll be watching your account like a hawk. I don't know if I'll be able to send more, so only buy what you need."

I took the envelope with a sigh and shoved it into the glove compartment. This wasn't a "see you later," or "call me when you get there." Neither of us knew when we'd see each other again. Maybe never.

I felt my chest tighten as I climbed into the car. Despite the windows being rolled down, I could hardly breathe. Everything about this was wrong. We should be making this trip together. But her life was here now. All I had was this junky red Focus and an old pink suitcase filled with nothing but broken dreams.

"I guess this is it then," I said, though part of me was still hoping she'd change her mind.

Katherine raised her hand in protest. "I've never been good at goodbyes, and I'm not about to start now." It was true. The night she left Windhaven, she vanished into the dark like a ghost, leaving nothing behind but a note on the kitchen table—one that Gran found the next morning.

I wanted to say something, anything, to stop her. To ask her to stay, to tell her that I couldn't do this alone.

"I've got to go," she added, as if the words were somehow easier than the silence.

Before I could respond, she leaned in through the window and kissed me on the forehead—a quick peck that felt more like a dismissal than a farewell.

And just like that, she was gone.

I watched her disappear in the rearview mirror until all that remained was my own reflection. I was a stranger. I barely recognized myself anymore—bruised, battered, and utterly defeated.

I felt the tears start to spill again. I wiped them away angrily, as if erasing them would make it all go away. But it didn't. Nothing would.

I was alone. Completely alone.

I shifted into reverse and slowly pulled out of the parking lot. When I first arrived in San Diego, it felt like the beginning of a fresh start. But now, I had overstayed my welcome. It was time to go home.

Fourteen

Gravel crunched under my tires as I turned onto the winding driveway, flanked by a canopy of magnolia trees. Sunlight filtered through their thick leaves, casting dappled patterns on the ground and illuminating the soft pink and white petals above. Ahead, the farmhouse emerged from the rolling hills, barely visible at first, then more recognizable as I drew closer.

"Home sweet home," I muttered under my breath.

I'd imagined this moment a thousand times on the drive here—the way the sun would catch the freshly painted clapboard, the porch swing swaying gently in the breeze. But as I drove closer, reality hit me.

The roof sagged, missing a few shingles like teeth in a weathered smile. The once-pristine white paint had peeled away, leaving patches of raw wood exposed. The barn was gone now. All that remained was a scattered ruin of wood and memory.

I parked the car beside the ruble, the engine humming softly as it came to a stop. Gran's urn, carefully packed in its box, sat next to me. When I'd picked it up in Charleston, something about stowing it in the back seat felt wrong, so I buckled it in beside me like a strange passenger. I grabbed it from the seat and slammed the door shut behind me, the sound startling a flock of birds into the distance.

Taking a deep breath, I let the crisp mountain air fill my lungs, a welcome change from the staleness of a thirty-six hour car ride. Holding Gran's urn tightly, I walked towards the front porch. Papas rocks were gone, and I wondered if that was Grans doing—or someone else's.

On the porch, I dodged loose nails and warped boards, the wood groaning under my feet. Chipped, empty flower pots sat abandoned on the railing, and the swing Gran once used to watch the sunrise clung desperately to its broken chain.

This wasn't the warm welcome I had imagined. The house, once so well-kept by Gran, now stood in a state of quiet decay. Cobwebs hung like forgotten tapestries from the archways, and thick flakes of peeling paint crunched beneath my feet.

It was as if, when she died, the house died too.

The screen door swayed loosely on its hinges. As I tugged it open, one hinge snapped with a sharp crack, and the door swung wildly before settling askew against the frame.

"Well. . . that's something," I murmured, half-expecting the rest of the house to come crumbling down on top of me. But to my relief, the main door opened smoothly.

Stepping inside, I inhaled sharply.

Everything was the same.

The floral sofa, its ruffled skirt sagging and worn, sat untouched near the stone fireplace. My eyes fell over the crocheted blanket draped over its side, and I was instantly brought back to the memory of cold nights, the scratchy threads biting into my skin as I huddled beneath it for warmth.

Even the way the sun streamed through the kitchen window, casting its rays across the original hardwood floors, evoked a flood of memories.

I swallowed hard, my throat dry as I closed the door behind me. Gran's presence lingered in every corner, woven into the very fabric of the house. I set her ashes down on the coffee table, next to a pile of incense ash and a towering stack of old magazines.

The familiar scent of aged wood and stale air filled my lungs, and for a moment, I almost expected her to call me into the kitchen, asking if I wanted tea.

But the silence that followed was deafening. The house was no longer the bustling, warm place it once was. It had become something else. Something hollow.

I stood there for a while, staring at the urn. How strange, to hold someone's remains in something so small. It felt wrong somehow, like the rest of her had been forgotten, discarded like the piles of junk around the house.

I shook my head, trying to push away the thoughts. This wasn't the time.

Instead, I went to the kitchen, where the faded curtains fluttered in the breeze. The once-gleaming countertops were now stained and chipped, the sink filled with dishes that hadn't been washed in God knows how long. I turned back toward the living room, where Gran's urn sat.

All around me, the house creaked and groaned, the old wood shifting with time. It used to terrify me, but now it was a fragile comfort—a distraction from the thoughts I couldn't shake.

Thoughts that made me feel guilty.

Thoughts that made me want to run back to California.

The airport hummed with chaos as fellow passengers rushed by. Jackson stood beside me, his hand brushing my cheek, soft and warm. A touch that seemed to pull me into him. He was gentle, and for a moment I almost let myself believe it was real.

But then, his fingers began to drift lower, trailing over the delicate column of my throat. The softness hardened, turning rough, and suddenly, I felt the pressure building beneath my jaw, his fingers curling like steel around my neck.

Dread knotted in my gut. "What are you doing?" The words fell from my lips, a nervous laugh that morphed into a desperate, strangled gasp as his grip tightened. My hands flew to his, my nails scraping uselessly against his skin. "Jackson. . . stop. . . please. . . you're. . ." I couldn't finish. His grip was a vice now, cutting off my air, cutting off my words.

His eyes locked onto mine, glassy and distant. "I love you, Emily," he lured, his voice impossibly calm. "Don't you know how much I love you?" A malicious smile curled at the edges of his lips.

I tried to speak, to say the words that had once come so easily between us. "I. . . I love you, too," I gasped, my vision swimming, the world around me dimming as the pressure of his alleged love crushed me from all sides.

But he didn't stop. His hands tightened, both of them now, interlocking around my neck like a promise I couldn't escape.

"I love you, Emily. I love you," he repeated—a cruel chant that echoed in my head, like a lullaby of betrayal.

The world blurred as the crowd continued to surge around us, unaware of the danger closing in. Through the haze, I saw Rita, moving quickly, Mia trailing close behind. They didn't glance back as they fled from me, from the nightmare unfolding right in front of their eyes.

And there, standing in the distance, was Gran—her eyes heavy with grief, her face etched with a sorrow that cut deeper than anything I had ever felt. She didn't need to speak. I already knew. I had broken her heart.

The overhead PA crackled to life. Katherine's voice broke through the chaos. "She's gone," it echoed throughout the terminal. "She's gone."

I couldn't hold on any longer. My body went slack, collapsing beneath the weight of his hands, still holding on, still choking the life from me.

"Did you ever love me?" I croaked as my gaze met his. But there was nothing there. His eyes were black, vacant craters.

Jackson didn't answer. He didn't need to.

This wasn't love. This was never love.

This was a dangerous lie.

Fifteen

I JOLTED AWAKE, GASPING FOR air. My hands shot to my throat, frantically pulling the lilac-colored sheets that had somehow wound around my neck.

A sharp, cool breath filled my lungs as Kat's voice, a distant echo, still lingered in my ears. I shook my head to clear it.

Across the room, the curtains billowed with the cool mountain breeze. A shiver ran through me as I noticed the quilted comforter, discarded in a heap on the floor beside my pillow. Stretching, I pushed myself upright, the old wood floor groaning beneath me as I tossed the quilt back onto the bed.

Dawn broke over the eastern horizon, a faint glow illuminating the dark silhouette of the Appalachian mountains, still bathed in the soft light of the moon.

I glanced at the clock on the nightstand. 6:45 AM.

My fingers traced the hollow of my throat, and another shiver wracked my body. There was no way in hell I could fall back asleep—not with the heavy reminder of what was waiting for me. I yanked open my suitcase, slipped into my robe, and hurried down the hallway.

Gran's family had owned this house for generations—long before the Civil War. Over time, modern additions had been made—new appliances, electricity, but the farmhouse's timeless charm had always remained. . . until now.

It broke my heart to see it like this, knowing how bright, vibrant, and well-loved it had once been.

I stepped into the kitchen. The wood floors beneath my feet were scarred and worn, the grain nearly erased in places. I sighed, the weight of guilt pressing on me. If I had never left, if I had stayed—would things have turned out differently?

Peering out the kitchen window, the shattered remains of a hand-painted gate lay scattered across the backyard. Standing on tiptoes, I leaned over the sink, my eyes tracing the sullen, overgrown patch of earth. What had once been a lively, flourishing garden was now a wild tangle of weeds.

I closed my eyes, blinking back the tears. The blue twilight of dawn was beginning to fade, and I wasn't going to waste the morning drowning in self-pity.

Shaking off the sorrow, I forced myself into motion. I yanked open the cupboard door and grabbed the first mug I could find. The ceramic handle was painted blue, adorned with two smudged pink handprints twisted into a lopsided heart. Beneath each print were mine and Katherine's initials. Another sob caught in my throat, threatening to break free.

I set the mug down and spun the lazy Susan, searching for the coffee. Everything was exactly where it had always been. My gaze landed on the small red tin of instant coffee nestled between the flour and sugar.

Reaching for it, I stopped. Something behind the oats and cornmeal caught my attention. I could see its shadow. Kneeling, I peered into the cupboard's dark corner. The shadow blinked.

A scream tore from me as a large squirrel shot across cans of baked beans, knocking over a bag of flour in its frantic escape. I fell back onto the floor, slamming my hands down as a massive cloud of white dust exploded into the air, temporarily blinding me. The squirrel, leaving a trail of tiny white paw prints, disappeared around the corner.

I coughed, sending more flour into the air as I struggled to sit up. Flour coated my hair, my robe, even my eyelashes. I looked like I'd been in a fight with a bakery.

Staring at my dusted hands, something inside me shifted. A laugh bubbled up, deep and booming, shaking my whole body. It echoed through the small kitchen, but just as quickly as it came, it faded into a heavy sob. Tears streamed down my flour-streaked face, carving dirty trails through the powder.

What a fucking mess.

My shoulders trembled as I spiraled into a full-blown breakdown. When the shaking finally eased, leaving nothing but a dry heave, I wiped my sleeve across my face, only smearing the flour further.

I sat there for a moment, breathing heavily. I could hear the low hum of the house settling, the creaks and groans of its tired bones—as though the walls were mourning with me.

I took a deep breath, trying to steady myself, and stood up slowly. My body felt heavy, like I was dragging the weight of everything—every mistake, every regret, with me.

With a shaky hand, I reached for the mug, not bothering to wipe away the flour on my face, and poured hot water over the instant coffee. The steam rose in a slow spiral, filling the kitchen with the familiar, comforting scent. It didn't fix anything, but for a moment, it was enough to make me feel human again.

Warm sunlight poured through the window, casting a soft halo of light over Gran's urn where it rested on the coffee table.

"I'm going to fix this," I whispered, a small spark of hope, stirring in my chest. "The house, myself, everything."

It wouldn't be easy, but I was ready. And for the first time in a long time, I actually believed it.

One hour of intense scrubbing later and the kitchen was finally clean. After dealing with the flour mess, I spent fifteen minutes battling years of stubborn grease on the oven, ten more tossing out spoiled food, and a solid half hour cleaning out the fridge. The last five were dedicated to wiping down the counters.

My arms ached, my back protested, but overall, I was proud of myself for this small victory. Unfortunately, the same couldn't be said for myself. Sweat clung to my skin, gluing my hair to my powdery face. Grease stains marred my robe, and there was an odd smell coming from somewhere I couldn't identify.

I'd already emptied the trash and double-checked the fridge for anything moldy.

That's when it hit me. I *was* the smell.

It shouldn't have been a shock. I hadn't bothered to shower last night, and after thirty-six hours cooped up in a car with only brief rest-stop bathroom breaks, it was bound to catch up to me.

My hair was a mess, and a prickling sensation crawled across my skin, like a thousand tiny spiders dancing beneath the surface.

I needed a shower.

The thought of hot water rushing over me felt like heaven. I shot back upstairs, grabbing a pair of faded jeans and a loose cotton shirt, then padded down the hall to the bathroom.

Setting my clothes aside, I placed my hands on both sides of the porcelain sink and stared at myself in the mirror. Even through my floury mask, my face was noticeably thinner, not by much but enough to make a difference. My cheeks held a brighter pink, and my once faded freckles now danced vibrantly over the bridge of my nose.

I looked. . . like myself. The me before Jackson. It had been so long since I'd seen her, but I'd recognize her anywhere.

Taking a deep breath, I pulled back the shower curtain and twisted the knob, eager to feel the warmth of water against my skin. A pathetic whisper of a trickle emerged from the faucet, barely enough to wet my fingertips, let alone my entire body.

"Shit," I groaned, my voice tight with frustration. I faced the sink again, flooded with disappointment when I realized this was clearly more than a faulty fixture.

Sighing, I realized I'd have to brave the basement. Gran kept a junk bin in the linen closet, and I reluctantly grabbed a flashlight before making my way back downstairs.

The basement door creaked open, revealing a steep staircase that seemed to drop into darkness. The uneven, dirt floor stretched out beneath me. I swallowed hard, my heart thudding with dread.

Somewhere, something clanged. My stomach lurched. I gripped the flashlight tighter. Suddenly I was eight years old again, Kat and I daring each other to brave the dark.

"You're a grown-ass woman," I told myself. "You can do this."

The wooden steps groaned under my weight. My heart pounded in my chest. Another clang rang out from somewhere unseen, and I jumped, nearly tripping on the last step. Dust swirled in the beam of the flashlight, casting long, eerie shadows across the jagged stone walls. I swallowed, licking my lips as I forced myself further into this dreaded hell.

The smell hit me then—a mixture of damp earth and mildew, followed by the unmistakable sound of something dripping. I swept the flashlight across the exposed pipes, their rust-eaten surfaces catching the weak light. Nothing looked broken, but how the hell would I know?

The dripping grew louder, feeding my irrational fear. I could call a plumber—I *should* call a plumber, but in my stubbornness, I was determined to figure this out myself, to prove I could handle it.

My flashlight landed on a dark puddle in the corner near the furnace, revealing a watery mess snaking its way across the dirt floor. The drip was coming from above, where a loose bolt held two pipes together.

Simple enough, I thought.

Across the basement, a rusty toolbox sat on a shelf, half-hidden by cobwebs. Its red paint was peeling like sunburned skin, and the metal hinges were so old they looked ready to disintegrate.

Inside, buried beneath random tools and scattered screws, I found a small wrench. Gripping it tightly, I braced myself against the pipe, the cold metal biting into my palm.

With the wrench in hand, I reached up to tighten the bolt. A low groan echoed from the wall, followed by a sickening crack. Then, with no warning, the pipe exploded.

A geyser of water shot through the broken pipe, soaking me from head to toe. I staggered backward.

Through the freezing spray, my numb fingers fumbled along the wall until I found the valve. I twisted and yanked, but the ancient wheel refused to budge. Desperation clawed at me as I wrestled with it. Finally, with a sharp twist, the water stopped.

I coughed, wiping water from my face. For a moment, I stood there, drenched and frozen in shock. Mud clung to my bare feet, and water dripped from my hair.

I didn't know whether to laugh or cry.

I wiped the mud from my cheeks, grimacing as the basement's musty stench clung to my skin. I didn't even want to think about what I looked like. Clearly, I wasn't going to fix this mess on my own—and at this point, a shower wasn't a luxury. It was a need.

With what little dignity I had left, I dragged myself upstairs, picked up the phone, and did the one thing I swore I wouldn't.

I called for help.

Sixteen

"WHAT DO YOU MEAN YOU can't get here until next week?" I snapped into the phone. "I can't go a whole week without water."

The man on the other end was losing his patience, but I didn't care. "Look, lady, I'm sorry, but we're booked solid until Monday. You'll have to find someone else."

"There *is* no one else!" I shot back, frustration creeping into my voice. I exhaled sharply. "I'm sorry, it's been a hell of a day, and I really need this fixed." There was a long pause. "Hello?" I called out, sure he had hung up on me.

"I'm still here. You said you're in Windhaven?"

I nodded without thinking, realizing he couldn't see me. "Yes, that's right."

"A friend of mine owns a contracting company nearby. He might be able to help. I'll call him. He's pretty flexible, might be able to come out today or tomorrow," he offered with fraying patience.

I pinched the bridge of my nose, exhaustion weighing on me. Tomorrow was better than Monday. "Thank you," I said, a sense of relief settling in.

"Don't thank me yet," he warned. "And for the love of God, don't tighten any more bolts, ok?"

The trickle from the faucet was barely enough to dampen the rag, but it was all I had. I scrubbed my arms and chest, working to eliminate the grime that clung to my skin, but my hair remained a tangled mess of grease. Digging around under the bathroom sink, I found a can of cornstarch—one of Gran's old tricks. I sprinkled it generously over my hair, and like magic, the worst of the oiliness disappeared. With a sigh of relief, I braided it tightly and let it rest over my shoulder.

I couldn't bring myself to put on anything nice, so I slid into a worn pair of jeans and grabbed an oversized t-shirt I only ever wore to bed.

Afterward I marched through the house, yanking open windows like I could chase the heaviness out with the wind. The scent of fresh earth and blossoming flowers filled the rooms, sweeping away the mustiness that had settled in.

It struck me then, how long it had been since I'd felt the change of seasons. San Diego was always the same—mildly chilly winters, but mostly hot, dry, and sunny every day.

I spent the next few hours cleaning—battling dust bunnies with the broom, shaking out blankets, tossing whatever trash I could find. It was something to do, a way to keep my thoughts from spiraling.

After vacuuming the whole house, I focused on the large stone fireplace. It was original, one of the few things that hadn't changed since it was built. Gran used it often to warm the house during the harsh mountain winters.

Grabbing the last garbage bag, I made a mental note to pick up more as I knelt in front of the hearth. Gran kept an arrangement of tools nearby. I picked up the small iron shovel, along with the broom and started clearing away the ashes.

Everything was coated in black soot. I scraped at the back of the fireplace, using the shovel to pry away stubborn debris clinging to the ancient stones. It was easier than I expected—until a loose stone tumbled free. White dust billowed up like snow, settling with a dramatic *thud* into the ash pile.

I coughed, waving away the dust cloud. First, the flour explosion in the kitchen, now this. My clothes were already dusted with soot. At this rate, I was starting to resemble a ghost in a low budget horror film. I threw a glance over my shoulder at Grans urn.

"No offense," I mumbled, more to myself than to her memory. The last thing I needed to add to my mounting list of problems was talking to the dead—or offending them.

Once the dust settled, I reached into the dark opening, halting when my fingers brushed against something unexpected. A dark leather strap stuck out from a crack in the stone where it had fallen away. Moving carefully to avoid disturbing the ash further, I tugged gently. The strap gave way, revealing more of whatever was hidden on the other side.

Curious, I pulled again, dislodging another stone. I worked slowly, shifting more rocks until all that remained was a deep, shadowy hole. My breath caught as I finally freed the strap completely, uncovering a small, worn leather satchel.

I stared at the unfamiliar object now in my hands. "Where the hell did this come from?" I whispered. The strap was frayed, the bag faded. Its brass buckles were tarnished with age.

My hands trembled as I unbuckled it. Inside, nestled among the cracked leather, was a bundle of envelopes tied with a faded ribbon. The faint scent of dried lavender mingled with the lingering smell of smoke as I carefully unfolded the top letter.

The script was elegant, a spidery dance of inky loops and swirls but still legible. The date at the top sent a shiver through me. They were written over several months, ending in late 1863.

A tremor of excitement ran through me as I began to read. *"My Dearest Charlotte. . ."*

Seventeen

December 27th, 1863
West Virginia

My Dearest Charlotte,

It has only been months since I saw your face, yet it feels like a lifetime. I dream of you often, but even in dreams, your voice slips away like wind through trees. Your death was a cruel fate, but the hollowness of your absence lingers. I write to you not out of hope, but habit. Writing to you brings me solace, though Finn mocks me for it. He says it's a waste of time, but time is all we have. Time to wait, to wither, to die.

Do you remember that spring by the Sycamore Grove, where the wildflowers tangled around your ankles and you told me you feared nothing so long as I stood beside you? I've carried that moment with me through every blood-soaked field and silent night. It reminds me of something worth surviving for.

I sometimes imagine you waiting there still, knees tucked to your chest, sunlight in your hair, humming that tune your mother used to sing when the sky turned amber with dusk. I try to hum it now, though I fear I've forgotten the words.

The war has taken so much, Charlotte. Brothers. Futures. Sanity. But I refuse to let it take you. Not truly. So long as I write, you remain. So long as I remember, you live.

I write from the cold ridges of the Appalachians, where the Confederacy creeps northward. Winter bares its ugly teeth, and already I feel its chill settle in my bones. These mountains are as deadly as they are beautiful, and we've lost many men to their wrath. Still, we march. Between the cold and the threat of attack, the days are long and unforgiving, but in every breath, I carry your memory. Whether peace finds me, or death claims me first, I pray it brings me back to you.

Your loving husband,
James

Twelve love letters, all achingly beautiful, sat sprawled out before me on the living room floor. They overflowed with passion, with a tenderness so profound it felt almost wrong to read them. But I couldn't help myself. A love like this only existed in books and movies, and yet these two clearly shared a connection that defied even death.

I didn't know what it felt like to be loved like that—to be cherished so deeply, that your spirit finds solace even when the world around you is crumbling.

I carefully refolded the letters, their paper crackling with age. Slipping them back into the satchel, I hesitated—briefly tempted to return them to the fireplace, to let them rest beside the spirits of Charlotte and James. But something about that felt wrong, like snuffing out a fragile light. A local museum would be perfect—maybe one dedicated to the memory of the Civil War. Perhaps they could even track down any living descendants. For now, I placed the satchel on the kitchen table, twelve silent witnesses to a love story that had outlived a century.

An ache stirred in my stomach as late afternoon melted into evening. I rummaged through Grans cupboards only to be met with empty shelves—save for a lonely jar of pickled onions and a dented can of something that vaguely resembled beans.

I must've tossed out more expired food than I realized during my manic cleaning spree.

I could order a pizza, but that didn't solve the rest of my problems. I was still in need of things like shampoo, trash bags—maybe even a bottle of wine or two. A trip into town was unavoidable.

Upstairs, I found the envelope my sister gave me and tucked a few twenty-dollar bills into my pocket. Anxiety tightened in my chest as I refolded it. This wouldn't last. Not forever. Eventually I'd need to get a job—something I hadn't had in years. I thought back to my last summer in Windhaven, working at the local Frosty Boy flipping burgers and scooping ice cream. What kind of job could I even get now? My resume was practically a blank page.

The thought of going into town filled me with cold dread. News of Gran's death had surely made the rounds by now, but in Windhaven, old news lingered like humidity. Still, eleven years had passed since I left. Time had carved its changes into me. I was older now—heavier. The sharp lines of my youth had softened, blurred by years of trying to hold myself together. I looked like someone still halfway between who they'd been and who they were trying to become.

With a sigh, I reached for my keys, the jangling sound loud in the quiet house. I wouldn't be in town for long. And besides, who would recognize me anyway?

Eighteen

Before

G RAN LIVED ON THE OUTSKIRTS of town—sheltered by the mountains and magnolia trees hugging her never ending driveway. You couldn't see the old farmhouse from the main road, but you knew it was there.

Everyone in Windhaven knew it was there.

Gran had a reputation. She was a spiritual woman, an eccentric woman. She spoke to the earth as if it were a living thing, and she threatened us with Karma instead of God. She danced in the rain, carried crystals in her pockets, and insisted on consulting her tarot cards before making any big decisions.

The squeak of my sneakers echoed loudly on the linoleum. Kat, her hand in Gran's, trailed behind me. My eyes darted to the aisle crammed with cheap toys and candy.

"Can I get a toy?" I asked Gran, batting my eyelashes.

With a smile, she glanced back and nodded. "What about you Kitty Kat? Want to tag along with your sister while I grab what we need?"

Kat shook her head. "I'd rather stay with you."

Gran gave her hand a firm squeeze, before turning to me. "Don't stray," she instructed, "I don't want to have to hunt you down later."

With a gleeful squeal, I skipped over to aisle twelve, where the Barbie knockoffs and generic Hot Wheels were waiting. However, I skidded to a stop a few feet away. A girl with hair as bright as sunlight was examining a miniature castle containing a tiny fairy princess.

"Hi," I approached, excited. "That's a really cool castle."

She looked up, her blue eyes mirroring the vibrancy of her hair. "One day, I'm going to live in a castle just like this," she smiled, revealing a gap toothed grin.

"My names Emily," I told her. Gran's reputation made it difficult to make friends. My closest pals were Katherine, and whatever salamanders I managed to catch beneath the floorboards in the old barn.

"I'm Lilly," she replied, her gaze returning to the castle. We stood there for a moment, both of us lost in its miniature world.

"Do you think she's real?" I whispered, a mix of playful curiosity and genuine wonder.

Lilly's eyes stayed fixed on the princess. "I hope so," she breathed.

"My Gran says magic is everywhere," I confided. "People just don't see it. Maybe she comes alive at night, eating all the candy and having tea parties with the other toys!"

Lilly giggled, and that made me giggle too.

Then, a woman with eyes like chipped steel appeared, yanking Lilly away with a harsh tug. "It's time to go," she snapped, her unfriendly gaze lingering on me. "Now."

"But mom," Lilly protested, "This is my new friend, Emily."

Her mother didn't even try to lower her voice. "That's Mae Hart's granddaughter. You are not to associate yourself with them. Do you understand?"

Lilly's eyes filled with sad understanding. "Yes Mommy," her struggle ceasing as her mother dragged her away.

Something cracked in my chest, like someone had dropped a heavy stone on it.

"Emily?" Gran's soft voice startled me. I blinked back tears as I picked up the miniature castle, carefully setting it back on the shelf. "Don't you want it?" She asked. I shook my head, unable to speak without crying.

Katherine gently slipped her hand into mine. "Come on, let's go."

The car ride home was quiet. Gran didn't push me to talk, but she kept glancing at me, concern etched on her face. Everything she'd said about magic felt pointless now. After what happened, I couldn't help but wonder if there was any magic powerful enough to change how people saw us.

That's when I realized we lived on the outskirts of town for a reason—because we were never truly welcome in it.

Nineteen

I navigated the old Ford Focus into the small parking lot outside Hank's grocery store, grabbing a basket from the metal corral before heading inside.

A wave of nostalgia slammed into me as I scanned the familiar aisles, the faded signage dangling from aluminum rafters under buzzing fluorescent lights.

I kept my gaze forward, doing my best to avoid eye contact as I started tossing random items into the cart. Macaroni and cheese. Bread. A jar of peanut butter. I needed to stretch the cash Katherine had given me, but I also wanted to avoid another trip as long as possible.

Moving quickly, I crossed off items from the crumpled list I'd stuffed in my pocket before leaving the house. Shampoo. Trash Bags. Bottled Water.

Once I was done, I rolled toward the back of the store. Hank's was the only place in town that sold beer and wine—anything stronger meant a trip to Charleston, which I wasn't interested in making.

I didn't bother reading the labels as I grabbed three or four bottles of wine, lining them up in the cart before heading for the register.

The cashier, a young woman with fiery red hair held back by a pink headband, scanned my items.

"That'll be $46.87," she said, snapping her gum as I pulled out three twenty's and my ID. "California, huh?" I nodded impatiently. "Always wanted to go to California," she added with another pop.

I gave her a tight smile, waiting for her to hand over my change.

"Emily Hart. . . is that you?" A thick, syrupy voice cut through the air. I stiffened. "Oh my *gosh*, it is. Alabama, look who it is—the infamous Hart girl."

Georgia Baker, arm-in-arm with her twin sister Alabama, sauntered to the end of the register.

"I heard a little rumor you were back in town, but I just couldn't believe it," Georgia purred. "Where's your sister? I don't think I've ever seen one of you without the other."

The cashier finally handed over my change. "Katherine couldn't make it," I said, turning to face them.

"Couldn't? Or didn't want to?" Georgia chuckled. My hands clenched tighter around the cart handle. "Oh, lighten up," she sighed, tossing her dark hair over her shoulder. "I'm only joking."

Alabama blinked, her brown eyes magnified behind her bottle-thick glasses. "We heard about Mae," she mumbled, like simply saying her name was a sin. "Sorry about your Gran."

Georgia gave me a pitying smile. "Yes, so very sorry. What a tragedy."

Something in her tone said she wasn't sorry at all.

"Thanks," I said, trying to squeeze past them, but Georgia stepped in front of me, blocking the way.

"If it makes you feel any better, we host a prayer group on Thursday nights over at the church," she said, her voice dripping with sugar. "We'd love to add your Gran to our prayers. You could come too, if you'd like."

Now it was my turn to choke back a laugh. Gran hated church—and made no secret of it. She used to say religion was the most successful cult the world had ever known.

"I appreciate the thought, but Gran's dead. I don't think she's in much need of prayer anymore."

Georgia's bright expression faltered. "Well, Emily, that may be true—but even the dearly departed can still use a few prayers." Her gaze flicked down to the bottles of wine in my cart. "Some more than others, it seems."

Of all the people I could've run into, why did it have to be the Baker twins? Their dad was the town preacher, all fire and brimstone. Their mother, a beloved Sunday school teacher, loved Jesus in public, but in private she worshipped other spirits—namely Jack and Jim.

Alabama adjusted her glasses. "In case you change your mind," she said, offering me a white pamphlet with a little black cross on the front.

I took it—not because I wanted to, but because I desperately needed this encounter to be over.

"Well, this has been a lovely surprise, but Allie and I need to get going. We're in charge of this year's church potluck and there's still so much to do." Georgia looped her arm through her sister's. "It was really great seeing you, Emily. We should catch up again soon."

I stood still, watching as they disappeared through the first set of doors and out of sight. Once they were gone, I stepped into the breezeway, slipping my buggy into place with the others. I gathered my bags, looping them over my arm carefully, when I heard Alabama's voice drift in from outside.

"Do you think she'll come?" she asked, her voice quiet and unsure.

I stood rooted to the spot. I didn't want to listen, but I didn't want them to see me either.

"Of course she won't," Georgie replied.

"Then why'd you invite her?"

"Because I was being polite," Georgia bit out, irritated. "I swear Allie, sometimes I wonder if the Lord forgot to give you a lick of sense, or if I'm the one being punished for it."

"Daddy always says—"

"Daddy would invite the devil himself to supper if he thought it'd get him somewhere," Georgia said with a snort. "Honestly, it's a blessing that old woman's gone. That family's never brought anything but trouble. I heard from Ruth, down at Betty's Salon, that Katherine ran off to California, and then Emily followed her out there, only to wind up married to one of the richest men in the country."

Alabama cleared her throat. "If she's so rich, what's she doing living back at that run-down farmhouse?"

Georgia gave a shrug. "Beats me. But I didn't see a ring on her finger, did you?"

"I wasn't really look—"

"Oh shut up, Allie," Georgia snapped, her voice sharpening. "Something's off about that whole situation, and I'm gonna find out what."

Twenty

The screen door slammed shut behind me, echoing the rage boiling in my chest. Georgia's words slithered back into my mind.

That family's never brought anything but trouble.

I rolled my eyes. Suddenly I wasn't very hungry anymore.

I dumped the groceries onto the counter, searching for the one thing that might take the edge off. The wine bottle was heavy in my hands as I yanked the cork free. I didn't bother with a glass, but instead, tilted the bottle straight to my lips, letting the wine carve a hot, bitter trail down my throat.

When it was clear one sip wasn't enough, I chased it down with another, then another until the edges of the world softened and my anger numbed. I was never much of a drinker. Especially not after watching Jackson slowly drown himself in the stuff night after night. But wine?

Wine was made from grapes, so technically I was just keeping up with my daily fruit intake.

Looking out the kitchen window, I surveyed the garden, now soaked in amber and violet hues of the setting sun. The mountains in the distance cast long shadows across the earth, silhouetted against a rich colored sky.

Another swig. This time, it went down like water.

I turned away, pressing my back to the sink as my eyes landed on the table where several love letters sat, addressed to a woman who would never read them. The wine buzzed through my veins as I pushed off the counter and made my way over, collapsing into a dining chair with a graceless *thud*.

"You and I. . . we're not so different, are we?" I slurred, speaking to the ghost of James. A hiccup slipped out, and I lazily licked a trail of red merlot that had dribbled down the neck of the now half-empty bottle.

I picked up one of the letters, taking care not to stain the paper. James's handwriting curled across the page like ivy clinging to stone.

"Your wife died. My husband turned out to be a raging asshole," I mused, my voice thick with wine and bitterness. "But hey. . . he's gone now, so, same difference."

Jackson hadn't died, but he might as well have. He died to me. It didn't really matter—the result was the same.

A wave of nausea, unrelated to the alcohol, hit me.

James, with his grief etched into every word, poured his heart out—knowing, deep down, that there would never be an answer. No reply. No comfort. No closure.

And me? I was nursing my own kind of heartbreak—a slower, more corrosive kind. Less tragic, maybe, but just as ruinous.

The bottle tilted dangerously close to empty and my head was swimming.

Fuck it.

I lurched to my feet, knocking the chair over behind me. Tearing open Gran's junk drawer, I rifled through old batteries and takeout menus until I found a pen and a crumpled pad of paper. I wouldn't get closure. But maybe one of us could.

I gathered James's letters and set them aside, careful not to tear them. My hand trembled as I focused on the page, trying to make my handwriting neat—not like it mattered, he'd never read it. But this wasn't for him, it was for me. An opportunity to shed my emotions, to process my own grief.

The wine had gone sour on my tongue as I pressed the pen down and began to write.

May 12th, 2023

Dear James,

You don't know me. I mean, I'm writing this nearly 200 years in the future, so. . . yeah, not exactly a typical introduction. I found what I think was your old bag hidden in my grandma's fireplace, and inside were your letters to Charlotte. I read them all. I know I probably shouldn't have, but I did.

I don't know exactly what you went through, but I get it. I've lost everyone I've ever loved. My mom, my gran, my sister. . . even my husband. That last one was probably for the best, though. You spend so long clinging to people just to keep yourself from floating away, and then one day, you look around and realize there's no one left to tether you anymore. That's where I'm at. Floating alone. Now I'm trying to figure out how to be okay with that.

I can't stop thinking about how much you loved her. I don't think I've ever had that. I don't think I've ever really loved myself either, which sounds dramatic, but it's true. Now that I'm alone, I'm kind of realizing I don't even know how. I hope, wherever your wife is, she knows how deeply she was loved. I think we all deserve to know that kind of love at least once in our lives.

It's strange. I never believed in fate before. But now, holding your letters, it feels like I was meant to find them. Like I was meant to find you. I don't know what ended up happening to you, but I hope wherever you are, you and Charlotte found each other again.

Your words reminded me that even when everything falls apart, something beautiful can still remain. Thank you for that. I needed it.

Your friend from the future,
Emily Hart

Twenty One

My head throbbed. Sunlight stabbed through a gap in my curtains, landing hard on my face. I groaned, rolled onto my back, and ran my tongue across my wine-stained teeth. My mouth tasted like something had died in it. Classic hangover.

"Fuck," I groaned, my voice a gravely rasp.

Water. I needed water.

Slowly, I pushed myself upright—trying to keep the nausea I was feeling at bay. *Why did I do this to myself?* I already knew why, but sometimes excuses are easier to swallow than the truth.

I hugged my arms to my chest and shuffled down the stairs. Spring in the Appalachians can be very temperamental, and I hugged myself tighter as the morning chill glazed over my skin.

"Water and coffee," I mumbled, my eyes squinting against the haze of sleep as I stumbled into the kitchen.

The rich scent of ground coffee bloomed beneath my nose as I scooped a generous spoonful into the filter. I grabbed the handmade mug from the counter, added a splash of cream, and hovered by the machine, willing it to brew faster. When it was finally done, I cradled the cup in both hands like something sacred.

Steam curled up in lazy tendrils as I took that first, blissful sip. My gaze drifted over the rim of the mug, scanning the kitchen—until it landed on the leather satchel, still resting on the table. My memory slowly trickled in—followed by a hot flush of embarrassment.

I had written a letter to a Civil War soldier. A *dead* Civil War soldier.

If my head wasn't still pounding, I would have laughed. Desperation doesn't get much clearer than that. At least no one else was here to see it.

I set the mug down and walked to the table. Maybe it was time to pack all this away. I'd call around this afternoon and find a museum to donate them to. That was where they belonged. But first, I needed to burn the one I had written. The one no one was ever meant to see. I didn't even want to see it again.

I reached for the satchel and unfastened the clasp, fully expecting to see my crumpled, wine-stained letter nestled inside.

It wasn't there.

Instead, a fresh envelope rested at the bottom with my name written across it in delicate, spidery script.

My heart lurched. How much had I actually had to drink?

I stared at the letter, the buzz of my hangover fading beneath a creeping chill.

"This isn't happening," I whispered.

I looked down at the satchel again, a coil of dread tightening in my chest. "I've officially lost my mind."

I brushed my fingertips over my name. It didn't seem real—like touching a bruise I hadn't known was there.

The rational part of my brain—the part that usually functioned, even if haphazardly, scrambled for answers. It pointed to the wine bottle, the throbbing headache, the haze of a morning hangover. It offered up simple explanations like an elaborate prank, or a rare form of temporal displacement induced by. . . well, I wasn't entirely sure, but cheap alcohol seemed like a solid culprit.

I should open it, right? I mean, it *was* addressed to me after all. It would be rude *not* to read it.

Hesitantly, I tore the envelope open. The brittle paper crackled like dry autumn leaves beneath my fingers.

"Dearest Miss Hart. . ."

I sucked in a breath.

Nope. No way. This wasn't happening.

I pressed my thumb and forefinger to the bridge of my nose and closed my eyes. I needed to sit down. I needed to breathe.

I set the letter on the table and dropped into the nearest chair, letting my head fall in my hands. Maybe if I counted backward, I'd snap out of whatever hangover induced hallucination this was.

"Ten. . . nine. . . eight. . . seven. . ." I cracked one eye open.

My name still stared up at me.

"Six, five, four, three, two, one," I rattled off in a rush.

Nothing happened. I was still awake and still insane.

A sudden crunch of gravel, followed by the low growl of an engine, cut through the silence. My head jerked up.

Shit.

I jumped to my feet and shoved the letter back into the satchel, trying to dial down the panic fluttering in my chest. Yanking the fridge open, I shoved the satchel inside and slammed the door before I could second-guess myself.

A white pickup barreled down the driveway, kicking up a cloud of dust before it rolled to a stop beside the Focus. *LG Contracting* was stenciled across the side in bold black letters.

Still wearing yesterday's clothes, I looked like shit and smelled like a bar. Thank God I wasn't trying to impress anyone.

I stepped out onto the porch, bracing against the sharp morning breeze as I carefully shut the half-broken screen door behind me. Shading my eyes with one hand, I squinted at the windshield, ready to give some halfhearted smile and a *sorry-I'm-a-mess* apology.

But the second the driver stepped out, my smile withered.

A jolt of nausea twisted in my stomach. The truck door slammed, and I stopped breathing.

He was tall, always had been, but the lanky frame I remembered had filled out with thick muscle.

A nervous heat crept up my neck, as I watched him walk toward me.

The morning sun kissed his chestnut skin, casting golden light over the stubble lining his jaw and I blinked several times, hoping this ghost of a man would disappear, but it only brought him closer.

"Emily?" he said, voice rough with age but still familiar.

The sound of it nearly knocked me off my feet, and I grabbed the porch railing to steady myself.

"Logan?" I choked, disbelief coating my throat like syrup.

Then he smiled—those damn dimples still carved into his cheeks. "It's been a long time."

Twenty Two

Before

THE SILVER BELL ON MY bike jingled as I pedaled towards Mr. Abernathy's hardware store. The sound of it clashed with the chime of loose change stuffed inside my pocket as I made a sharp left turn onto Main Street.

Today was allowance day, and once a week Gran would let us ride our bikes into town to purchase penny candy at the local hardware store. Usually, Katherine would ride beside me, our tires in sync like always. But today, she stayed behind.

"I'm fourteen now, Emily. I'm too old for penny candy," she glanced up from her magazine and rolled her eyes. "You're getting too old too."

So I rode alone, the sun pressing hot against the back of my neck as I fought off the disappointment of my sister's absence. She'd been distant lately—too focused on herself to pay any attention to me.

I reached the store and slipped my bike into the rack out front. The bell above the door gave a merry jingle as I stepped inside. Mr. Abernathy offered a quick nod from behind the counter before turning back to the customer he was helping.

The air smelled like sawdust and oil as I made my way through the store. Toward the back wall stood the candy display—fully stocked and waiting. I took my time picking the perfect mix. Three strawberry bonbons, a marble-sized jawbreaker, and a chewy grape lollipop. I added a few of Kat's favorites too, just in case she changed her mind.

"That'll be twenty-five cents," Mr. Abernathy said, his voice warm. He reminded me of Santa Claus, with snow white hair and soft blue eyes that crinkled when he smiled.

I placed two dimes and a nickel on the counter and waited patiently as he slid the candies into a small paper bag and handed it over.

"Thanks," I said, already trying to decide which sweet to unwrap first as I stepped back into the sun.

Outside, a group of kids leaned against the brick wall. I didn't know their names, but I'd seen a few of them around school.

"Well, well, well. Look who it is," a blonde girl sneered, her voice carrying across the quiet street. "If it isn't the orphan freak." I flinched when her eyes met mine. "Going solo today? Where's your babysitter?" The others laughed behind her.

I swallowed hard, my mouth suddenly dry. "Leave me alone," I mumbled, trying to steer my bike past them.

She stepped forward, still smirking. "Sure, I'll leave you alone. . . if you give me what's in the bag."

I held the paper sack tighter. "No," I said, shaking my head.

She moved in front of me, blocking my path. "Give me the candy, freak."

"No way!" I shot back. "Get your own."

Her lips curled into a mocking grin. "What are you gonna do? Cry to your mommy? Oh wait. . . that's right. You don't have one."

Tears stung my eyes, but I lifted my chin and held them back.

"Aww, are you gonna cry?" she mocked, and her friends laughed again. "Is the little orphan freak gonna cry?"

"Come on, Maddie, give it a rest," a boy's voice cut in. He was taller than the others, but with a softer face that made him look younger. "Leave her alone."

Maddie turned and glared at him. The rest of the group went quiet.

"Whatever," she snapped. "I was getting bored anyway. Let's go."

I gave the boy a grateful smile and mounted my bike, but before I could escape, Maddie spun back and shoved me to the ground.

I hit the sidewalk hard. The paper bag tore open, scattering my candy like confetti across the dusty pavement. Blood bloomed at my knee, and grit clung to my elbow as I struggled to sit up.

Everyone laughed. Everyone except the boy.

Crying, I jumped back on my bike and pedaled home as fast as my legs could carry me—leaving the candy behind.

"What happened?" Gran asked, lightly dabbing my bloody knee with a tissue.

I didn't want to tell her about Maddie and her friends. I didn't want her to know that they'd called me a freak. I didn't want her to know that I was angry—not just at them, but at her too. Angry at the world for mom dying and sending us here, and how I hated that people thought we were weird because Gran *was* a little weird.

"It's nothing," I said, wiping the tears and snot from my face. "I just fell off my bike."

Gran raised an eyebrow, but didn't push.

"I hate it here," I huffed, crossing my arms over my chest. "I want to go home."

"You *are* home," she said gently, pressing the Band-Aid down over my scrape. "There, all better."

I slid off the kitchen chair and stomped toward the door, anger still bubbling in my chest. My bike was lying in the middle of the driveway and Gran had warned me that next time I left it out, she'd run it over. Gran never made empty threats.

I heard the crunch of tires and turned to see the boy from earlier pedaling down the driveway—a fresh, paper bag clutched tightly in his hand.

"I'm sorry about earlier," he said, rolling to a stop. "That wasn't cool."

I stared at him, unsure what to say.

"I tried to get the same stuff you had, but they were out of jawbreakers. I hope you like Lemonheads," he grinned, holding the bag out to me.

I took the bag slowly, peeking inside at the rainbow of candy. "Thanks."

"I'm Logan," he continued without me asking.

"Emily," I replied, slipping a strawberry bonbon into my mouth. I held out the bag. "Want one?"

He took one and we sat down together on the porch steps, the warm wood creaking softly beneath us.

"Your friends aren't very nice," I said, twisting the wrapper between my fingers.

"They're not my friends."

"Then why do you hang out with them?" I asked, watching him closely.

Logan shrugged. "It's better than being at home."

The way he said it made my chest hurt a little. There was more to that story, but I figured he'd tell me when he was ready.

I popped a sucker into my mouth, letting the tartness settle on my tongue. "So that Maddie girl. . ." I started. "What's up her butt?"

Logan glanced down at his scuffed sneakers, the laces frayed and uneven. "Her name's Madeline McBride. She's the mayor's daughter. Her mom's on the city council, so their family pretty much runs this town."

"Oh," I tilted my head slightly. "Isn't she going to be mad at you now?"

The late afternoon sun cast long, golden shadows across the porch. Logan stood, wiping his hands on his jeans. "Maybe," he said, reaching for his bike. "Guess I'll find out." He straddled the frame, "Listen, I gotta go, but maybe I'll see you at school?"

I nodded, watching as he pedaled down the driveway, the wheels kicking up tiny clouds of dust as he disappeared behind the curtain of magnolia trees.

The screen door creaked open behind me and Gran poked her head out. "Where'd your friend go?"

I climbed the porch steps, ignoring the sting in my knee as I passed by her. "Home," I said, a hint of a smile in my voice. "But he'll be back."

Twenty Three

Now

LOGAN'S HANDS SMOOTHED OVER THE last of the repair tape, patching up the broken pipe.

"It's just a temporary fix," he said, catching me staring. "You're going to need to replace these pipes. But the epoxy should hold for a bit."

Eleven years. That's how long it had been since I'd last seen Logan Graham. And now, here he was, coming to my rescue again.

"Thanks, Logan." My voice wavered a little more than I liked.

"I heard you were back in town." He straightened, his eyes meeting mine briefly before turning to gather his tools. "I'm sorry to hear about Gran."

I cleared my throat. "Yeah, well. . . that's life, I guess."

"She was a good woman," he offered kindly. "Made the best damn pot roast I've ever had." That made me smile. "So, when's the funeral?"

"No funeral," I said with a shrug. "She didn't want one. Said she wanted to be returned to the earth the natural way."

"Sounds like her," he said with a short laugh, and we started up the stairs together.

When we reached the landing, Logan set his toolbox on the kitchen counter. "Mind if I bother you for a glass of water? I want to make sure everything is working the way it should."

I nodded, grabbed a glass from the shelf, and turned on the tap—nearly crying with relief when the soft sound of water sputtered from the faucet.

Logan thanked me as I handed him the glass. "Doing some remodeling?" he asked, glancing at the pile of stones still on the floor near the fireplace.

I thought about the satchel still in the fridge, then quickly shrugged it off. "Sort of. More like a distraction really. It gets pretty quiet when you're here by yourself."

His gold-flecked eyes met mine as he set the empty glass on the counter. "Where's Katherine? I figured she'd be helping you with all this."

"Kats with her family. It's just me," I said simply.

"Alone?" he asked, tilting his head.

A flicker of irritation rose in my chest. "Why are you asking so many questions?"

He gave a slight smirk, clearly amused by my annoyance. "Didn't realize I was poking a bruise."

I crossed my arms over my chest. "What's that supposed to mean?"

"Nothing," he chuckled—reaching for his toolbox again. "It's just good to see some things haven't changed."

"Excuse me?" I shot back. "You don't know anything about me."

Logan raised an eyebrow. "Are you sure about that?"

I started to respond, then thought better of it. "So, you're a contractor now?"

He glanced down at his dirt-covered khakis. "Pays the bills," he shrugged.

Now it was my turn to raise a brow. "You're going to have to give me more than that."

I didn't have to spell it out—he knew exactly what I meant. The pause that followed said enough. He ran a hand ran over his head, a nervous habit, and guilt crept up on me for pressing.

"I got out of the Army a few years ago. Did two tours in Iraq before being discharged." He let out a short laugh, but it didn't carry any real humor. "After that, I figured I'd spend my time fixing things rather than tearing them apart. So. . . here I am."

Here he was, eleven years later, the same Logan—yet somehow entirely different.

"Anyway, good luck with all this," he nodded toward the mess of stones. "You should probably get a plumber out here sooner than later. Broken pipes aren't really my thing, and trust me, that's not something you want to let sit."

I searched for something to say—anything that might keep him from leaving. But nothing came. So I just nodded instead.

I watched as he eased the door open, bracing himself as a gust of wind ripped through the front porch. The hinges gave way and the screen door tore free, crashing to the floor with a sharp, metallic thud.

Logan froze, staring at it, before turning to me. "Seriously? How long's it been like that?"

"Since I got here," I admitted, embarrassed. "Honestly, the whole place is falling apart."

He sighed, bending down to prop the screen door against the side of the house. His eyes slowly moved to the warped boards on the porch steps. "I'll see about getting a new one. Might need to fix a few of these boards while I'm at it."

I fidgeted, uncertain. "Logan, you don't have to—"

"I want to," he cut in. "For Gran."

"Okay," I agreed, though part of me was still unsure. "For Gran."

Logan gave me a soft, almost sad smile. "It's good to see you again, Emily."

I nodded, swallowing the lump rising in my throat as I watched him head back to his truck.

He disappeared through a cloud of dust, and just like that, he was gone—leaving me alone with the memories I'd spent years trying to forget.

Turns out, some things, unlike busted pipes and broken doors, are surprisingly more difficult to fix.

Twenty Four

January 22nd, 1864
West Virginia

Dearest Miss Hart,

I scarcely know how to begin, for my hands tremble more from the weight of your words than from the cold. I found your note nestled within my satchel, though how it came to be there, I cannot say. The bag had been resting at my side for hours, yet when I reached for my tobacco, your letter was there, folded with great care, as if it had always belonged. I must admit, I find myself utterly bewildered. The date you penned, 2023. Can it truly be? Or has madness finally claimed me, as Finn so often warns? If it has, I will not fight it. I have done enough fighting for one lifetime. And so, for tonight, I choose to believe you are real.

This satchel was a gift from my late wife, Charlotte, God rest her soul. It was the last thing she placed in my hands before I left for the war. I have carried it with me every day since, through cold dawns and blistering marches, through hunger and gunfire and grief. It has weathered nearly as much as I have. How it ended up in your grandmother's hearth, as you say, I do not know. It baffles the senses. Yet, perhaps there are forces at work in this world, unseen threads that bind souls across time and sorrow.

When I first saw your letter, I confess I feared it a message from beyond the grave, Charlotte's spirit reaching back to me with some final word I had missed. Were it not for the difference in your penmanship, I might have cursed the thing and cast it into the fire, thinking it some cruel trick of memory. But your words were kind, laced with ache and honesty, and though I cannot explain how your letter reached me, I cannot deny the comfort it has brought me.

You spoke of your losses. Your mother, your grandmother, your sister, and your husband. Such sorrow, such hollowing. I am sorry beyond measure that you walk this world so burdened. But know this, to feel such pain is proof that your heart still beats with love. It may not feel like it now, but you are not broken. You are surviving. You are still here. That is no small thing. I cannot offer you wisdom, only this, loving someone with *your whole soul changes you, even after they are gone. That love does not vanish. It lingers in the spaces we do not expect.*

I will refrain from inquiring about the future, tempting as it is. Hope is a fickle thing, and I dare not carry more of it than I already do. Instead, I ask, who are you, truly? What led you to write to a man long dead, if dead I truly am?

Write again, if you are able. I am not certain if I am dreaming or if God has seen fit to open some strange door between our worlds. But I have known stranger things in war. Until then, know that I shall wait for your reply with great anticipation and a heart that, against all logic, feels a little less alone tonight.

Your friend in madness,
Captain James Percival Walker
2nd Regiment, Union Army

My eyes wandered across the swirling patterns on the ceiling. The clock on the nightstand glowed, *10:15.*

I had moved into Gran's room shortly after arriving, hoping the larger bed might offer more comfort. But after lying here for over an hour, I still couldn't sleep. I was restless—the familiar ache of unshed tears blooming in my chest.

Logan's face wouldn't leave me alone. Our awkward, abrupt exchange. That maddening smirk. The way he looked at me, like he recognized me and didn't all at once.

I turned onto my side, the clock's red glow bathing my face as thoughts spun wildly in and out of my mind.

What had he thought of me? Had he noticed the years gone by, etched into my face, or the extra weight I carried now? Or did some shadow of the girl he once knew still linger?

Each thought left behind a splinter of anxiety inside my chest. Time alone was time to think, and I couldn't stop myself from replaying every word over and over again until all that was left was a blur of regret.

Unease burrowed under my skin until I couldn't bear it any longer. I swung my legs over the side of the bed, shivering a little at the cold floor against my feet.

A week ago I was in San Diego—eager to escape a violent life. Now here I was, wondering if the cure might have been more harmful than the disease.

It wasn't *just* Logan—it was everything. My world shifted on its axis so quickly, leaving me to deal with the emotional whiplash.

I flicked on the lamp and crossed the room to the dresser where Captain Walker's bag sat, untouched. I had pulled it from the fridge as soon as Logan left.

Even now, standing there, rereading his words for what felt like the hundredth time, I still couldn't believe it. Things like this didn't happen. Not to people like me.

There had to be a logical explanation. Something that made sense. But logic was useless when the truth was staring me in the face.

A sharp crash splintered through the quiet house. I jerked my head toward the door. Another loud crack echoed down the hall.

I stood frozen, straining to hear, my heart hammering so loud it nearly drowned everything else out.

A creak, a light thud.

Oh god, oh god, oh god.

My eyes darted around the room, searching for anything to use as a weapon. The lamp was too heavy, and a framed photo of Katherine and I one youthful summer wasn't much better. My gaze settled on a heavy brass candlestick sitting next to the satchel on the dresser.

Good enough.

I grabbed it, the cold metal biting into my sweaty palms.

Be brave.

Moving slowly, I crept down the stairs, careful to avoid the creakiest floorboards. At the bottom, I tensed, every muscle tight. The front door was wide open, swinging in the wind, knocking against the frame.

"Hello?" I called out, voice cracking. "Is anyone there?"

Nothing. Only the low hum of the refrigerator bled through the silence.

Slowly, I edged closer and peeked outside. The moon hung low, throwing long, warped shadows across the porch.

"I've got a gun," I lied, holding the candlestick in a death grip as if it were enough of a defense against someone who might actually have one.

But there was no one there.

A cold breeze slipped past me, raising the hair on my arms. I stared at the door. Maybe I hadn't latched it properly. I was sure I had, but the old lock wasn't exactly reliable. Maybe a strong gust of wind had pushed it open.

It was a weak excuse, but it was something.

Still, I forced myself to step forward and yank the door shut, bolting it tight before hurrying back upstairs.

Sliding into bed, I gripped the candlestick against my chest. The logical part of me said it was just the wind, but the scared part wasn't so sure.

Every creak of the house, every shift of the wind outside, made me flinch. I squeezed the candlestick tighter.

"Be brave," I whispered over and over until, somehow, I finally drifted off to sleep.

Twenty Five

The Harrison County Animal Shelter sat on the outskirts of town, half-hidden by overgrown weeds. It resembled more of a neglected barn than a refuge, and could be easily missed if you weren't looking for it.

I stepped out into the glare of the afternoon sun, cicadas buzzing lazily somewhere off in the distance.

"This looks promising," I murmured, eyeing the chipped paint and grimy windows.

After last night, I'd decided that the whole "living alone" thing wasn't for me. Maybe it was time to get a roommate—one with fur and a bark loud enough to let me know if someone was creeping around.

I pushed open the heavy front door, the bell above it giving a half-hearted jingle. A chorus of barks erupted from somewhere down the hall, where a tall, slender woman appeared, looking slightly annoyed.

"Don't mind them," she said, sliding into a worn-out chair behind a cluttered desk. "We don't get many visitors here."

Her jet-black bob framed her face perfectly, but it was the vivid tattoos trailing down her arm and across her chest that caught my attention. At her feet, a hefty orange cat wove lazily between her legs.

"This is Henry," she said, scooping him up. "He's nosey as hell and has some. . . personal space issues. But he's neutered, so at least he won't pee on your pillow." She set him back down, scrunching her nose in a way that made the silver hoop in her nostril glint in the light. "He also smells kinda funky. It's a genetic thing—I think. He's been here a while, so he might have a hard time adjusting, but if you're interested, I'll waive the adoption fee."

Henry blinked at me, his butterscotch eyes narrowing before he let out what sounded like a disgruntled sigh.

"Uh, thanks," I replied, glancing between her and the cat. "But I was kind of leaning toward a dog."

"Oh!" the woman sprang up from her chair so quickly it startled Henry, who darted down the hall. She extended her hand toward me with a grin. "I'm Danielle, but everyone calls me Dani."

"Emily," I said, shaking her hand as we made our way toward the back of the building.

The inside was surprisingly in much better condition than the outside appeared to be. The large tile floors gleamed under the harsh fluorescent lights, and the lobby shelves were neatly stocked with leashes, food bowls, and other essentials for new pet owners.

"So, do you live in town?" Dani asked, glancing back at me as we walked. The barking grew louder, forcing us to shout as we turned down another hallway.

I adjusted the strap of my purse. "Sort of. I'm staying at the Magnolia House—"

Dani whirled around, her green eyes bright with excitement. "Shut up! You mean that creepy old farmhouse at the base of the mountains?"

I groaned. "Yeah, that's the one."

"That's so cool!" she gushed, practically bouncing. "I heard the woman who lived there was a witch, and now that she's gone, the place is supposed to be totally haunted."

I thought briefly of last night, then quickly shoved it away.

"That *witch* was actually my grandmother," I said, hesitantly. "She passed away a few weeks ago, so now the house is mine. As far as I know, it's not haunted—just old and kind of creepy."

Dani stopped. Turning to face me, her expression shifted. "I'm so sorry. I didn't mean anything by it."

"It's fine," I said, waving it off. "Honestly, I'm used to it."

A grin tugged at her lips. "Between you and me, I love that shit—witches, ghosts, all of it. I bet your grandmother was a total badass."

I smiled. People had called Gran a lot of things over the years, but 'badass' was definitely a first.

"You're not from around here, are you?" I teased as we approached a gray steel door.

"What gave it away?" Dani laughed, shoving her weight against the door.

The moment it swung open, the barking and howling amplified. I clapped my hands over my ears as Dani pulled the door shut. Stretched out before us, was a long, narrow corridor. Dozens of kennels lined the walls, each holding one or two dogs.

"How many do you have?" I shouted over the noise.

"Right now we have forty-eight. But our max is supposed to be forty, so we've had to double up," Dani called back.

I crouched in front of a kennel where a small rat terrier bounced eagerly against the gate, his muddy brown eyes pleading for attention. I reached through the bars to scratch his head.

"What happens when you run out of room?" I asked, my heart breaking a little as I looked around at all the hopeful faces.

Dani crouched beside me, stroking the terrier behind his ear. "We used to euthanize them," she admitted sadly. "That was before I got here. It took a lot of fighting with the county and a lot of changes, but we're a no-kill shelter now." She offered me a small, tired smile. "Honestly, I wonder how much longer we can keep it that way. People are dumping them faster than I can find homes." Her voice was heavy. "We spay and neuter every animal that comes through, and I've got fosters from out of state who help when they can. But it's just me here, and there's only so much I can do." She stood and wiped her hands on the faded denim of her overalls.

I gave the little dog one last scratch under his chin before rising to join her. "And if you can't find homes for them?" I asked. "What happens then?"

Dani shrugged, her expression tight. "The county will pull their support, and I'll be forced to start euthanizing again." Her voice cracked, and for a second, she looked as worn down as the shelter. "I wish people would stop getting animals they can't afford or care for. But people are selfish, and there's nothing I can do to fix that." The barking around us softened, as if the dogs could sense their potential fate. "Speaking of which," Dani continued. "I assume you've got a big yard?"

"There's plenty of space," I nodded. "To be honest, it's been a long time since I've had a pet. We had a cat when I was little, but I barely remember her." My mind wandered to Sushi, scratching at the door where Mom lay, motionless. I forced the thought away. "My grandmother said it was cruel to own another living being. She said every soul belongs to the earth—mosquitoes and spiders too."

Dani laughed. "I don't know about mosquitoes, those things are the devil. But, I admire her logic." She smiled. "As for dogs, I think they own you, not the other way around. It just depends on what you're looking for."

"I need a guard dog," I admitted a little too quickly. "I live alone, and the mountains can be a little overwhelming at night."

"Makes sense. You want something that makes you feel safe." She nodded toward a large black-and-brown shepherd sprawled in a nearby kennel. "Ruger would be perfect for that. German Shepherd and Rottweiler mix. Serious muscle. Serious bite. You can't get any better than that."

I crouched down. "Is he. . . friendly?" I asked, a little wary.

Dani gave a half-shrug. "Depends what you mean by friendly. He's loyal, sharp as a tack, and once he bonds with you, no one will get within five feet without him ripping their face off."

I thought of Logan, and immediately pulled away. "He's impressive. But I'm not sure I'm into the whole face-ripping off thing." Ruger gave a soft huff and sat back on his haunches, studying me with dark, intelligent eyes. "What else do you have?"

Dani grinned. "Brutus might be more your speed. He's a boxer-hound mix. He won't tear anyone apart, but he'll let you know if someone's creeping around who shouldn't be."

The large dog cocked his head as we approached, studying me with curious brown eyes.

"He's cute," I said, crouching to offer my hand for a sniff. "How long has he been here?"

Dani tapped a finger against her lips, thinking. "About a year, give or take. His owner passed away, and none of the family wanted to take him in."

Brutus licked his massive paw, watching me with a slobbery, lopsided grin. Drool dripped from his jowls, and my face twisted in disgust.

"Yeah. . . he does that," Dani said.

I rose to my feet, disappointed. Maybe getting a dog wasn't the brilliant idea I thought it was. I turned, ready to apologize for wasting her time—when I saw him.

At the far end of the hall, tucked into a corner kennel, was a smaller, quieter dog. His coat was the color of a thunderstorm, clashing against the bright blue of his soft eyes.

Dani followed my gaze. "That's Winston. Purebred Australian Shepherd. Not much of a guard dog. He's more of a herder, really."

But I was already kneeling, my hands reaching toward him. "What's his story?" I asked.

Dani hesitated, chewing on her lower lip. "He came in about a month ago. Rescued from a. . . bad situation."

I pulled my hand back, frowning. "Bad like he attacked someone or something?"

She dropped her gaze, her sneaker tracing a line along the tile. "Bad like he was attacked. By his owner. Multiple times."

Understanding slammed into me, knocking me back on my heels.

He'd been abused.

"He's quiet, and a little skittish. I don't think he's what you're looking for," Dani added. "Brutus, on the other hand, would make a great guard dog."

Winston's eyes, though hesitant, met mine, and in that moment, I knew. This gentle, sad-eyed dog needed me. And I needed him.

"I'll take him," I said, my voice steady with certainty. The truth was, Winston's quiet wariness mirrored my own. We were both survivors, scarred but not broken.

Dani blinked, clearly surprised. "You're sure? Because this isn't Target. There's no return policy or anything. Once he's yours, he's yours."

"I'm sure. Absolutely sure," I said, straightening.

A wide grin broke across Dani's face. "Alright then. I'll get the paperwork started."

Twenty Six

May 22nd, 2023

Dear Captain Walker,

This feels completely insane. Somehow, our letters are slipping through time, like this bag is some kind of portal. Do you think it disappears with each letter? Like it only lets one through at a time before slipping back into whatever space it came from? I have no idea if that's even possible. Honestly, it sounds ridiculous just writing it. Part of me thinks you're just some kind of hallucination, like something out of a bad sci-fi movie, or the kind of dream you wake up from and try to explain, only to realize it never made sense to begin with.

And yet, here we are.

I'm so sorry to hear about your wife. Just reading her name in your letters made me ache in places I thought I'd sealed shut. I can't imagine what it was like, to lose her in the middle of a war, with death already so close around you. But I think I understand a small piece of that pain. Loss is loss, no matter the century.

You asked who I am, and the truth is, I don't really know. Not anymore. A few weeks ago, I left a marriage that was, for lack of a better word, brutal. Honestly, I stayed longer than I should have. Out of fear, mostly. Fear of what came next, of being alone. And maybe part of me believed I deserved it. Karma, maybe. But this time was the last time, and so I packed up and moved into my Gran's old farmhouse, here in the small town of Windhaven. It's tucked away at the foot of the Appalachians, surrounded by magnolia trees. I have no idea if it exists in your time. Maybe it hasn't been settled yet. Or maybe our letters are proof that it does. Maybe you've walked the same hills I look out at now. Wouldn't that be something? Two strangers staring out at the same horizon, separated by lifetimes, but somehow. . . connected.

Part of me wants to know everything about you. I want to ask what you're like, what you dream about when the fighting dies down, what kind of man you were before the war stole you away. But another part of me wants to crumple this whole thing up, *toss it into the fire, and pretend it never happened. Because what kind of sane person writes letters to the past and expects a reply?*

It feels like I'm writing to a ghost. Maybe I am. Or maybe you're real, and I'm the ghost. Either way, it's nice not feeling so alone, even if it's completely nuts. Whatever the truth is, your letters found me. And that has to mean something right?

So I'll keep writing, at least for now. Because for the first time in a long time, it feels like someone's actually listening.

Sincerely your crazy, curious friend,
Emily Hart

Monday morning arrived like a clenched fist—gray and overcast and speckled with rain. I was working my way through my third cup of coffee when the familiar rumble of an engine shattered the morning quiet. Winston's ears perked up and I gave him a reassuring pat on the head before heading to the door.

Logan stood there, rain clinging to his jacket. "Hey," he said, his eyes flicking from Winston to me.

"Morning," I replied, stepping aside to let him in. "Are you sure you still want to do this?"

"I'm here, aren't I?" He set his toolbox on the table with a metallic *thud*, then gave Winston another wary glance. "Nice dog. Where'd you get him?"

"I adopted him from the shelter." I smiled down at Winston, who thumped his tail against the rug, oblivious.

Logan raised his brows. "You think that's a smart move?"

I felt a jab of irritation rise in my throat. "A few days ago, you were worried I was alone. Now that I'm not, you've got a problem with that too?"

He hesitated. "I meant. . . you know what, never mind. It's not my business."

"You're right—it's not." My voice was sharper than I intended. Sensing the tension, Winston settled onto the couch, his head resting on his paws.

Logan went to work on the door, unscrewing the old hinges and setting them aside.

"He's a good listener," I offered, trying to break the heavy silence. "Winston, I mean. Not as good as a human, of course, but he does the job."

Logan let out a quick laugh. "He seems to have impeccable couch-potato skills," he said, nodding toward the couch with his drill.

I tilted my head and smiled. "Have you always been this mean? Or did that come with age?"

"I prefer *grumpy*," he said wryly. "Sounds better."

I rolled my eyes, suppressing a laugh as Logan straightened, lifting the new screen door into place.

"Want a cup of coffee?" I asked, already drifting toward the kitchen.

He shook his head. "Appreciate it, but no thanks. Never been much of a coffee guy."

"Maybe that's why you're so *grumpy*," I teased, eyeing my own half empty mug before deciding three cups was probably enough.

Once he finished mounting the door, Logan opened and closed it a few times. "That should do it," he assured, testing the alignment. "Everything feels solid."

I hesitated. "What about the other door?"

"What about it?"

"Is it. . . sturdy?" I asked carefully.

He rapped his knuckles against it. "This is solid oak. Doesn't get much sturdier than that."

My eyes widened.

"What happened?" he asked, suddenly suspicious.

"The other night. . ." I began slowly, the unease still lingering, "I woke up and the door was open. It was probably nothing. I'm sure I just forgot to latch it all the way."

Logan studied the lock. "It's definitely old," he said, running a thumb over its worn edges. "I'll replace it with a new one—something a bit more durable."

I opened my mouth to argue, but one look at his face told me not to bother. Instead, I offered a small, genuine smile. "Thank you, Logan. Really. It means a lot that you're doing all this."

"It's no trouble," he said, wiping the sweat from his brow. His hand gestured toward Gran's urn. "So, when do you plan to. . . ?"

I rocked back on my heels and sighed. "Soon," I said. It was the truth. Gran didn't want to spend eternity in a jar and every day I put it off—the guiltier I felt.

"Do you know where?" he asked.

"Not exactly," I admitted. "Maybe the garden, once I get it cleaned up. She loved that place. Spent most of her time there." I left out the part about not having the heart to do it in the state it was in. The thought of it all felt like another layer of unfinished business weighing on me.

Logan must've seen the defeat on my face. "I'm sorry," he said. "I shouldn't have brought it up."

"No, it's okay," I said quickly. "It's just. . . I've had so much going on lately."

"You know," he said after a moment, "if you want help fixing up the garden—for Gran, I'd be happy to lend a hand."

My pulse quickened. I hadn't expected the offer. I hadn't even realized how badly I needed it.

"Yeah," I whispered. "I'd like that."

I looked at him then, really looked at him—and for the first time I noticed the fine lines etched into the corners of his tawny eyes. The hint of silver dusted along his dark roots. At some point, the boy I once knew had become this man I didn't know. We might as well have been strangers now.

"How's your mom?" I asked, desperately clinging to a thread of our shared past.

He shifted, his eyes dropping to the floor. "Wouldn't know. Haven't seen her in six years."

"What?" I blinked. "Why? Is she okay?"

He shrugged, still avoiding my gaze. "She's probably fine. We were never close. . . you remember."

I did. He and his mom were like oil and water—always clashing. But Logan had a habit of shutting people out when things got hard. And for him, things were almost always hard.

I followed Logan out onto the porch, the rain still falling steadily from angry gray clouds. He stepped down onto the front steps and pried at a warped board. A loud crack split the air as the wood gave way.

"When I got back, she was in rough shape," he said, shaking his head. Another sharp crack echoed between us as he wrenched loose a second board. "The bank was days from foreclosing, and she couldn't stay sober long enough to give a damn." He paused, gripping a third board tightly in his hands, the rain running in thin rivulets down his back. "I didn't know what else to do. I took what little I'd managed to save and brought the mortgage current. On one condition. . . she had to go to rehab."

His voice trembled, and I watched him blink rapidly, trying to hold back tears. Or rain. Or both.

"She went," he continued. "And for a while, things were great. She even managed to get a job over at Connie's."

"The truck stop diner off 59?" I asked, surprised.

Logan gave a bittersweet laugh. "Yeah. That's the one. Started in the back washing dishes, then moved up to waiting tables. She was proud of herself, hell, I was proud of her." His smile faded as quickly as it had come. "But then she met this guy. A long-haul trucker who loved Oxy more than she did."

My stomach knotted as I stood in silence, watching Logan methodically replace the old boards with the new ones he'd brought.

"After that, she started missing shifts," he said, his voice growing more distant. "And then one day, I found her in the cab of his truck—high as a fucking kite and barely able to stand. Turns out, she never really quit, she just got better at hiding it."

He went quiet again, his brow furrowed, sleeves rolled to his elbows as his hammer met the wood in steady rhythm. The scent of fresh pine mingled with the cool mountain air, and for a moment, the world narrowed to the creak of the porch and the sharp clink of nails.

I stood by, unsure if I should offer help or just stay quiet—the silence between us stretching taut like a rope neither of us was ready to pull.

I didn't know what to say. The image of his mother, slumped in some stranger's truck, eyes glazed over, lost to a haze she'd chosen over everything else, including her own son—made me sick.

Finally, Logan took a step back, admiring his work. "That was the last time I tried to save her. After that, I stopped showing up. I figured. . . if she didn't want it, why should I keep wanting it for her?"

Tears burned at the corners of my eyes, but I blinked them back. I wanted to reach for him, to comfort him—to be there for him the way I should have been this whole time but I remained frozen, stiff with guilt and aching with regret.

"She lost the house after that," he said, ashamed. "It all happened so fast—like watching a building crumble into dust, only the building was our life." He turned to me then, and the raw, hollow look in his eyes was something I'd never seen before. "I couldn't do it anymore, Em," he confessed. "I couldn't keep fixing things."

"Logan. . ." I began, then stopped. What could I say?

"I'm fine," he said quickly, swiping a hand across his face as if to erase everything he'd just shared. He glanced down at his watch. "It's already after eleven," he mumbled, changing the subject, "and I haven't eaten yet. Do you want to grab some lunch?"

"Yeah. . . sure," I said, though the idea of food made my stomach turn.

"Meet you at Connie's in twenty?" he asked, tossing his jacket over his shoulder.

I stared at him. "Seriously? After everything you just told me, you still want to eat there?"

Logan gave a half-smile and shrugged. "What can I say? I'm a sucker for their burgers."

Twenty Seven

FROM IT'S GRIMY WINDOWS, TO its peeling paint, Connie's Diner wasn't much to look at. The faded neon sign flickered intermittently, casting a weak glow over the cracked pavement. The parking lot out front was littered with eighteen-wheelers and a few scattered cars, their hoods dusted with remnants of the afternoon rain. It was the kind of place people passed by without a second thought—quiet and forgotten. Another pit stop along a road that never really seemed to go anywhere.

Inside, fluorescent lights buzzed overhead, underscored by the clatter of silverware and the low hum of conversation.

Across the table, Logan licked grease from his fingers before devouring another bite of his burger. I nudged a piece of lettuce from one side of my plate to the other.

"What's with the salad?" he grunted, mouth full.

"I like salads," I said, spearing a tomato.

"Nobody *likes* salads," he snorted.

I shrugged. "I do."

"No. . . you don't," he argued, flagging down the waitress.

A weathered woman with a permanent scowl and a voice held hostage by years of cigarette use shuffled over. "Yeah?" She croaked, hands on her hips.

"Can I get another burger?" he asked, his eyes lingering on me with quiet amusement.

She snorted, muttered something under her breath that sounded suspiciously like "*bottomless pit*," then turned on her heels and shuffled back toward the kitchen.

"Another one?" I asked. "Do you even know how many calories are in one of those?"

"No, but I'm sure you're about to tell me." He smirked. "Besides, it's not for me. It's for you."

"I'm not eating that," I replied sharply.

He ignored me, pushing away his plate as he leaned back into the vinyl booth. His eyes met mine. "Why are you here?"

I stared at him, confused. "You said you wanted to eat here."

"No." His voice dropped. "I mean why are you *here*. . . in Windhaven?"

My fork clinked against the plate. "Gran died. I thought that was obvious."

"I get that," he said. "What I don't get is why you're *still* here." I stared down at my plate—at that lonely scrap of lettuce I couldn't even bring myself to eat. "If you came back to bury Gran, where's your sister?" He leaned in. "And your husband—shouldn't he be here too?"

My head snapped up. "How did you know I was married?" I asked, frowning. "Have you been keeping tabs on me?"

Logan shrugged, like it was the most natural thing in the world. "I might have checked in on you once or twice."

I blinked, bitterness rising on my tongue. "How da—"

"Can I get you anything else?" the waitress cut in, sliding a plate between us.

Logan shook his head, and she trudged off. "Eat up," he said, his gaze locked on mine.

I shoved the plate away. "I lost my appetite."

"Seems you've lost more than that," he shot back.

I sighed. "What do you want from me, Logan?"

"The truth would be nice," he said, folding his arms across his chest.

"I told you already," I mumbled, tired of repeating myself. "I came back for Gran."

It wasn't a lie. Not exactly. But the way his eyes narrowed told me he wasn't buying it—and I hated how that made my stomach twist.

"You expect me to believe that?" he asked, shaking his head.

My jaw tightened. "I didn't ask you to believe anything."

Logan rolled his eyes. "You always were a terrible liar."

I opened my mouth, but nothing came out. The truth was too big, too raw. I traced the edge of my plate with my fork, avoiding eye contact.

"It wasn't perfect," I finally confessed. My throat felt tight, as if a fist were clenched around it. "I . . . I couldn't stay. Not anymore." My voice cracked. I wanted to run—to disappear under the booth.

"What happened, Em?"

My heart lodged itself in my throat. What would he think of me when he learned the truth? My hands trembled as I drew in a breath.

"Jackson was abusive," I finally said. "Emotionally and physically. This last time. . . he almost killed me. As awful as it sounds, Gran's death was my way out."

Silence fell between us. I shut my eyes, cheeks burning with shame. How had I let it get this far? How could I have allowed myself to become so broken?

Logan's hand settled over mine, and the ease of it surprised me. My first instinct was to pull away, to retreat behind the walls I'd spent the last few weeks building. But instead I let him comfort me.

For a while, neither of us spoke. My confession hung between us like a fragile piece of glass, threatening to break. Part of me wished I could take it back. But the other part, the stronger part, finally felt relieved.

"Say something," I whispered.

Logan stared at the untouched burger, then at me—his expression a tangled mix of shock and concern. I waited, bracing myself for whatever came next.

"Oh Emily. . . ." His voice was so low I could bare-ly hear him.

"I know it's a lot," I admitted, feeling the need to ex-plain. "But I don't want you to think less of me, or worse, that I—" my voice faltered "—that I deserved it."

His grip tightened. "I could never think less of you." He let go of my hand, and for a moment, I felt a quick sting of dis-appointment. Then, without warning, he slammed his hand against the table. "That motherfucker!" he hissed.

I flinched. Around us, heads turned.

Logan's face softened the second he saw my mine. "Shit. I'm sorry. I just. . . I didn't know."

"How could you have?" I asked, tucking a loose strand of hair behind my ear. "Besides, it's my own fault anyway."

"How could you even say that?" He asked, his voice still slick with anger. "None of this is your fault. Do you under-stand? None of it. He's an asshole and he deserves whatever's coming to him."

I let out a dry laugh. "Is that a threat?"

"Maybe," he shrugged.

An unsettling feeling washed over me. "You don't under-stand. Jackson's untouchable. He does what he wants, when he wants, to whoever he wants."

"Everyone has a weak spot," Logan replied stiffly.

"Please don't," I pleaded, realizing now that Logan might actually be serious enough to do something reckless. "I mean it, Logan. He probably already knows where I am, so it's only a matter of time before he shows up here. I have nowhere else to go, nowhere else to hide. Please don't make this worse than it already is."

"Emily, I can't—"

"Promise me," I begged, cutting him off. "Promise me you won't do anything stupid."

I watched as his confidence shattered, replaced by a flicker of something I couldn't quite place.

Logan nodded. "I promise."

And somehow, that was enough. For now,   it was more than enough.

Twenty Eight

January 27th, 1864
West Virginia

Dearest Miss Hart,

Night has fallen heavy here. The kind of darkness that settles into your bones and makes even the stars feel far away. The camp is quiet now, save for the occasional cough, the soft jingle of a harness, or the distant rumble of thunder that may or may not be cannon fire. I sit by a dying fire with your letter in hand, the paper worn from how many times I've read it.

You are right, writing to someone in the future feels like madness. And yet, your letters are a strange comfort in a place where comfort is scarce. Like you, I cannot explain how they find their way to me. I place mine in my satchel, and by morning, they vanish, replaced by your words come nightfall. It feels like witchcraft, but there is no malice in it, only mystery. I cannot explain how or why this happens, but I have chosen not to fear it. Too much of my world already defies reason.

What I do know is this. You are no hallucination. If you are, you are a vivid one, and far too clever to be conjured by a weary soldier's mind. War carves loneliness into a man's bones, and even an unexplainable presence such as yours is a welcome reprieve. I find myself looking forward to your words with an anticipation I can hardly admit aloud.

I was sorry to read of your husband. Let me assure you, such cruelty is not strength, but cowardice. I have seen what true courage looks like, and it is not in the hand that strikes. A man's duty is to protect, not to control or harm those he is sworn to cherish. I admire your courage, for it is no small feat to leave behind such cruelty and step alone into the unknown.

Allow me to take a small liberty. If we are to continue this unexplainable friendship, I insist upon you calling me James. And may I be so bold in asking to call you Emily? It feels strange to refer to you so formally when your words have already taken up such space in my thoughts.

As for me, I am an educated man. I carry a worn copy of Plutarch's Lives in my coat pocket, and I read it when sleep won't come. I have no children, for Charlotte passed before we might bear any. Before the war, I was a carpenter. Now, I lead good men into battle, and each day I pray I will not lead them to their deaths. I miss the simple things, such as walks at dawn, and the sound of a banjo on a warm summer night.

My younger brother, Finnigan, fights beside me. He is the only family I have left, and a steady light in this ever-changing hellscape of blood and mud. If we are to be honest with one another, I must confess, he has saved my life more than once. Without him, I fear grief would have claimed me long ago.

Perhaps our correspondence is a miracle, or perhaps it's the ramblings of two souls unmoored in time. Either way, I will write again, if you'll have me. Ghost or not, your ink is real. Your words are real. And in a world so full of loss, that feels like something worth holding onto.

Until next time, Your faithful friend,
James P. Walker

P.S. What, pray tell, is a sci-fi movie?

Five days. That's how long it had been since Logan and I last spoke over lunch at Connie's. Five days of unanswered calls, and unread texts—despite all my efforts.

I tried to distract myself with meaningless tasks, but nothing stuck. Anxiety curled in my stomach like a serpent, gnawing from the inside out until all that was left was dread.

I never should have told him about Jackson. I knew better. And yet, I did it anyway. How could I have been so careless? Yes, there was history between us but that was a long time ago. I knew Logan as a boy, not as the man he'd become. It was entirely possible that he'd gone off and done something stupid—like confront Jackson. Or. . . was it me? Had I changed so much he could no longer see the girl he once knew in the woman I was now?

My thumb drifted along the edge of James's last letter, my eyes drinking in the elegant curves of his inked script. I couldn't decide which was worse. That James, fighting a war in another century, still carved out time to write to me. Or that Logan, who was just across town, couldn't be bothered to return a single call.

I needed to move. To get out. To stop sitting here, replaying what was already said and done. I needed something simple, something solid—anything to calm the rising panic in my chest. Charleston was only an hour away. Maybe the drive would help.

"Want to go for a ride?" I asked Winston.

He lifted his tail just enough to give it a slow, approving wag.

An hour later, we stood at the foot of the Charleston Public Library. Its towering brick exterior cast a long shadow beneath the sharp West Virginia sun.

I gripped Winston's red leash and crouched until our noses were nearly touching. "I need you to be on your best behavior, okay?"

His response was a wet, unapologetic lick across my cheek.

"Good boy," I praised, wiping the drool against my jeans with the back of my hand as we climbed the wide stone steps to the heavy wooden doors.

Inside, the air smelled like old pages and dust. Sunlight streamed through the high windows, warming my back as I stepped into the spacious entryway. The woman at the front desk looked up with a polite smile that quickly vanished when her eyes landed on Winston.

"I'm sorry, but dogs aren't allowed in the library," she said, peering at me over wire-framed glasses perched precisely at the bridge of her nose.

I looked down at Winston. He tilted his head, as if to say, *Who, me?*

"He's not my dog," I said slowly, the lie forming as I scrambled for an excuse. "He's my emotional support animal."

"Whatever he is, he can't be in here." She pointed to the desk sign—a red circle with an X over a cartoon dog.

I chewed the inside of my cheek. *Think fast.*

"I understand, but Winston isn't *just* a pet," I pressed. "He's a service animal."

Her gray brows drew together. "And what service does he provide?"

Damn it. I hadn't planned to get this far.

"I'm, uh. . . partially blind," I blurted out. "He helps me read."

"He helps you read?" she repeated, unamused.

I nodded. "It sounds crazy, I know. But it's true. Winston can read just about anything. Poetry, romance. . . even fantasy."

The woman stared at me, stone-faced, as if trying to decide whether I was dangerously unwell or just deeply annoying.

"Right," she said flatly. "And does he have his library card?"

I opened my mouth, half-ready to double down on the lie, but the edges of her mouth twitched—just slightly. Not quite a smile, but not full disdain either.

"He's working on it," I said, letting a small grin slip through.

She exhaled sharply. "You've got ten minutes. Keep him on a leash and off the furniture. If I hear so much as a bark, you're both out."

Winston sneezed in response. But before she could reconsider, I turned to leave—then paused.

"Where can I find books on the Civil War?" I asked, glancing back over my shoulder.

She eyed me for a moment, then nodded. "Head down that hallway and take a right. You'll find about four shelves dedicated to that section. Let me know if you're looking for something specific."

We made our way down the main aisle, paws tapping softly on the tile. The library was a cathedral of stillness—high ceilings, soft lighting, the faint rustle of pages turning. A place where people came to disappear into stories that weren't their own.

Soon, rows of books stretched out before me, their titles promising stories of battles and bloodshed. I let my fingers trail along the spines, the raised lettering cool against my skin.

Confederate Strategy. Life in the Trenches. Charleston Under Siege. Each one caught my eye, stirring something I couldn't quite name—longing, maybe. Or regret. Whatever it was, it sat heavy in my chest.

I chose all three and carried them to a quiet corner. The chair creaked softly as I sank into it, and Winston curled over my feet like a warm blanket.

The first book read like a textbook, all dates and generals and maps that blurred together before I reached the second chapter. I flipped a few pages, hoping for something to catch, but it was all logistics and fort locations—more about troop movement through Virginia than anything remotely personal.

Winston shifted with a thump beneath me, as if to say, *Seriously? This is what we came for?*

The second book wasn't much better. Judging by the cover, it promised grit and heartache, but it mostly detailed rations, the weight of wool uniforms in the West Virginia heat, and how many men died of dysentery. Important, sure, but nothing that stirred anything in me beyond a yawn.

I leaned back in the chair, exhaling hard through my nose. Sunlight slanted through the high windows, catching the dust in lazy spirals. For a moment, I wondered why I'd bothered coming at all.

Then I reached for the third book.

It was older than the others, bound in faded navy cloth with no dust jacket and only it's title etched in gold on the spine. The moment I cracked it open, something shifted. The pages smelled older, mustier. I turned to a chapter halfway through, and began to read.

It wasn't just history, it read like real voices. Real people. A woman describing the way the cannon fire rattled the china cabinets. A boy, no older than twelve, tasked with carrying messages between soldiers. Letters written in trembling hands to husbands who never came home.

Something about the voices in the pages pulled at me. I could see it all. *Feel* everything. The soot. The fear. The way time bent under pressure.

The pages fluttered under my fingertips. I turned another—then stopped.

There, pasted crookedly between two brittle pages, was a black-and-white photograph. A group of Union soldiers stood in tight formation, posed in front of a canvas tent. Underneath, their names were listed neatly, just below the photo. **Samuel S. Johnson. Patrick M. Meyers. Finnigan J. Walker.**

I blinked. That name. My heart skipped.

Finnigan.

It echoed in my head, pulled straight from James's last letter. I stared at the man in the photograph—young, with a crooked smile. His hand rested lightly on the shoulder of the man beside him.

My gaze shifted and my heart hammered hard against my ribs.

The soldier next to him was striking—dark hair, a neatly tailored uniform, and a calm, unwavering expression. Something about his eyes felt unsettlingly familiar.

The name beneath him read: **Captain James P. Walker.**

My breath caught.

It wasn't just the name. It was the certainty in my gut—the instant, impossible recognition. As if some part of me had always known what he looked like. As if I'd seen his face before. . . somewhere behind my eyes, in sleep, or maybe memory.

Winston whined quietly at my feet.

I leaned in, my eyes locked on James's face. He wasn't just handsome, but *familiar.* Too familiar. Like a word on the tip of your tongue, or a song you know before the first note plays.

Captain James P. Walker—I read again, over and over until the letters began to bleed together. This man, the one I'd been writing, was no longer just a name on a letter, but a face.

A face I couldn't shake.

The edges of the room seemed to blur as a strange weight pressed down on my chest—an invisible pull, like gravity had shifted and I was no longer anchored to the present. The air turned thick, electric, the way it does before a storm.

I blinked hard, but the photograph didn't change. James's eyes stared back at me with that same quiet intensity—calm, measured, and yet somehow knowing. My fingers trembled as I brushed them over his features, tracing the sharpness of his jaw, the line of his mouth.

I'd never seen this picture before. Couldn't have. And yet—*I had*. Not in any conscious way, and certainly not in any way that made sense.

Déjà vu clamped down like a vice.

I pressed a hand to my chest, my heart thudding beneath my palm like it was trying to escape.

How could I know this man?

The letters had been one thing, but this? This was something else entirely. And it terrified me. Because if I knew him, then everything I believed about time, and memory, and what's possible, had just cracked open at the seams.

After a quick glance to make sure no one was watching, I ripped the photo from the page. I knew it was wrong, but I'd make peace with karma later.

Then I shot to my feet, nearly tripping over Winston as I rushed to return the book to its shelf.

"Time to go," I said, fumbling for his leash.

The woman behind the counter glanced up, concern creasing her brow as I hurried past. "Are you okay?" she asked. "You look like you've seen a ghost."

I think I have, I thought, the weight of the photograph burning like a brand against my thigh.

"I, uh. . . just remembered I left the oven on at home," I said. The lie rolled off my tongue a little too easily—it was starting to scare me how natural it felt. "Thanks for all your help."

I stepped into the fading daylight, the chill brushing my skin like a warning. Winston stayed close, his usual tug replaced by a hesitant pace as if he, too, sensed something had changed.

In my pocket, the photograph seemed to pulse with a quiet urgency.

I didn't know what any of this meant—not the letters, not the pull in my chest when I saw his face. But something was unraveling. Not just around me, but *inside* me.

And for the first time, I wasn't sure if I was chasing the past. . . or if it was chasing me.

Twenty Nine

By THE TIME I made it home, darkness had already settled in. I opened the car door, and Winston hopped out, tail wagging as he trotted alongside me. We started up the porch steps together, but as we neared the front door, he let out a soft whine.

"What is it?" I asked, kneeling beside him. His body was rigid, ears pinned flat against his head. He wouldn't look at me—just kept staring straight ahead, unmoving, like he saw something I couldn't.

I unlocked the door and stepped inside. "See, everything's fine," I reassured him.

My hand brushed the wall as I searched for the light switch. The lamp in the corner flickered on, casting light over the living room and spilling into the kitchen.

My heart stopped.

A hole, the size of a softball, had been smashed through one of the living room windows. Tiny glass shards were scattered across the floor, the trail leading to a large rock sitting in the center of the room. From the porch, Winston let out a low growl.

"It's okay boy," I whispered, trying to calm both him and myself. "Everything's fine."

But it wasn't fine.

I slowly approached the rock, crouching down to pick it up. But as I reached for it, a voice from behind made me jump out of my skin. I spun around, ready to hurl it at whoever had snuck into my house, when I saw Danielle's wide green eyes, wild with shock.

"It's just me!" she shouted, hands raised in surrender. "I didn't mean to scare you. The door was open, and I saw Winston outside—" Her gaze shifted to the rock in my hands, then to the shattered window. "Whoa, what happened?"

I set the rock down and leaned against the wall. "Some asshole threw a rock through my window," I said, still trying to process it.

Dani's eyebrows shot up. "Oh, fuck." She stepped closer, glancing at the broken glass. "Did you call the cops?"

I hesitated. "No. Not yet."

"Why the hell not?"

I shook my head. "Because I don't know what I'd even tell them. I didn't see anyone. Winston and I just got home and this is what we walked into."

Dani frowned, her voice lower now. "You think it was just some kids pulling a dumb prank or something?"

"I don't know," I shrugged. But I did know. I swallowed hard, trying to shake Jackson's name from my thoughts.

With Dani here, Winston finally decided it was safe enough to come inside. He crept in cautiously, sniffing every corner before curling up on the couch. Even then, his ears stayed alert, tail rigid.

"Got any duct tape?" She asked, inviting herself the rest of the way inside. "And maybe a broom?"

"You don't have to do that," I said, already opening the closet door. "What are you doing here anyway?"

She took the broom from me as I dug through the junk drawer in search of tape. "Well… I told myself Winston might want his kennel blanket. You know, something familiar to help him settle in. But honestly? That was just an excuse. I really just wanted to see your place."

"Not much to see," I said, glancing over my shoulder. "Unless you're into peeling paint and creaky floorboards."

Dani gave me a sheepish grin. "I saw you pull in and didn't want to seem like some creepy stalker, so I waited until you got out of the car." She bent down, sweeping the broken glass into a neat little pile. "I'm sorry, I should have called first."

I tore off a strip of duct tape with my teeth and pressed it over the broken window. "No, it's fine, really. It's just been a long day."

"Well, how do you feel about unwinding a bit tonight?" Dani emptied the dustpan into the trash and propped the broom against the counter. "There's a great band playing down at the Tavern. Thought maybe you'd want to come with?"

The Old Mill Tavern was a dive bar tucked in the center of Windhaven. It used to be the town's original train station back when it was first founded. Over the years, it had morphed into all kinds of things—a bookstore, an ice cream shop, even a tattoo parlor—although that one didn't last long.

I bit my lip, glancing between Winston and the now duct-taped window. "I don't know. . ." I said, hesitant. "I'm not sure how I feel about leaving him alone, especially after this."

"I get it," Dani nodded. "I just figured I'd ask. You seem like a cool person, and, well. . . I don't have many friends around here. Just the dogs and Henry, and I'm pretty sure the bar won't let them in."

A sense of familiar longing twisted in my chest. Here was this girl, practically a stranger, reaching out for friendship. It had been so long since anyone had done that, and my first instinct was to say no. But moving back here was supposed to be a new start. That meant stepping outside my comfort zone. And truthfully, if Jackson *had* been the one behind that rock, I didn't want to be alone in case he decided to come back.

"You know what?" I said, reaching for my purse. "I'd love to come."

Dani's face lit up. "Really?"

I nodded, offering a small smile as I slung my purse over my shoulder. "Yeah. Why not?"

She waited by the door as I gave the living room one last glance. Winston was curled up on the couch, head resting on his paws.

When I turned back, Dani held the door open like it wasn't a big deal—like this wasn't the first time in a long time someone had asked me to come along just because they wanted me to.

The night air brushed against my skin as we stepped out onto the porch. I paused, just long enough to swallow the unease rising in my throat. Leaving Winston alone after what had just happened didn't feel right—but I turned the key anyway, the lock clicking into place behind me.

Thirty

Before

RAIN STREAKED ACROSS THE CAR windows, turning the streetlights into glowing smears as Gran's old Crown Vic tore through town like a bat out of hell. The pulse of heavy music thudded through the brick walls of the Old Mill Tavern. Gran slammed on her brakes, the force of it, throwing me against my seatbelt.

"Stay here," she ordered, slamming the door behind her.

Katherine had snuck out. One month shy of her eighteenth birthday, her rebellious attitude had become worse with the shadow of adulthood lurking around the corner. She and Gran were constantly fighting, and the two of us no longer spent afternoons chasing butterflies in the field or searching for earthworms in the garden.

Still, sneaking into the local bar was the last thing I expected. Sure, I'd caught her puffing a cigarette behind the barn once, and she'd admitted to allowing Eddie Preston to get to third base, but this was a whole new level of defiance. Even for her.

Gran was always about good vibes and gentle hands. That's why it shocked me to see her dragging Katherine out by the collar, one hand clamped around her neck like a vice. Katherine's hair was a mess, her cheeks flushed, her eyes glassy and distant. She didn't look at me as she slid into the back seat alongside me.

"What the hell am I gonna do with you?" Gran asked, gripping the wheel as we pulled away. It was the first time I'd ever heard her curse.

"Nobody asked you to save us," Katherine slurred, the heavy stench of booze rolling off her in waves. I watched them both carefully, holding my breath.

"What were you gonna do?" Gran shot back. "Go live with your father?"

Silence followed. I could see the regret hit her the second the words left her mouth.

"I hate you," my sister hissed.

"Yeah? Well, I'm not your biggest fan either," Gran said, eyes locked on the road.

When we got home, Katherine stormed upstairs. A moment later, our bedroom door slammed so hard it rattled the walls as the sound echoed down the hall.

Gran lit a few incense, the spicy-sweet scent curling through the air as she sank onto the couch, pressing a hand to her forehead.

"She's just like your mother," she mumbled—more to herself than to me. It was the first and only time I'd ever heard her mention Mom. "You can sleep in my bed if you want," she added after a moment, her light brown eyes dull with exhaustion. "I'll stay out here tonight."

I didn't answer—just turned and padded up the stairs. But instead of slipping into Gran's room, I quietly opened the door to ours.

Katherine was on her side, facing the window and I crawled into the bed across from her. After a while, her voice drifted over my shoulder.

"I'm moving to California. As soon as I turn eighteen."

I turned to face her.

"I'm going to be an actress," she continued with a yawn. "And I'll live in a big house next to the ocean."

"What about me?" I asked, tears already welling up at the thought of her leaving. "You said we'd always be together."

"And we will," she mumbled, her voice thick with sleep and cheap booze. "As soon as you're old enough, you'll come live with me. Everything will be perfect."

"You promise?"

"I promise," she murmured.

I clung to her words like a lifeline. "Pinkie swear?" I whispered, holding out my smallest finger.

She blinked slowly, then hooked hers around mine with a lazy smile. "Pinkie swear," she echoed, before rolling over and drifting off.

I stayed there long after she fell asleep, staring at the ceiling, memorizing the sound of the fan clicking above us, the way the curtains swayed in the breeze. I wanted to believe her—I *needed* to. But somewhere deep in the quiet, I felt that heavy, gnawing doubt.

Promises made in the dark didn't always survive the daylight.

Thirty One

Now

THE OLD MILL TAVERN HADN'T CHANGED MUCH over the years. The brick exterior had grown more weathered, and the roof sagged slightly in the middle. The hand-painted sign out front still displayed the same familiar brushstrokes, and the parking lot remained riddled with potholes.

Inside, a band I'd never heard of was setting up on what passed as a stage. It was really just an open patch of floor a few feet away from the restrooms. A banner reading, *The Quiet Revival* hung overhead, and the soft strains of a fiddle drifted through the air as a woman and two men took their places.

"They're from my hometown." Dani said, sliding a cold beer across the table. "I used to date the singer's younger brother." She gave a quick wave to the woman at the mic, who returned the gesture with a smile.

"And where's that at, exactly?" I asked, eyeing the beer in front of me. I could feel the weight of curious stares from nearby tables—regulars who clearly knew we didn't belong here.

"A little town called Gretna, Nebraska," she said, lifting her glass and taking a long sip. "God, this tastes like shit."

I hesitated before tasting mine. It was like drinking stale water that had been left to bake in the sun.

"What brought you all the way out here?" I asked, fighting the aftertaste as I took another reluctant sip.

"The thriving nightlife," she joked, waving a hand over the dim bar around us. On the makeshift stage, the band had started playing—a soft, bluesy tune layered with a bluegrass rhythm.

"Obviously," I grinned. "But seriously, why the hell would you come here?"

Dani took a long pull from her beer before setting the glass down. "I didn't have anywhere else to go. Both my parents died when I was a kid, and as far as I know, there's no family left."

I didn't know what to say. Part of me couldn't believe how similar our stories were—two people shaped by loss, stumbling through a world we never asked for.

"I got into some. . . bad shit," she confessed. "Started out selling weed, but when that didn't cover enough I started hitting medicine cabinets. Sometimes from friends, sometimes not. I kept telling myself I just needed to sell enough to get by. But then I stole from the wrong person. Turned out, he was a cop. The judge gave me two options—a year in jail with probation after, or pay back every cent and get the hell out of town. Needless to say, it wasn't a hard decision."

"So where are you staying now?" I asked, leaning back into the booth.

"The shelter," Dani said casually, like she was telling me what she'd had for lunch. "There's a couch in the breakroom and a microwave. Honestly, it's not a bad setup."

I blinked, trying to hide the ache creeping into my face.

"It's just temporary," she added quickly, a faint flush rising to her cheeks. "Until I get things sorted. You know. . . until I land on my feet again."

I couldn't help it, I was speechless. She was broken in a way I understood. Different wounds, maybe, but broken things always have sharp edges, and they cut just the same.

"I was afraid of that." Dani pointed her finger at me. "You've got that look on your face—like you're judging me."

I shook my head quickly. "No. No judgment. I'm just surprised by how much we have in common."

Her eyebrows lifted. "You used to deal too?"

"No, of course not. I mean. . ." I winced. "I lost my mom at a young age and I never knew my dad. After she died, my sister and I moved here to live with our grandmother."

Dani ran a hand through her hair. "Damn. Yeah, that'll do it."

I nodded, unsure what to say next. "Gran had her quirks, but she took us in. Kept us fed and put a roof over our heads."

"That's more than most," Dani replied. She leaned back. "I bounced around a lot. Group homes, foster families. No one really stuck. Eventually, I figured out it was easier to rely on myself."

I met her gaze, the quiet between us suddenly charged—like we were both tiptoeing around a shared ache neither of us knew how to name.

"Guess we both learned early how to survive," I admitted softly.

Dani raised her glass. "To surviving first and trusting later."

Our glasses clinked, and we both drank quickly, trying to catch the beer before it spilled over the edge and onto the table.

"Pretty sure I broke the seal way too soon," she winced, suddenly rising from her seat. "Be right back."

As she made her way to the bathroom, I let my gaze drift over the unfamiliar faces, scanning the crowd for someone I knew wouldn't be there. Logan would never set foot in here, and yet, his absence was like a small hole in my chest—one I wasn't ready to admit was there.

"Are you expecting someone?" Dani asked, returning a few minutes later.

I shook my head, clearing Logan's face from my mind. "Nobody important."

Dani slid back into her seat, eyeing me curiously. "Good," she said, taking a sip of her drink. "Because this place doesn't exactly scream 'warm welcome.' Did you know the toilets are shaped like actual buckets? Seriously, who signed off on that?"

I laughed, and for the first time in a long while, I let myself enjoy it. It felt good. It felt *normal*. I hadn't had someone to laugh with, to talk to, to just *be* with in what felt like forever. Dani wasn't the kind of person I would've hung out with back in California—with her messy eyeliner and chipped black nail polish, but I liked her. She was unapologetically herself. And in some strange way, she reminded me of Gran.

"Thank you," I said, realizing I'd been staring. "For inviting me out. I forgot what it felt like to have a friend."

Dani gave me a crooked smile, like she wasn't sure what to do with something so sincere. "Yeah, well. . . you looked like you needed one."

I looked down at the table, the honesty in her voice catching me off guard.

"I mean that in a good way," she added quickly, taking another sip. "You just have this vibe—like you've been carrying too much for too long."

I let out an unsteady breath. "Yeah. Something like that."

Behind us, the front door swung open, and a familiar voice sliced through the music.

"Oh my God. . . I *knew* it," came Georgia's thick drawl. "Allie, didn't I tell you there was something off about Emily?"

Alabama nodded silently beside her.

"Can we help you with something?" Dani asked, her eyes flicking between the sisters and me.

"What are you doing here?" I asked, just as stunned to see the Baker twins inside a bar as they were to see me.

"The church potluck's tomorrow," Alabama said, gently smoothing an invisible crease from her sundress. "The tavern's donating some of their famous cornbread."

"Friends of yours?" Dani asked, straightening a little.

"Oh, I wouldn't go so far as to call us friends," Georgia said, loud enough to draw attention. "But Emily and I go way back. In fact, everyone in town knows the Harts." She leaned in slightly, eyes gleaming. "What I *didn't* know was that little Miss Emily here is a lesbian."

"A what?" I blinked, unsure I'd heard her right.

Georgia gave a dramatic sigh. "You heard me. What else would you be doing at the bar at night with the town queer?" She nodded toward Dani. "I knew something was off the minute I saw you at Hank's without your wedding ring. This here's just proof in the pudding."

"I am *not* dating Dani," I said, rising a little in my seat. "Georgia, you are *completely* out of line."

"You're married?" Dani asked, her voice calm but clearly surprised.

"*Was* married. It's. . . complicated."

"Oh, I bet it is," Georgia smirked, arms crossed like she'd just won a game no one else was playing. Behind her, Alabama let out a soft, awkward chuckle.

I turned to Dani, realizing she never denied the accusation. "Wait. . . are you? I thought you said you dated the singer's brother?"

Dani smiled. "What can I say? Life's better when you have options." She turned to Georgia. "Not that it's any of your business, but Emily and I are just friends. Unless, of course. . . *you're* interested?"

"I beg your pardon?" Georgia recoiled like she'd been slapped. "I'll have you know I'm a daughter of the Lord, and your kind of lifestyle is—"

"A sin?" Dani cut in smoothly. "Yeah, I've heard that one before. The thing is, the Lord's not here tonight—but the band is, and so is the beer. So unless you're planning to grab a drink and pull up a chair, I suggest you move along."

Georgia's mouth fell open but all she managed was a dramatic scoff. She grabbed Alabama by the arm and stalked off toward the bar, snatching up the cornbread boxes before heading out the door.

"That was incredible," I said, turning back to Dani. "I don't think anyone's ever told her off before."

She shrugged. "It's not my first run-in with a narrow minded asshole. Won't be the last."

"I'm sorry," I said, realizing how this all must have felt for her. "I wasn't trying to—"

"Don't apologize," she interrupted. "You didn't know." In the background, the band switched songs to something more lively. "So. . ." Dani said, her eyes gleaming with curiosi-

ty. "This complicated ex-husband of yours—I'm sensing dra-
ma. Spill it."

I tipped back the rest of my beer, the burn giving me
courage. Then I set the glass down, leaned into the table, and
started from the beginning.

Thirty Two

May 27th, 2023

Dear James,

I keep catching myself rereading your letters, like there's some-thing hidden between the lines I might've missed the first time. Maybe it's the way your words feel familiar, even though they shouldn't. Or maybe it's just that hearing from you makes every-thing feel a little less heavy.

The past few days have been a bit of a blur. I adopted a dog. He's an Australian Shepherd named Winston. Your letters have been wonderful, but I'd be lying if I said it doesn't still get a little lonely out here. He's not much of a talker, but he's an excellent cuddler, so I'm not complaining. Also, kind of scary, but someone threw a rock through my window the other night. Winston's not exactly a guard dog, but having him here makes me feel a bit safer.

I haven't read Plutarch's Lives, but now I'm curious. Maybe I'll grab a copy next time I'm in Charleston. Speaking of which, I stopped by their library the other day. I'm not sure what I was hoping to find, maybe something to make you feel more real. I was about to give up when I came across an old photo of you and your brother. I stopped breathing for a moment. You have this look, like you know more than you let on. It's. . . distracting. Is it weird to say you're incredibly handsome? Probably. But I haven't been able to shake the feeling that I've seen you before, like in another life or some half-remembered dream. Not that I'm thinking about you all the time or anything, it's just nice to finally put a face to the name.

I'm glad you have your brother. That kind of bond is rare. What is he like? I have an older sister, Katherine. But after our mom died, she became more of a mother than a sibling. I think part of her resents me for that. Our relationship suffered because of it and eventually she moved away. I followed, hoping to fix things, but it's never been the same. Too many old wounds that never fully healed, you know?

Oh, and since I've seen you, it's only fair you see me. I'm in-cluding a photo. It's a few years old, but considering you've got 160 years on me, I figure we're even.

Anyway, it's late and I should probably sleep. Write when you can. Your words have a way of finding me when I need them most.

Yours truly,
Emily

P.S. A sci-fi movie is a glimpse of a world that doesn't exist yet, but maybe could. Funny enough, I guess that's kind of what our letters are, too.

The shrill ring of my phone yanked me out of sleep. Beside me, Winston barked, just as startled by the noise as I was.

"What was that?" my sister's voice crackled through the speaker.

"Katherine?" I croaked, my voice heavy with sleep.

"Who else would it be?"

I glanced at the unfamiliar number on the screen. "Where are you?"

"I'm on a payphone at a gas station near Mission Bay." She paused, like she wasn't sure what else to say. "I'm sorry I haven't called. I meant to. It's just. . . Are you okay?"

I didn't know what surprised me more—Katherine calling out of nowhere or that she was using a payphone.

"I'm fine," I said, sitting up. "Why? What's going on?"

There was a beat of silence, followed by her unsteady voice. "Jackson called Grant a few nights ago."

A chill ran through me.

"It's bad, Emily. I told Grant I hadn't heard from you, that I didn't know where you were, but I don't know how much longer I can keep lying to him. And once he knows, it's only a matter of time before he tells Jackson. You know he's awful at keeping secrets. Remember when I found out—"

"Where is he?" I asked, now wide awake.

"I don't know. Grant doesn't either," Katherine said, panic slipping through. "But he said Jackson sounded. . . unwell. Ranting and raving. Grant couldn't understand what he was saying. Jackson's losing his mind and no one knows where he is. You haven't seen him. . . have you?"

I thought back to the shattered window downstairs.

"No," I said, shaking my head.

"Good," she breathed, clearly relieved. "Honestly, Em. . . maybe this whole thing wasn't such a great idea, you being out there alone."

"I'm not alone," I ran my hand over Winston's head. "I've got a dog."

"You got a—? You know what, we'll circle back to that later."

"And then there's Logan. . ." I began.

"Logan?" she repeated, surprised. "You're not—"

"No, nothing like that," I said, cutting her off. "He stopped by to help fix a few things around Gran's house. You should see it, Kat—it's falling apart. Anyway, I haven't seen him in over a week, which is probably for the best. . ."

Please deposit fifty cents to continue this call, an automated voice interrupted.

"Listen, I've gotta go," Katherine said, her voice suddenly rushed. "I'll call you again as soon as I can."

I hadn't spoken to my sister since the day I left the hospital. I didn't want to admit it then, but I'd been so angry at her for leaving me again. For making me go through this alone. And now, with her voice fresh in my ear, I didn't want to let her go.

"Kat. . . ?" I whispered, unsure if she was still there. But I could feel her on the other end—almost like she didn't want to let go either. "I miss you," I admitted quietly.

"I miss you too." Her voice was heavy with longing. "I'll call again soon."

Then the line clicked. And she was gone.

I sat there for a moment, phone still pressed to my ear, listening to nothing. Winston leaned into my side, his warm body steadying me.

I rose and crossed the room, pulling back the curtains just enough to peek outside. Morning sunlight filtered in, casting a golden haze over a cloudless sky.

But the beauty of it didn't settle anything in me.

I turned away from the window and looked down at my phone, Katherine's last words ringing in my head.

It's bad, Emily. . .

Maybe Jackson had finally realized how far things had gone. Maybe he regretted it—regretted everything. Maybe us being apart made him understand how much he still loved me.

I headed downstairs, but the moment my foot hit the last step, my eyes landed on the broken window.

. . . Or maybe he just wanted to finish what he started.

Behind me, Winston let out a low whine, circling near the front door.

"How about a walk?" I asked, reaching for his leash. "We could both use some fresh air, don't you think?"

Thirty Three

Winston bounded ahead, his leash draped loosely in my hands. We'd wandered to Appalachian Point—a public trail not far from the house. Gran used to bring us here when we were kids for days of scavenger hunts. We'd search for vibrant leaves, oddly shaped rocks, and anything else that caught our eye.

Eventually, it changed over the years. Paved paths had replaced the old dirt ones, and a steady stream of tourists gave it a more polished, less wild feel. We stopped coming after a while. Gran preferred the quiet trails behind her house, and so did we.

The air around us buzzed with the steady roar of rushing water. Waterfalls dotted the mountains—some thin like ribbons, others crashing in powerful sheets. I'd seen them before, but could never get over how enchanting they were. The way the sunlight caught the spray made them look like something lifted from the pages of a fantasy novel.

Winston paused to sniff at a large moss-covered boulder while I leaned against the trunk of a wide oak tree—its thick branches giving little relief from the impending heat of June lurking around the corner. Up ahead, a couple walked hand in hand, chatting quietly, and for some reason. . . it made me think of James.

Since Charleston, I hadn't been able to get him out of my head. Some nights, lying in bed, I'd re-read his letters—the smell of earthy wood smoke clinging to the pages. I couldn't help but wonder if that's what he smelled like.

I closed my eyes and let the sun warm my skin. It was strange—James was technically dead, and yet I kept catching myself wondering where he might be right now. In this exact moment. Could he have walked this trail? Stood where I was standing? Basked in the beauty of these same waterfalls?

I still had no idea how his bag ended up sealed behind Gran's fireplace. Did he hide it there himself? Or had Gran? Had she even known it was there?

The leash went taut in my hands and I glanced up to see Winston eyeing a squirrel. If he lunged, I could easily end up tumbling down into the stream below. I wrapped the leash tighter, bracing myself.

"Don't even think about it," I warned, giving him a look. He sat back, pretending to listen, but the glint in his eyes said otherwise.

The squirrel, realizing it was being watched, made a break for it—darting down the tree and across the path. That was all the invitation Winston needed. He took off like a shot, yanking the leash from my hand and dragging me down in the process. One second I was upright, the next I was on the ground, watching him disappear around the bend.

I groaned, brushing dirt and tiny gravel from my palms as I sat up. My elbow throbbed where it had met the ground, but nothing felt broken—just scraped and a little bruised. Winston was already a blur in the distance, tail flying like a flag of rebellion.

"Winston!" I shouted, scrambling to my feet. "Get back here!"

He didn't, of course. I took off jogging down the trail, heart pounding—not just from the sprint, but from the thought of him crashing into some poor hiker or flying straight off the edge of a ridge.

The path curved sharply, and I rounded it just in time to see Winston skidding to a stop near the base of a small, tiered waterfall. The squirrel had vanished, but Winston remained, panting and pleased with himself, as if he hadn't just caused total chaos.

"What the hell is wrong with you?" I scolded, grabbing the leash and bending over to catch my breath.

Winston wagged his tail like we were old pals reunited after years apart, completely unfazed by the mayhem he'd caused. I snatched the leash off the ground and gave it a slight tug—not enough to hurt, just enough to let him know I wasn't amused.

We started the slow climb back up the trail, the sky already beginning to change. The light had shifted into a strange, golden hue that made the woods feel more dreamlike than real. I wrapped the leash twice around my wrist and kept my eyes on the path ahead, trying not to focus on the tight ache in my knee or the sting of gravel still embedded in my palm.

That's when I noticed how quiet it had gotten.

Earlier, when we arrived, the parking lot had been nearly full. But aside from the couple I'd seen earlier, that had been it. No joggers. No dog walkers. No distant hum of laughter. Nothing. Just Winston and me, alone on a trail that had suddenly turned unfamiliar.

There were two unspoken rules about the mountains: Never go in after dark. And never go in alone.

I glanced behind me. Still nothing. But when I turned back, something flickered at the edge of the path—a sudden shift, like someone slipping behind the trunk of a tree just out of sight.

I froze. Winston froze, too, head tilting, his ears alert.

I held my breath, waiting for another sign of movement. A small rabbit shot out from behind a bush, vanishing into the undergrowth. I let out a shaky exhale, then shot a warning look at Winston.

The farther we walked, the more the woods seemed to close in. The sun filtered through the leaves in strange angles, casting shadows that shifted as if they were watching. A branch cracked to our right. I stopped, heart stuttering.

"Probably a deer," I whispered, but my voice didn't sound convinced—not even to me.

We kept walking, my grip on the leash tightening until my knuckles turned white. That's when I heard it—footsteps behind us. Not fast, not close, but steady. Deliberate. A pause. Then a crunch of leaves. Another step.

I spun around. Nothing but trees.

"Hello?" My voice echoed in the thick silence. "Is someone there?"

No answer.

Just the slow creak of a tree swaying in the breeze. . . and then the unmistakable snap of another branch behind us.

Winston let out a low whine, his body tensing.

That was all I needed. I turned and started walking faster, almost dragging him behind me. I didn't look back again.

The walk home felt twice as long as the hike out. Part of it was the limp, my leg still stinging from the fall. Mostly it was Winston, who had suddenly declared war on every bird and squirrel he saw—forcing me to keep a tight grip on his leash.

Sweat slicked my palms as we rounded the corner onto the driveway. I always knew we were close when the thick, heady scent of magnolias hit me—rich, sweet, and impossible to ignore. A soft breeze rustled the branches above, sending a white petal with a blush of pink drifting down into my hair. Another landed right on Winston's nose. He sneezed, loud and dramatic, forcing a laugh from me as we slowly ambled the rest of the way.

We were about halfway up the drive, where the trees began to thin, when a flicker of movement caught my eye. My stomach did a little flip.

There, sitting on the front steps, with his head in his hands—was Logan.

Thirty Four

Before

THE FIRST PEBBLE PINGED harmlessly against the window, followed by another—a little harder this time. I drew back the lace curtains and smiled when I saw Logan standing below, his face half-lit by the moon, the rest of it swallowed by the night. Carefully, I opened the window, wincing as it gave a soft groan.

"Hey," he called up.

"Shhh!" I hissed, glancing over my shoulder at Katherine, who was fast asleep in the bed behind me. "Are you trying to get caught or what?"

Even in the dim light, I could see Logan roll his eyes. "A bear could tear through your room and your sister wouldn't flinch."

He wasn't wrong. But Gran was still awake—I could hear the low hum of her TV through the bedroom door. She liked Logan well enough during the day, but a midnight visit might be pushing it.

Quietly, I eased myself through the window and onto the roof. Logan was already scaling the thick, vine-covered lattice running up the side of the house. A moment later, he hoisted himself up beside me.

"You're getting good at that," I grinned.

"Practice makes perfect." He flopped down next to me, and we both leaned back on our elbows, gazing up at the stars.

"Why weren't you at school today?" He asked after a few quiet minutes had passed.

"I wasn't feeling well," I said, tugging at a loose thread on my pajamas. It was a lie. A weak one, and he knew it.

"Weird. You don't look sick to me."

I rolled my eyes. "Why are you always so pushy?"

"Why are you such a bad liar?" he teased.

I laughed. "Would you rather I wasn't?"

"It would make things easier," he smirked, nudging me with his elbow.

I drew in a deep breath, catching the sweet scent of wildflowers drifting up from Gran's garden. "I didn't feel like dealing with Maddie and her entourage today."

"Ah," Logan murmured. "Have you ever tried ignoring her?"

I sat up, fixing him with a sharp glare. "Gee, Logan, what a great idea. Why didn't I think of that? I'll be sure to keep it in mind next time she shrink-wraps my locker or dumps water on my chair."

"I know she can be difficult—"

"*Difficult?*" I cut him off. "Madeline McBride isn't *difficult*. She's a full-blown menace. A tyrant. A sociopath. A—"

"And very very lonely," he interrupted gently.

I stared at him, heat rushing to my cheeks. "Are you *seriously* defending her right now?"

Logan shook his head. "I'm not defending her, I just. . . see things a little differently, that's all. That *entourage* of hers? They're not *really* her friends. They're just looking to get something out of her. Her parents are never home, and when they do show up, they're too busy curating their perfect image to notice her. Honestly, I think she goes after you because she's jealous. She probably sees something in you that she wishes she had."

I snorted. Maddie McBride, queen bee and social royalty—jealous of me? The idea was laughable.

"Jealous of what?" I pushed back. "She has a house the size of a hotel and actual parents. My dad bailed before I was born, my mom's gone, and everyone in town thinks Gran's one séance away from a padded room. You're the only friend I have. Maddie's not jealous—she's cruel."

"*Perspective,*" Logan said, tapping the side of his head. "You're brilliant, Emily. Funny. Strong. Kind." He paused, his gaze locking with mine. "Sometimes I wish you could see yourself the way I do."

The look he was giving me made my stomach flutter. Suddenly the rooftop felt too small.

"How do you see me?" I whispered, inching closer. His breath ghosted over my skin and I could smell the subtle scent of his cologne as the overwhelming pull of his gaze dragged me in.

"Like this. . ." His fingers brushed mine, a feather-light touch that sent a jolt of electricity into my very soul.

Speechless, I couldn't move. The flutter in my belly had suddenly erupted into a wildfire—lighting me up from the inside.

"Emily. . ." he said my name like it was something delicate, like it was something meant to be cherished.

My heart pounded so loud I was sure Gran could hear it from inside.

But before I could answer, before I could say *yes* or *wait* or *what are we doing?* a light flicked on downstairs.

We both froze.

Logan pulled back a fraction, just enough to break the spell. "Gran?" he whispered.

I nodded, already shifting toward the window. "She gets up sometimes for tea or to yell at the news."

We both held our breath, listening. When the light finally dimmed, Logan exhaled sharply. His hair was slightly mussed, one dark curl flopping over his forehead. I fought the urge to brush it back.

"You should go," I whispered.

He nodded, the soles of his shoes scraping the worn shingles as he made his way back down. I watched until the dark swallowed him whole, the vines trembling in his wake.

Once inside, I pressed the window shut and turned the lock with a soft *click*. Then I eased back into bed, heart still thundering, thoughts racing. I wasn't sure what just happened. I only knew everything had changed.

And nothing would ever be the same again.

Thirty Five

Now

LOGAN DIDN'T SAY A WORD as I approached. He just sat there, shoulders slumped, head buried in his hands.

"Hey," I said, loosening my grip on Winston's leash.

He looked up. "Hey." His voice was low, laced with sorrow. He stood as I stepped past him, struggling to secure my keys. "Here, let me help you. . ."

"I've got it," I said sharply, the keys slipping from my hand and clattering to the porch.

Logan bent to retrieve them. His gaze drifted to the dried blood on my arm. "What the hell happened to you?"

I snatched the keys from his hand. "What are you doing here, Logan?"

He ran a hand over his face. The sharp edges of his features were dulled by exhaustion. Dark circles ringed his tawny eyes. He looked. . . broken.

"Emily," he began, his voice a rough whisper, "I'm so sorry."

A wave of hurt washed over me. The righteous fury I'd been nursing over the past week still blistered over my skin. But seeing him like this—the bone-deep weariness etched onto his face, made my heart ache.

"What happened?" I asked.

Logan leaned against the porch railing, his shirt creased and dusty. He stared at his calloused hands. "Something came up," he mumbled, the words barely audible over the sound of birds chirping. "But that's no excuse. I shouldn't have left you hanging like that. I—" He stopped, swallowing hard, the effort visible in the tightening of his jaw. "It's complicated," he finished, shaking his head.

I started to reach for him but stopped. Whatever was going on with him, I didn't want to complicate things further.

"It's ok," I whispered. "I get it."

A flicker of relief passed through his eyes.

I gave him a faint smile. "Do you want to come in?" I asked, gesturing toward the door.

He shifted awkwardly, then nodded.

I jammed the key into the lock, the metal scraping against the bolt as Logan hovered behind me like a shadow.

"I bought a replacement," he offered, like that somehow made up for everything. "I've got it in my truck, I can switch it out today."

"Sure," I agreed, pretending I'd forgotten all about it. "That would be great."

The door creaked open and Winston shot through it, nearly toppling us both. I dropped the keys on the table and headed straight for the kitchen, searching for a glass of water.

"What's with the window?" Logan asked, eyeing the duct tape stretched across the broken pane.

I downed half the water in one go. "Someone threw a rock through it," I shrugged, as if it were another Tuesday.

He turned to me, eyes wide. "What? Who?"

I shrugged. "Take your pick. My family doesn't exactly top the popularity charts around here."

He studied the taped glass, jaw tightening. "Why didn't you—"

"Call you?" I cut in.

Logan flinched. "I'm sorry."

I crossed my arms, lifting my chin with false confidence. "I didn't need your help anyway. The duct tape works fine. And Dani was here to—"

"Dani?" he interrupted. "Who the hell is Dani?"

I paused, catching the edge in his voice. Was that jealousy? The audacity made my blood rise. What fucking right did he have to be jealous of anything? He'd vanished for almost a week without a word, and no real excuse. Besides, it's not like we were anything more than friends anyway. And even that felt like a stretch.

"Danielle," I corrected. "She runs the county shelter. That's where I adopted Winston." I nodded toward the fury menace now snoring on the rug, his earlier chaos forgotten. "She stopped by that night and helped me clean up the mess."

Logan's eyes narrowed, but the tension in his shoulders eased at the realization that Dani was, in fact, a Danielle. Still, suspicion lingered on his face as he turned back to the window.

"Duct tape's not a real fix," he said, running his fingers along the peeling edge. "Honestly, it's not even a decent temporary one. They're calling for heavy storms next week—this'll peel right off." He paused, then added, "I have to head into Clarksburg this afternoon. I can pick up some plastic sheeting while I'm there. It'll hold up better until I can get a replacement."

I chewed on my bottom lip.

"Why?" I asked, studying him like I was seeing him for the first time.

Logan tilted his head. "Why what?"

I set the glass down on the table and crossed my arms over my chest. "Why are you offering to help me? And don't say it's for Gran because I don't buy that. Is it guilt? Or is it pity? Because if you feel sorry for me, let me save you the trouble. I don't need your sympathy."

"It's because I want to," he replied. "Look, I know I screwed up. I should've called. I should've said something. But you know how I am—"

"Used to," I blurted out before I could stop myself. "I *used* to know how you were. But we're not those people anymore. We've both changed—shaped by things clearly neither of us are ready to talk about."

Logan rocked back on his heels, face tightening. He didn't argue, nor did he deny it either. And that told me everything. He knew I was right.

"So let's get to know each other again," he said after a moment. "Come with me to Clarksburg. Spend the afternoon with me. I promised I'd help you restore Gran's garden, we can grab the supplies while we're out. Maybe grab dinner after?"

I hesitated, wondering if this was such a good idea.

"Please," he insisted. "Let me make it up to you."

I glanced over at Winston, still sprawled in the exact spot he'd collapsed in earlier. "Okay…" I said, shifting slightly. "But can you give me a minute to clean up first?"

Logan smiled, the tension in his face easing. "Take all the time you need."

As he stepped outside to wait, I closed the door behind him and pressed my back against it, exhaling slowly.

Maybe it was a mistake.

Maybe it wasn't.

Either way, I was already moving toward something I wasn't sure I trusted yet—but couldn't quite walk away from either.

Thirty Six

THE DRIVE TO CLARKSBURG WAS AWKWARD. NEITHER OF us said much, just sat there listening to the wind whip through the open windows. Logan kept apologizing for the AC being broken. He kept meaning to fix it but hadn't gotten around to it yet.

The heat had died down, but the humidity lingered, and the air was thick enough to make my clothes stick. I was relieved when we'd finally stopped in Bridgeport, at a small nursery a few miles outside of town.

Once inside, Logan started chatting with the owner—a round man with dirt under his nails who looked like a potted plant himself.

Afterwards, we spent the next half hour wandering the aisles, making small talk as we passed rows of bright, blooming flowers.

"What about roses?" Logan suggested, holding up a vibrant crimson bloom.

Memories of Jackson flooded back—how he'd used bouquets of them as a cheap attempt to gloss over his violence.

"No roses," I said, my words sharper than I intended.

Logan raised an eyebrow. "You've got something against roses?"

"Just never been a fan," I mumbled, avoiding eye contact. Naturally, he picked up on the edge in my voice but, thankfully, didn't press any further.

It didn't take long to fill the cart. By the time we wheeled it out, we'd grabbed a little of everything—marigolds, black-eyed susan's, even a buddleia bush that Logan insisted would attract butterflies.

"I don't remember you ever having a green thumb," I teased, helping him load the back of the truck.

"I don't," he admitted with a grunt. "But I helped Gary out with some repairs on the nursery last summer," he added, nodding toward the building. "The first crew he hired ran off with a bunch of his money. Almost put him out of business. I offered to do the work for free, but he wouldn't let me. So now I send folks his way, and he does the same for me. Fair trade."

"That's actually really thoughtful of you," I said, handing over a pot of zinnias.

Logan hopped down from the truck bed. "You sound surprised."

"Maybe I am." I meant it as a joke, but it landed wrong. I winced. "Gran would say we're going totally overboard with all this," I added with a laugh.

"And she'd be right," Logan chuckled as he lifted heavy bags of soil, compost, and fertilizer into the back of the truck with ease.

I glanced over, noticing the way his arms tensed beneath the weight, a bead of sweat trailing down his sun-warmed skin. When did he get so. . . solid? The boy I'd grown up with was leaner, a little clumsy and a bit awkward. But the man standing in front of me now was more grounded, more sure of himself. And, well, he looked good. Really good.

"Like what you see?" he teased, a slow grin spreading across his face.

I rolled my eyes. "You've got dirt on your face," I said, motioning to my own cheek before climbing back into the truck.

We rumbled back onto the road as we pulled away from the nursery. Clarksburg was only ten minutes out. Silence settled in again, soft but not as awkward this time. The windows were still down, letting in warm air now thick with the scent of fresh soil and sun.

Logan drummed his fingers against the steering wheel, glancing over once or twice like he wanted to say something but hadn't quite decided how.

"You know," he said eventually, "I don't think I've been back to Clarksburg since that day your Gran got a wild hair up her ass and made us drive all the way out here to buy copper plates from that weird little shop."

I looked out the window, watching the blur of green roll by. "Yeah. She was convinced they would help 'cleanse the air' or whatever."

He laughed. "She was a good woman. Scared the hell out of me when I was a kid though."

"She scared everyone," I replied with a sigh. "But yeah, she was pretty great."

We both fell quiet for a moment.

"Feels weird, doesn't it?" he asked, his voice softer now. "Coming back when so much has changed."

"Yeah," I said. "It does."

As we turned onto the main road, Clarksburg opened up around us, bustling with life and sun-drenched streets. Storefronts came into view alongside faded billboards. Up the hill, an old gas station sat with its flickering "Open" sign still clinging to life. Somehow, the city had managed to hold onto its small-town charm, even with the buzz of modern life swirling around it.

Logan immediately pulled into a shaded office plaza—the kind with a jumble of places like a dentist office, and a nail salon. A low key tax office sat tucked in the corner. When he parked in front of a law office, I gave him a curious look.

"Business stuff," he said, rubbing the back of his neck. "My lawyer dropped the ball last week. I've got to sign some paperwork for a contract in Charleston. It's why I needed to come out this way. I won't be long, I promise."

Once he disappeared inside, I rested my head out the window, watching the slow rhythm of people moving through their daily lives—families with strollers, couples carrying iced coffees. It struck me how *normal* we must've looked together. Like a regular couple out running regular errands on a sunny afternoon.

That was something I never had with Jackson.

I blinked the thought away. I didn't need to go there—not now, not again. And besides, this whole thing was temporary anyway. I was only staying at Gran's until things settled down. Once the dust cleared with Jackson, I'd be gone again.

Unless it never cleared. Then what?

I leaned back in my seat, arms crossed, eyes fixed on nothing in particular. The sun had shifted just enough to cast a warm glow across the dashboard. It should've felt peaceful. Instead, I felt like I was standing at the edge of something I didn't know how to name.

Katherine said no one knew where Jackson was. But he wouldn't stay hidden forever, not with his name and money on the line. Sooner or later, he'd show his face. And when he did. . . would he expect me to come running back? All smiles and forgiveness? Because that wasn't going to happen.

If Jackson wanted to fix things, it would take real change. Not just him saying what he thought I wanted to hear, but actually proving it. And I did want to work things out with him. . . didn't I?

A small part of me believed I'd go back. That Jackson would change, that things would settle. But deep down, I knew better. I knew what settling with him meant—apologies that didn't last, promises stretched thin, walking on eggshells even when things were good.

And yet, the idea of leaving for good still felt impossible, terrifying, even. Not because I wanted him. But because I didn't know who I was anymore without that constant pressure, that low-grade survival mode. I'd forgotten what it was like to breathe without bracing for something.

Logan's truck smelled faintly of flowers and dirt, and I found myself clinging to it like an anchor. Being here—doing something as mundane as waiting while he ran an errand, it felt safe. Familiar, in a way that didn't make my stomach tighten.

But safety was just an illusion, wasn't it? There was always a risk to feeling safe, to allowing myself to be happy, because it never seemed to last. Sooner or later, the other shoe would drop, and this time, I needed to be ready.

I took a deep breath, my eyes wandering across the cab of Logan's truck. A vanilla-scented pine tree hung from the review mirror, faded from the sun. Below it, random coins laid scattered across the center console where a frayed piece of rope peeked out from a small compartment.

Curious, I lifted the lid, my heart squeezing in recognition at the small heart-shaped rock wrapped neatly in twine.

Suddenly the driver's side door swung open and Logan climbed inside. "You hungry?" he asked, throwing the truck into drive.

But I couldn't speak—couldn't find words as I held up the small bracelet I'd made for him so many years ago.

"You kept this?" I managed, finally finding my voice. "All these years, and you kept it?"

Logan's face shifted, a mix of embarrassment and mild irritation at me digging through his stuff. "Of course I kept it," he said. "Hell, I wore it every day until a couple years ago. I only took it off 'cause I didn't want to risk breaking it."

He opened his hand and I dropped it into his palm, but instead of tucking it back into the center console, he carefully slipped it over his wrist.

"I'm sorry I snooped," I mumbled, feeling a bit guilty.

"It's alright. Honestly, I probably would've done the same thing." He grinned. "Find anything else interesting?"

I shot him a playful look. "Oh, you know, a few condoms, an old bottle of whiskey. . ."

"Ah, so the usual," he chuckled, and I couldn't help but laugh too.

In that moment, something clicked. Maybe I didn't want to work things out with Jackson after all. Maybe everything I'd been looking for was sitting right in front of me all along.

Thirty Seven

WE STOPPED FOR CHILI DOGS on the way back—some cute little shack with a yellow roof that had been around since the '50s.

"No salad?" Logan teased, the two of us perched side by side on the tailgate of his truck.

"No salad," I grinned, polishing off my second one.

By the time we rolled into Windhaven, night had settled in, and I was more than eager to see Winston. It was the longest I'd been away from him since I brought him home.

"You need to replace that bulb," Logan said, nodding toward the lightless porch.

As we pulled into the drive, I heard Winston barking from inside, but something else caught my attention. The rear tire on my car was completely flat.

"Damnit," I muttered, climbing out of the truck.

Logan came around, crouching beside me to get a better look.

"Think it's patchable?" I asked, already bracing myself for the cost of a replacement. I still had plenty of cash tucked away, but a new tire wasn't how I wanted to spend it.

He shook his head. "Not unless you can patch a crater."

"What are you talking about?"

He pointed to a gash in the rubber. "This wasn't an accident. Someone slashed it."

I shot up and ran around to check the others but immediately froze. The word *SLUT* had been carved into the passenger side of the car in big, angry letters—each one jagged and deep, like whoever did it wanted to hurt more than just the paint.

"What is it?" Logan asked, alarm creeping over his face as he came to stand beside me.

I didn't answer right away. My stomach had dropped, the air sucked clean out of my lungs. I just pointed, my hand trembling slightly.

Logan followed my gaze. His jaw clenched when he saw it. "Jesus," he muttered, stepping closer for a better look. "Who the hell—?"

"I don't know," I said, voice low.

He turned to me then, something dark flickering behind his eyes. "This wasn't random."

No. It wasn't.

From inside, Winston let out a howl.

I turned and sprinted for the front door with Logan calling after me.

But I didn't stop. My hands shook violently as I jammed the key into the lock and shoved the door open. Winston launched toward me, his paws thudding against my chest as I knelt to greet him.

"Stay here," Logan said, stepping into the darkened house. Minutes dragged by before he finally returned. "It's clear," he said. "Winston must've sensed someone nearby. They probably took off just before we got back." He scanned the darkness beyond the porch. "I'm going to take a quick look around—make sure no one's still out there."

I nodded, my mouth dry, as I coaxed Winston back inside. From the window, I watched Logan's flashlight cut through the night—the narrow beam sweeping across the house and over the collapsed barn toward the open field. When he came back, I'd finally steadied myself enough to speak.

"Find anything?" I asked, my voice weary.

He shook his head. "Nothing. Whoever it was, we must've scared them off."

"Why would someone do this?" I whispered, though the answer was clear.

This was rage. This was anger.

This was Jackson.

Warm tears slipped down my cheeks before I even realized I was crying. "I'm sorry. Jesus, I'm so sorry."

Logan's hands settled firmly on my shoulders. "What the hell do you have to be sorry for?"

"This is all so fucked up," I sobbed. "I didn't mean to drag you into this."

"You didn't drag me into anything," he insisted, his face inches from mine. "I *chose* to be here. And thank God I was—because if I hadn't been, who knows what could've happened."

The thought paralyzed me. I knew *exactly* what would've happened. Logan knew too.

"I'm staying the night," he said firmly.

"You don't have to do that," I argued.

"Yes, I do," he replied, already heading toward the hallway.

"You're overreacting," I insisted. "I'll be fine." It was a lie—and we both knew it. But the idea of him sleeping over stirred something in me I wasn't ready to face.

Logan grabbed a pillow and blanket from the linen closet and tossed them onto the sofa. "I'll sleep on the couch," he said without looking at me. "I'll be gone by morning. You won't even know I was here."

I rolled my eyes. *Yeah right.* Still, as much as I hated to admit it, the thought of him close by, just in case, eased the fear and anxiety mounting in my chest.

"Fine," I relented. "But then what? You can't sleep on my couch every night trying to protect me."

A brief image of Logan sleeping over, hair tousled and shirt-less every morning sent a warm flood through my veins.

Logan turned to face me. "You're right. I can't. But I don't like the idea of you being out here alone. Especially with. . ." He paused. "Your situation."

"My *situation*?" I repeated, surprised. "I'm not some damsel in distress, Logan. I don't need you to rescue me. For fuck's sake, how do you think I've survived this long?"

"I don't know, Emily!" he snapped.

His sudden anger caught me off guard and I flinched.

Logan exhaled slowly, the fire in his brown eyes dimming. "I don't know," he repeated, softer now. "And it scares the hell out of me."

Thirty Eight

THE FLOORBOARDS GROANED AS I CREPT downstairs. I couldn't sleep with the scent of Jackson's possible intrusion still thick in the air.

Every creak needled my nerves. Every shadow made me flinch. Even with Logan here, the idea of Jackson lurking outside gnawed at me like something feral. What if I hadn't locked the door? Would he have hurt Winston? Ransacked the house? Waited in the dark to attack me once I was alone?

But Jackson didn't want confrontation. He wanted control. To leave his mark. To violate me in a way only he could. This was a game to him—one he intended on winning.

This house had once been a refuge. A sanctuary. Now it felt tainted—robbed of everything it once offered.

Logan didn't stir when I entered the living room, his face cast in soft amber hues from the fire crackling in the hearth. At some point in the night, he'd built a fire. The stones on the floor were gone, and for a brief moment, I was oddly irritated that he'd moved them back.

"Couldn't sleep either?" I asked, shifting my weight from one foot to the other.

He shook his head, lifting a half-empty glass of wine. "I hope you don't mind. It felt. . . necessary."

I settled into the worn armchair across from him. "Actually, I think I'll join you, if that's okay?"

"The more the merrier," he murmured, tilting his head back for a slow sip.

Passing me the bottle, I slowly raised it to my lips and let the bitterness burn its way down my throat.

The flames crackled, throwing soft amber light against the walls as the silence stretched. I wasn't sure who would speak first—maybe neither of us would. Maybe we'd just sit here, pretending the past wasn't clawing its way to the surface.

"You ever wish things had gone differently?" I asked finally, my voice barely louder than the crackling fire.

His eyes didn't leave the flames. "Every damn day."

I swallowed hard, unsure if I was relieved or devastated to hear it.

"Yeah," I said quietly. "Me too."

He took a long drink then finally turned to face me. "Eleven years," he said faintly. "Since the last time we saw each other." He placed his now empty glass on the coffee table, and I refilled it without asking. "Not once did I think you'd actually leave."

I sighed. He wanted to do this now? Fine.

"You left first," I challenged, but the sting wasn't there.

"But I came back," Logan countered, his voice thick. "I came back, Emily. For you. If I'd known you were going to leave. . . if I'd known it would be over a decade before I saw you again—I never would've left."

I swallowed hard, the warmth from the fire suddenly too much.

"You didn't give me a reason to stay," I whispered.

Logan leaned back, the couch sighing beneath his weight as he sank into it. "I wasn't the same man when I came back, you know."

The fire popped, sending up sparks like fleeting stars drifting into the night.

"I did things," he went on. "Things I can't take back. Things I'll never forgive myself for. The training, the deployments. . . they strip you down. Numb you. Chipping away until all that's left is reflex and survival."

He stared into the flames, haunted by memories I couldn't begin to understand. I could feel the weight of his pain pressing down on me like a storm cloud ready to burst.

"But you made it through," I said, a sad attempt at comfort.

He nodded slowly. "I did. And the only thing that got me through—the only light in all that darkness, was you. The idea of you. Coming home to you. That was what I clung to. On the nights when my thoughts were too loud, the days when I didn't even feel human. . . it was always you." He paused, his expression tightening. "And then. . . fuck, you were just gone. No letter. No goodbye. Nothing."

"Logan. . ." I tried, but the words collapsed inside my mouth. How could I answer that kind of pain? How could I measure his suffering against the glamourous, albeit, violent life I'd built?

I reached toward him, my hand hovering across the coffee table, but I couldn't bring myself to touch him. There was an invisible barrier between us now, between the years that had swallowed us whole.

"Why didn't you call?" I asked, even though I already knew.

He looked at me, his face worn. "You know why."

"Tell me anyway."

Logan exhaled slowly. "I almost did. When I first got back. For a second, I let myself believe maybe we could pick up where we left off. I knew you'd moved away, but I thought. . . if I could just see you, talk to you, maybe you'd come home." He paused, jaw tightening. "Then I found out you were married. To Jackson Bishop, of all people. How was I supposed to compete with that? My head was a mess. I was a mess. And you. . . you had everything you'd ever wanted. You were happy. All I had to offer was a broken man and some distant memories. What kind of a life is that to give someone? What kind of love?"

Tears stung my eyes, blurring the edges of the room. My silence wasn't hesitation—it was habit. A wall I'd built over years of swallowing my voice, brick by agonizing brick.

"Why him, Emily?" Logan asked, his voice strained. "And why didn't you leave when things…" He broke off, unable to say the rest out loud.

I couldn't look at him. Instead, I traced the wood grain of the coffee table with an unsteady finger, trying to ground myself in something solid.

"He wasn't always like that," I admitted after a pause. "In the beginning, everything was perfect. Too perfect. Then it wasn't. I didn't want to admit it, but the picture I'd painted of us started to crack. His protectiveness turned into control. Then came the isolation, the gaslighting, and eventually, the physical abuse."

My heart slammed against my ribs like a frantic bird trapped inside a cage of bone. This was it. There was no going back now. The truth was a festering wound that had silently poisoned my life and I was desperate for an antidote.

"Katherine warned me—*begged me* not to marry him. But I was already in too deep. And by then, walking away wasn't simple. He made sure of that." I finally met Logan's heavy gaze, my eyes red rimmed, my lips tripping over my confession. "And the worst part? He made me believe I deserved it."

Logan's face darkened, rage splashing across his features like fire burning over dry brush.

"You should've called me," he said, voice sharp. "You should've let me help."

"Look around you, Logan," I said, my voice catching on the lump in my throat. "Protecting me from him wouldn't have stopped any of this." I motioned toward the shattered window. "He didn't just break and bruise my body, he broke my fucking spirit."

The tears came fast in hot, relentless rivers down my cheeks. My marriage to Jackson hadn't been a sudden collapse. It had been a slow, agonizing descent into a darkness I hadn't known existed. A darkness woven together by threads of control, manipulation, and a creeping insidious violence.

Jackson fed on fear. On silence. On the pieces of me he'd broken and claimed as his own.

Silence stretched between us. I shut my eyes and a kaleidoscope of images bloomed from memory—Jackson's face, twisting into a mask of rage. The cold glint of the belt buckle, sharp against my back.

Beside me, the fire popped and I jumped.

"I'm so sorry, Emily," Logan said at last, his voice a pained, low rumble.

I looked at him. The firelight danced in warm shadows across his face, highlighting the worry etched around his chestnut eyes. He wanted to fix it. He wanted to fix *me*.

But some things aren't fixable.

"Don't you *dare* say you're sorry," I snapped, the heat in my voice surprising even me. "It's not your responsibility to shoulder another man's demons—and trust me, his are heavy enough to crush him."

The truth was, I didn't want his pity. I needed something else—something I couldn't name, let alone ask for.

My gaze drifted toward the broken window again. Beyond it, a single star burned defiantly above the dark line of the mountains. And for a moment, I couldn't help but wonder if stars ever felt the weight of the world too.

"Even if Jackson apologized—and he won't, I *know* he won't, I don't think I could ever forgive him," I admitted, the words tasting as bitter as I felt.

Logans voice, usually soothing, now grated on my raw nerves. "What Jackson did—that's not a reflection of you. It's *him*. His sickness. His need to control."

"*Stop*," I choked out, my voice fraying at the edges. "Stop trying to explain it away. Stop trying to minimize it. You weren't there. You don't understand." Tears continued to stream down my face. "I'm broken, Logan. *Irrevocably* broken. And no amount of comfort or well-meaning words is going to glue me back together."

"No," he said, his voice wavering with emotion. He reached for my hand, but I recoiled, his touch falling short in the growing space between us. "You're not broken. You're strong, Emily. Stronger than you know. You survived."

"*Survived?*" I spat the word back at him, my voice venomous. "You, of all people, should know that surviving isn't living. You don't know what it's like to be carved into pieces by someone who swore they loved you. You don't know how that kind of control seeps into your soul and hollows you out."

"I want to know," he said, his voice breaking under the weight of it. "I want to understand. I want to help. I want to—"

And then it hit me.

"Is that what this is?" I asked. "Some twisted rescue mission?"

He faltered, hurt flickering across his face. "No," he said quickly. "No, of course not."

But I wasn't done. I needed the truth, even if it shattered whatever fragile thread we had left.

"Then *what*, Logan?" I demanded angrily. "What is it about me that keeps pulling you back and dragging me from my own wreckage over and over again?"

"Because I fucking love you!" he burst out, the words ripping free like they'd been trying to claw their way out for years.

My breath hitched—swallowed by the silence that followed his outburst. I opened my mouth to argue, to tell him he was wrong, that loving me was a mistake. But before I could speak, he'd already closed the distance between us. His hand cupped my face, thumb brushing away the tears as he brought me closer to him.

"I always have," he whispered. Then his lips crashed into mine.

The kiss wasn't soft. It wasn't careful. It was a wild storm, a hurricane of longing and undeniable need. It was fierce and heavy, held together by years of silence, and missed chances. It wasn't the tender kiss I'd once dreamt about—but a reclamation shaped by the wreckage we both carried.

I melted into him, my arms winding around his neck in instinct. The taste of him, the feel of him—it was an addiction I hadn't realized I'd been craving. I needed this. I *needed* him.

Pulling me closer, I inhaled his scent as he guided me gently toward the sofa. I couldn't let go—the only time I pulled away was to breathe.

The cushions dipped beneath us as he laid me down, his hands warm and deliberate. A shiver rippled through me as his mouth found the sensitive spot along my jaw.

I moaned, my fingers threading through his hair.

"Emily. . ." he breathed against my skin. I loved the way he said my name, the way it coated his tongue in sweet ecstasy.

"Say it again," I whispered, my hips rising to meet him.

He smiled against my neck. *"Emily."*

When his mouth found mine again, it was with a hunger that nearly unraveled me. His hand slipped beneath my shirt, fingers delicately trailing over the curve of my breasts. The heat of his touch seared into me, pulling a soft gasp from my lips. I could feel the urgency in him, the hard evidence pressed against me as he began to lift my shirt.

But just as quickly, doubt crept in. I shifted, pressing my palms to his chest.

His eyes searched mine, immediately concerned. "What's wrong?" he asked gently, his fingers hesitating at my waist.

I swallowed hard, shame blooming in my throat. "It's just. . ." I stumbled, unable to express the rush of insecurities threatening to swallow me.

Logan shifted back slightly, cradling my face in his hands. "Look at me," he whispered. His gaze locked with mine. "You are the most beautiful woman I've ever seen. Every inch of you—every curve, every line. But if you want to stop, we'll stop. I understand."

I blinked against the sting in my eyes. I wanted this. I *wanted him*. But the words were jagged on my tongue.

"I don't look the way you think I do," I revealed. I'd lost weight since Jackson, but was still heavier than I liked—my body still carrying remnants of the violence I'd survived.

Logan's thumb brushed against my cheek. "No, you don't," he smiled. "You look better."

I let out a shaky breath, the tightness in my chest loosening just enough for me to nod. "I want this," I said, voice small but steady. "I want *you*."

Something in him shifted then, as if my confession unlocked a door he'd been waiting years to walk through. He leaned in slowly, his lips brushing mine with a reverence that made my heart ache. This kiss was different—less urgency, more worship. It said *you're safe*, and *I see you*, and *you matter*.

As our bodies pressed together again, I let the tension melt away. His hands moved with purpose, exploring with a slowness that made every touch feel sacred. He lifted my shirt, pausing for my silent permission before peeling it away. His eyes drank me in—not with lust, but awe.

"You're stunning," he murmured, as if the word itself wasn't enough to capture what he saw.

I didn't push him away this time.

His fingers skimmed down my sides, leaving a trail of heat in their wake. He kissed the hollow of my throat, then lower, his mouth tender and patient. With every touch, he unspooled something tight and fearful inside me.

My hands roamed over his broad chest, memorizing every inch. His breath hitched when I ran my fingertips along the line of his ribs. Something primal and deeply human stirred between us.

There was no rush. No performance. Just presence. Just two people rediscovering a rhythm that had never really left.

Logan leaned back, muscles flexing as he peeled off his shirt, the low firelight casting warm shadows across his chest.

A slow smile tugged at my lips. His dark olive skin shimmered in the amber glow, and the way his hungry eyes locked onto mine sent a pulse of heat spiraling through me.

I propped myself up on my elbows, anticipation curling in my belly. But as I lifted my mouth to meet his, he leaned in too fast—and with a sickening crack, the two of us collided.

Stars burst behind my eyelids as pain bloomed across my forehead. Disoriented, I blinked, instinctively raising a hand to my face.

Across from me, Logan had recoiled to the other end of the couch, one hand clutched to his forehead.

"Are you okay?" he asked, his voice heavy with concern.

"I'm fine," I said, wincing as I pressed my fingers gently to my eye. Then I saw a thin line of blood trailing down his temple. "Oh my god, you're bleeding!"

Logan swiped at it and let out a short laugh. "Well, that's a first." He didn't seem the least bit fazed. "You might want to get some ice on that," he added, nodding toward my swelling eye.

"There should be a bag of frozen peas in the freezer," I said, easing myself upright.

He disappeared into the kitchen and returned a moment later, not with peas—but with two frozen dinner rolls.

"I couldn't find any vegetables," he said, grinning as he held one out. "These were the next best thing."

"Seriously?" I asked, raising a brow as I took it and pressed it to my face.

"Hey," he shrugged, mimicking the gesture with the other roll, "at least we'll have a hell of a story."

I couldn't help it, I burst out laughing. One minute we'd been wrapped in heat and hunger, ready to burn the house down, and the next we were bruised, bleeding, and icing our injuries with frozen bread.

If that wasn't an accurate description of my life, I didn't know what was.

Logan chuckled along with me, though he winced when the roll shifted. "Well," he said, pressing it back into place, "I can't say our reunion has been boring."

"That's one word for it," I giggled, sinking deeper into the couch.

The laughter slowly faded, leaving behind a warm quiet. Not uncomfortable—just real. Like a curtain had dropped between us and we were finally seeing each other, bruises and all.

Logan turned toward me, resting the roll on his knee. "You know, I meant what I said earlier. I love you, Emily. I always have."

I looked down at the dinner roll clutched in my hand, now slightly thawed and damp with condensation. It was ridiculous, this whole situation—but maybe that was the point. Maybe love wasn't always neat and tidy. Maybe sometimes it was clumsy and bruised, patched together with frozen bread and unsaid words.

"I'm still trying to figure out who I am without him," I confessed. "I'm still trying to feel like I'm worthy of love."

Logan's voice was low but reassuring. "Then let me remind you."

I looked at him and saw the man who had waited, the man who had come back. Not to fix me, not to save me, but to stand beside me.

My heart cracked wide open.

"Okay," I whispered. "Remind me."

He leaned forward again—slower this time, and kissed me. Not out of desperation, or uncertainty, but with the quiet conviction of someone who knew exactly what he wanted. Me. Every wound, every sharp jagged edge.

He didn't flinch from the broken parts or shy away from the scars I tried to hide. He wasn't afraid of the darkness I carried. It was like he saw it and chose me anyway.

And in that moment, wrapped in the warmth of his arms and the hush of the firelight, I felt something I hadn't in years—safe.

Thirty Nine

MORNING LIGHT SLIPPED THROUGH THE windows, brushing the worn floorboards in soft gold. The living room smelled faintly of smoke, with whisps of it still curling over white ash in the fireplace.

For a few blissful seconds, I didn't remember where I was or how I'd fallen asleep—then it all came rushing back. The slashed tires. The keyed car.

Logan.

I blinked, my cheek stuck slightly to the throw pillow, and turned my head. A blanket had been tucked over me sometime during the night, and my neck ached from the angle I'd been curled in.

From the kitchen, I heard Logan's voice, half-singing some old song I couldn't remember. I sat up slowly, rubbing my eyes, and turned to see him standing by the stove, wearing one of my dish towels slung over his shoulder. Winston stood beside him, watching him slowly move around the kitchen—though I'm guessing he was less in it for the help and more in it for the bacon.

Logan glanced over and smiled when he saw me. "Morning."

I cleared my throat, my voice still thick with sleep. "Are you. . . cooking?"

"Trying to," he said, flipping something in the pan that might've been eggs. "I figured I owed you breakfast after making you sleep on that torture device you call a couch."

I pulled the blanket tighter around me and leaned back against the armrest. "It's a very stylish torture device, thank you."

He grinned and turned back to the stove. "You drooled on it. Just saying."

"Rude," I mumbled, though my lips curved upward anyway.

I watched as he tossed a slice of bacon in Winston's direction. "As promised," he said. Winston licked fervently at the grease spot left on the floor before cocking his head and begging for another. "I told him if he didn't wake you, he would be rewarded."

"A very fine reward indeed," I mused.

Logan poured coffee into the handmade mug before carrying it over.

"I wasn't sure how you take it anymore," he said, handing it to me.

I wrapped my hands around the mug, feeling the heat seep into my fingers. "Just a splash of cream. Nothing fancy."

He nodded and sat on the edge of the coffee table, balancing his own mug on his knee.

I tilted my head, eyeing him. "I thought you said you didn't like coffee?"

"I don't," he replied, grimacing at the mug before taking a cautious sip. "But you do. And I want to share the things you love, with you."

I smiled, cradling my own cup and breathing in the warm, comforting scent.

We sat there for a minute, drinking coffee and letting the quiet settle again. There was something about this moment that made my chest ache in a good way. Like hope, but quieter.

Logan reached out, brushing a strand of hair from my face. "I don't expect this to be easy." he said, breaking the silence. "I just want you to know I'm here. However long it takes."

I bit the inside of my cheek, the emotion rising too fast. "I don't know how to do this yet."

"You don't have to," he said, his hand finding mine. "You just have to trust me."

I set the mug down and gave him a half-smile. "I've always trusted you."

We ate in companionable silence, pausing to laugh at Winston who seemed to keep inching closer each time we took another bite.

"I should probably head out soon," Logan said after we finished. "Change into some fresh clothes, check on things. Maybe go to work."

I nodded, my heart sinking a little. "Yeah. Of course."

He watched me for a moment, then gave me a reassuring smile. "I'll come back tonight. If you want me to."

I squeezed his fingers. "I do."

Logan kissed my forehead gently and stood, wincing slightly as his hand brushed over his eye. I watched him walk to the door, hesitant to break the moment.

"Logan?" I called after him.

He turned, hand on the doorknob.

"What you said... last night? I feel the same way. Just, please be patient with me." The last time I told someone I loved them, it destroyed me. I knew I loved him, but once those words left my mouth, I couldn't take them back.

His expression softened. "I'll spend the rest of my life waiting, if that's how long it takes."

I looked down at my hands, then back up at him. "You mean that?" I asked, heart stumbling in my chest.

He crossed the room, stopping in front of me. Then, gently, his fingers brushed my cheek, like I was something fragile he wasn't ready to lose.

"I've never meant anything more."

His mouth found mine with aching slowness—no urgency, just truth. The kind that settled in your bones and made you forget how to breathe.

He kissed me like a promise. Like the years we lost didn't matter, because this moment was ours.

And I kissed him back, like I'd been waiting my whole life to remember how.

February 2nd, 1864
West Virginia

Dearest Emily,

The lantern burns low tonight, its flame flickering against the canvas walls as if it, too, is weary from all this waiting. Outside, the wind howls across the camp like a restless ghost, stirring up the scent of ash and cold earth. Most of the men have turned in, their breaths rising in clouds as they sleep, but I find myself awake once again. . . thinking of you.

It is a strange thing, to write to someone I have never met and yet feel tethered to in ways I cannot explain. Perhaps it is the nature of war that makes men speak truths they might otherwise carry to their graves. Or perhaps it is something else entirely. Something older. Something deeper.

You asked of Finnigan, and it's no simple thing to put him into words. My brother is as steady as an oak, firm-rooted and resolute in a way I have never quite managed to be. And yet, for all his steadiness, he is not without heart. I've seen him risk himself for men he hardly knew. I've watched him carry the wounded and bury the dead with the care of a brother. Where I tend to overthink and carry the weight of things too long, Finn moves with quiet purpose. Men follow him not because he demands it, but because he embodies a kind of strength they can trust. When we were boys, Finn was always the first to leap from the riverbank, the first to climb the highest branch, the first to throw a stone simply to watch the ripple. He was bold, not for the sake of bravado, but because the world seemed to welcome him. He has a fondness for stories, particularly the old ones told by our grandfather on winter nights, about kings and warriors and far-off lands. I recall how he'd sit at the hearth, eyes wide, absorbing every word as though it were truth carved into stone.

Though younger by three years, he leaves behind a wife and a small child. Emily, the thought of him not returning to them haunts me more than any bullet or blade. Of all the horrors this war has shown me, that possibility remains my greatest fear. To know him is to know loyalty in its truest form. And to lose him. . . I dare not let my thoughts go that far.

I must confess, when I first laid eyes on your photograph, something stirred within me, a sensation I can neither explain nor dismiss. It was as if your eyes were not new to me. As if I had seen them before, though in what world, in what life-time, I cannot say. The clarity of the image was so strik-ing that I felt as if I could reach out and touch you. It was al-most as though you were standing before me, so vivid, so real. In some confounded way, you were more than a photograph, as though the image itself was alive.

And the color, how astonishing to see you in such richness! The way the hues of the light captured your beauty, the way your skin seemed to glow with a fairness that made me pause, in awe. And your eyes. They are a depth I cannot begin to explain, rich and alive with something untold. I find myself transfixed by them, unable to look away.

Is it possible that such a thing could be? Could it be that my soul has somehow wandered between worlds, or that I am al-ready lost, trapped in a strange limbo between time? I do not know, Emily, but what I do know with certainty is this. I know you. Not just in my mind, nor in the words I write to you, but in something far more familiar. My soul knows you. It knows the warmth of a summer rain that lingers on your skin. The sweetness of honey in your hair. The constellation of freckles across your cheeks. I know them as though I've touched them, kissed them. I've held you in a way this life does not remember.

Please, do not think me mad, nor forward in my affections. I am simply a man who has nothing left to lose and no time for silence. Before I ride out again, I felt the desperate need to speak the truth that stirs deep within me. If you do not feel this strange connection, this pull between us, I will understand, though my heart aches at the thought. Perhaps it is madness, but then again, how else can one explain the way the universe bends, folds, and carries us along in strange currents we cannot control?

I leave tomorrow, and I may be gone for several days. We are surrounded, with no food, no medicine, and precious little time. Our plan is bold, almost reckless. We ride into confederate lines to negotiate what peace we can. The general and several officers will accompany me, and Finnigan will stay behind. He does not know of you, nor of the letters we've shared, but I have instructed him to write to you should I not return. My satchel, with all my thoughts of you, will remain with him.

Whatever happens, Emily, I want you to know this. I saw you. I saw you as though you were a part of me, a part I did not know I had lost until I found you. And something deep within me, something I cannot explain, remembers you.

Yours beyond time and space,
James

Forty

I SAT ON THE edge of the bed, reading James's letter again and again until the ink blurred into indistinct swirls and the words lost their shape.

I hardly knew this man, but I couldn't deny the familiar pull between us, no matter how crazy it made me feel. Everything about this was insane. Then again, so is writing to someone who died over a century ago, but here we were.

Still, I couldn't shake the sense that James was right. That somehow, impossibly, I *did* know him. Not in memory, but in the marrow of me. In a place that didn't reason with logic or time.

I set the letter down, then picked it up again.

My soul knows you. I've held you in a way this life does not remember.

The words sliced through me.

I pictured Logan—his hands tracing over my body, the heat of his mouth against mine. Guilt surged so sharply in my gut I thought I might be sick.

This was crazy. All of it. How had I found myself needing to *justify* feelings that had no place in reality? James didn't exist. Not anymore. He was a ghost.

Logan was here. He was real. He was alive.

And yet. . .

I couldn't deny the pull I felt every time a new letter appeared. Or the quickening of my pulse at the sight of my name written in James's hand. The unshakable feeling that the life I was living without him was somehow. . . incomplete. Like I was reading someone else's story.

I refolded James's letter and set it gently on the nightstand. He said he'd be gone a few days—maybe that would be enough time for me to clear my head.

But what if it was too late by then?

I grabbed my phone and dialed Katherine without hesitation. Fuck the risk. Fuck Jackson. He already knew where I was and I wasn't about to continue letting him decide who I could talk to, and when.

The line rang twice, then went straight to voicemail.

"This is Katherine. Leave a message."

I closed my eyes. "Kat, it's me. I need you. Call me back."

I hung up and started pacing, the phone still clenched in my hand. My eyes flicked between the folded letter and the mirror in front of me.

A bruise bloomed beneath my right eye, a swirl of violet and indigo. I reached up, touching it gently—and then I smiled.

This bruise didn't make me feel small or powerless. It didn't make me feel cheap or weak. But instead it reminded me that I was a woman worth loving. And that I too, deserved to be happy.

I re-dialed Katherine but again, it went straight to voicemail. Damn it.

I needed to talk to someone—*anyone* who wouldn't look at me like I'd completely lost it.

Winston let out a sharp bark from the doorway.

"Hold on, I'm thinking," I said, glancing up at him.

Then it clicked.

Danielle. A grin spread across my face. "Winston, you're an absolute genius!"

Like Gran, she was weird, and wild, and more open-minded than anyone I knew. If I told her about the letters, about James and Logan, she'd listen. She might call me crazy but she'd do it with a smile and most importantly, not from a padded room.

I wrapped my arms around Winston, still lingering in the doorway. He stood perfectly still, ears perked, head tilted in that impossibly wise way only dogs could manage.

I pointed a finger at him. "No squirrels this time, got it?"

By the time we finally reached the shelter, I was drenched in sweat. The sun was blazing overhead, and the humidity was somehow even worse than yesterday.

A chorus of barking rose above the jingle of the front bell, and I heard Dani's footsteps hurrying down the hallway.

"Sorry about that," she said, suddenly appearing. "I was just—oh my god. What the hell happened to you?"

"We. . . it's. . ." I panted. "Winston and I. . . we walked."

Beside me, Winston collapsed onto the cool floor, his tongue lolling out in exhaustion.

"You *walked* all the way here?" she asked, grabbing a bowl for Winston and handing me a water bottle from behind her desk.

I dumped some on my face before chugging the rest. Once my lungs stopped wheezing, I wiped the sweat from my forehead and managed a half-smile.

"Someone slashed my tires," I said, waving my hand to fan myself. "Among other things."

"Other things?" she echoed, refilling Winston's bowl as he drained it. "What kind of other things?"

Once I was sure I could speak without gasping, I gave her a quick recap of the night before—including everything involving Logan.

"Damn," she said. "People really don't like you much, huh?"

"Yeah. . . not exactly," I mumbled.

She gave a low whistle. "That bad?"

"If you think carving the word 'SLUT' into the side of my car is 'bad,' then yeah, I'd say it's pretty awful."

Dani leaned against the desk with her arms crossed, eyes narrowed like she was trying to solve a puzzle. "You gonna tell me who did it?"

I shrugged, though the movement felt like lifting a bag of wet cement. "I think. . . I think it was Jackson. I'm pretty sure he's the one who threw that rock through my window, too."

"Your crazy piece of shit ex?"

"Not *technically* an ex yet. But yeah, that one."

"Yikes." She uncrossed her arms, walked over, and gave Winston a gentle scratch behind the ears. "And you still walked here?"

I nodded. "I needed to talk to you."

"Sounds serious," she said, straightening.

I drew in a breath before letting it out slowly. "Remember when you told me you thought Magnolia House was rumored to be haunted?"

"Yeah. . ." Her green eyes sharpened. "Wait—did something happen?"

"Sort of," I admitted. "Honestly, I don't even know how to say this without sounding completely unhinged, but. . . here goes."

I spent the next half hour explaining everything. The letters, the stupid, impulsive decision to write back. My complicated history with Logan. When I finally finished, I handed her the photograph I'd stolen from the Charleston library—bracing myself as she studied it.

She didn't speak right away. She just stood there, staring at it like she wasn't sure it was real. Then, slowly, she exhaled through her nose and ran a hand through her short hair.

"Okay," she said finally. "That's. . . a lot."

I blinked. "Wait. So you believe me?"

"I've seen enough weird shit not to rule anything out," Dani said, handing me the photo back. "Can't say you have bad taste in men, though. He's hot."

I rolled my eyes. "He doesn't *exist*."

"Obviously he does if you're talking to him," she argued. "Maybe not here, not now, but somewhere, there's a very fine man—or two—pining after you. At least, that's what it sounds like to me."

I shot Dani a pointed look.

She grinned, a mischievous glint in her eyes. "Personally, I'd keep both. It's not considered cheating if one of them is technically dead."

"This is crazy," I said, my voice a little shaky. "I sound insane."

"No," she said firmly, stepping closer. "You sound like someone who's been through hell and is still trying to make sense of it."

I let out a dry laugh. "So what, you think I've been writing love letters to a ghost?"

"Maybe," she shrugged. "Or maybe it's someone you're connected to—like from a past life or something."

I stared at her. "Is that actually a thing?"

"Absolutely," she said, making her way behind the desk and sinking into the chair. From somewhere down the hall, Henry appeared, looking just as dissatisfied as the day I met him.

"Your soul's just energy," she continued, scooping him into her lap. "When the body dies, that energy has to go some-where. Think of it like, spiritual recycling."

I studied her. "So, reincarnation?"

"Exactly. Maybe you and this James guy have done this be-fore—been something to each other in another life. I've never heard of soulmates reconnecting *this* way, but hey, stranger things have happened."

I sat with that for a second, my thoughts spinning. "And what about Logan?"

She looked down at Henry, stroking his fur absently. "What about him?"

"I mean, where does he fit in? If James and I have this whole soul-connection thing, then what does that make Logan?"

Dani shifted slightly in her seat. "Wherever you want him to fit. Soulmates aren't always romantic. You can have more than one. Hell, I've had twelve in this lifetime alone. Some were partners, some friends, one was definitely my dog."

I raised an eyebrow.

"What?" she said, grinning. "He was emotionally available and always happy to see me. What more can you ask for?"

"Okay. . ." I said warily. "I came in here worried *you'd* think I was crazy, but now I'm starting to wonder if *you* are."

Dani smiled. "That's because it *is* crazy—but just because something is crazy, doesn't make it any less real."

I thought of Gran and her so-called *spiritual nonsense* that turned half the town against us. I thought of Papa's rocks, and the nights Katherine and I would lie in bed, listening to Gran whispering to someone who wasn't there.

What if she hadn't been crazy like everyone said? What if she was just more open in a world full of people too scared—or too stubborn, to see beyond what made them feel safe?

The phone rang on Dani's desk.

"Harrison County Animal Shelter, how can I help you?" she answered, her voice tight. "Uh huh. . . Are you kidding me? Okay, but you said that last time. I understand, but what am I supposed to do until then? Fine. Whatever."

She slammed the phone down hard and Henry leapt off her lap. Winston stirred beside me, barely lifting his head—too drained to even pretend he cared about chasing the cat.

"Everything okay?" I asked, tightening the leash just in case he changed his mind.

Dani pinched the bridge of her nose. "It's the damn supplier. I've been out of dog food for days. Someone donated a bag, thank god, but it barely covered anything. And now this *asshole*"—she snapped the word at the phone like someone might still be listening—"says he can't get here until next week."

"I can go get it," I offered.

Dani looked up from her desk, brow raised. "You walked all the way here. I'm not sending you right back out there on foot. And besides, I need more than you can carry."

I glanced out the window at the white Jeep Cherokee parked out front. "What if I take your car?"

She hesitated, chewing on her bottom lip.

"Come on," I said. "You helped me, let me return the favor."

After a pause, she sighed. "Alright. But be careful. I'm already pushing my luck with the brakes."

"No hard stops. Got it." She tossed me the keys, and I caught them midair. "Mind if I leave him here?" I asked, gesturing to Winston.

We both looked down at him, sprawled out and snoring at my feet.

Dani grinned. "I don't think you could get that dog to move even if you dangled a ribeye in front of him."

I turned to head out, the door jingling as I stepped into the sun, setting off another round of chaotic barking behind me.

Forty One

Rows of dog food blurred in front of me—lamb and rice, chicken and quinoa, salmon. I grabbed several bags of each, unsure which one Dani preferred or if she even cared.

Behind the counter, the girl with the gum was back. Her headband was blue this time instead of pink, and she didn't bother looking up as she rang me through.

"Still here?" she said with a pop.

I smiled. "Still here."

A young boy bagging groceries helped me load the heavy bags into the Jeep. I was about to head back to the shelter when suddenly, I had an idea. My fingers closed around the leftover change, jingling in my pocket as I crossed the street to the hardware store.

Mr. Abernathy wasn't there. In his place stood a younger version of him. He had the same kind eyes, but with shoulder-length dirty blonde hair instead of familiar white curls.

"Good afternoon," he greeted as I stepped inside. "Is there something I can help you find?"

I shook my head. "Just looking, thanks."

As I wandered toward the back, I was struck by how everything had changed and yet, somehow hadn't. New shelves gleamed under fresh fluorescent lights, and the hand-painted signs had been replaced with sleek, modern ones. The same red-and-white dusty tiles lined the floor, and the air still smelled like oil and sawdust.

The penny candy sat in its usual spot, though most of the stock had changed. I grabbed a few lemonheads, some bubblegum, and a few random pieces I thought Dani might like. The idea of sharing them with her made me smile but it also made me miss Katherine.

I was rounding the corner toward the register, still admiring my little haul, when I accidentally walked straight into someone.

My candy scattered across the floor.

"I'm so sorry," I apologized, dropping to my knees to pick it up.

"It's okay," the woman said, kneeling to help me. She drew in a sharp breath. "Oh my God. . . Emily?"

My head snapped up. It took me a second to recognize her. Her blonde hair was longer now but those sharp blue eyes hadn't changed, and the youth in her face was still the same.

Madeline McBride.

"Maddie, hi," I said, scooping up the last of the Double Bubble and rising to my feet.

"Wow," she said, standing with me. "What's it been, like fifteen years?"

"Eleven," I said, my voice tight.

She rose onto her tiptoes, peering over my shoulder. "Where's Katherine?"

"She's still in California. Husband, kids, you know. . . the whole family thing."

"Totally get it. If it weren't for my husband, I wouldn't be here either." She tossed a blonde curl over her shoulder. "Speaking of which. . ."

A shadow stretched across the tile, and I turned my head to see Logan walking down the aisle.

"I couldn't find the—" he started, but the words died in his throat. He slowed when he saw me, like someone had tightened an invisible leash around his neck.

"Babe, look who it is!" Maddie beamed as he stepped beside her.

"Logan. . ." I spit out his name like a seed I hadn't meant to swallow. "You two are married?" The question came out mechanical and hollow.

"Seven years this September," she chirped, curling a possessive hand against his chest. My eyes dropped to the gaudy ring resting on her perfectly manicured finger. "I know," she went on, catching my stare. "Some days I still can't believe it. I mean, who *actually* marries their childhood crush right? Stuff like that only happens in movies."

Logan's face had gone from chestnut brown to a queasy, mottled green.

"Are you okay?" Maddie asked, and for a second I wasn't sure if she was talking to me or him.

"Yeah," I said, my mouth dry. "Just a little lightheaded."

"Logan told me about your little accident," she said, gesturing to the bruise under my eye.

"He did?" I choked out in surprise.

"Of course. Something about the front door swinging open while he was helping you fix it?" Her eyes flicked to the scab on his forehead. "Looks like you got the worst of it, though. That's a nasty shiner." She leaned in slightly. "I'm so sorry about your grandmother, by the way. She was a lovely woman."

I nearly laughed. What the fuck was happening?

Maddie tilted her head, concern still plastered across her perfect face. Logan stood completely still, like he'd been turned to stone.

"I thought it was *so* sweet when he told me he was helping you fix up her house," she said, slipping her arm through his. "Isn't he the best?"

"The sweetest," I managed a smile, but it was thin and brittle.

"When Logan mentioned you were back in town, I was like, *Emily Hart?* No way! But here you are." She let out a soft laugh, shaking her head.

"Here I am," I echoed, the words sitting awkwardly in my mouth.

Logan finally looked at me, his eyes locking on mine like he'd just stepped off a cliff and realized there was no bottom.

"Well," Maddie said brightly, "we should catch up sometime. Do you have a number?"

I hesitated. "I'm only in town for a little while."

"Oh, come on," she laughed. "We're practically neighbors. I mean, we could do brunch or something. I'll drag Logan along—he'll hate it."

"I'm sure he will," I said before I could stop myself.

Her smile fell slightly, eyes flicking between the two of us. "Anyway," she said, her tone cheery again, "We should get going. We're supposed to meet my mother for lunch and she hates it when we're late."

She tugged on Logan's hand but he hesitated—just for a second.

"Emily. . ." he said, so soft I barely heard it.

I turned away.

They disappeared down the aisle, and I stood there for a long moment, staring at the spot where they'd been standing, still holding the candy.

I didn't remember walking to the counter. I just found myself there, sliding coins across the scratched surface, the young man's voice barely registering as he wished me a good day.

Outside, the air hit me like a slap. I leaned against the faded brick building, trying to breathe.

Eleven years.

Eleven years and the past still knew exactly where to find me.

Forty Two

Before

The grass was warm beneath my back, prickly in places but still soft enough to forget the world for a little while. Logan and I lay side by side in the field behind Gran's house. The sky above us felt wider somehow as clouds drifted lazily above.

"That one's definitely a dog," I said, pointing upward.

Logan's lips quirked. "Looks more like a misshapen rabbit."

I gave him a gentle shove. "You have no imagination."

He didn't argue, which was weird. Normally, he'd throw some witty comeback, something sarcastic and stupid that would make me laugh. But this time, he was quiet. Too quiet. I turned my head.

Logan now sat cross-legged beside me, picking apart a stem of grass—his shoulders slumped in a way that told me something wasn't right.

"What's wrong?" I asked gently. But he didn't answer right away. "Logan…" I pressed, sitting up beside him. A soft breeze blew through the field, brushing the hair from my face, but he still wouldn't look at me.

"I'm leaving," he said at last.

I blinked, confused. "What, like right now? But we just got here."

He turned, his dark eyes meeting mine. They were sad and distant, not the rich brown they had been earlier.

"I joined the Army."

A shadow swept across his face. Above, a tall cloud, drooping like a weeping willow, had moved in front of the sun.

"What?" I asked, confused. "Why?"

He didn't answer at first—just plucked a dandelion from the ground and rolled the stem between his fingers.

"Mom's getting worse," he said. "So the way I see it, I can either stay here and watch her slowly destroy her life, or I can go and try to make something of my own."

I tried to process what he was saying, my mind spinning in a dozen different directions. Katherine had been gone for four years now, married, with a baby on the way—a whole new life she built without me.

I thought of Mom—how thirteen years had passed since her death and yet Gran still refused to speak her name. I thought of the father I never met, who disappeared before I was old enough to even remember his face.

Why did everyone always leave?

I knew what Logan's mom was like—a tornado of a woman whose addiction destroyed everything she touched. I didn't want that for him. I didn't want him to suffer. But I didn't want him to leave me either. Did that make me selfish? Probably.

He was all I had left, besides Gran—and even she spent more time in her garden than with me these days. Sometimes I'd catch her in the flower beds late at night, the moonlight clinging to her silver hair, her hands deep in the dirt like she was trying to bury something she couldn't get away from.

"When do you leave?" I asked, trying to keep my voice from cracking.

He hesitated. "I ship out for basic tomorrow."

"Tomorrow?" I repeated, stunned. "But how is that possible if you just—" My words trailed off as realization clicked into place. "How long have you known about this?"

"Emily, you've got to understand—"

"How long, Logan?"

He stared at the ground. "Six months," he confessed, so quiet I almost didn't hear him.

"Six months?" An ache twisted in my gut. "You've known you were leaving for six months and you're just now telling me?"

"I didn't want to upset you."

"And you thought waiting until the *day before* wouldn't upset me?" I shouted, on my feet now.

The field was still, the clouds indifferent above us. But inside, everything was unraveling just like it always did.

Logan stood up slowly, brushing his hands on his jeans, not meeting my eyes. That made it worse somehow. Like he couldn't even face me after what he'd done.

"I wanted to tell you," he said. "I almost did. A dozen times. But every time I looked at you, I couldn't bring myself to say it. I didn't want to see that look on your face."

"What look?" I snapped, heart pounding.

He gestured vaguely at me. "*That* one. Like I've just ripped the ground out from under you."

I folded my arms tightly across my chest, trying to hold myself together. "Maybe you should see it. Maybe then you'd understand what this actually means."

Logan ran a hand over his face, frustrated. "It's not like I'm dying, Emily."

"No," I said coldly. "You're leaving. Just like everyone else."

He flinched. That hit the mark. Good.

"I'm not trying to hurt you," he said, softer now. "I'm just trying to find a way out."

"Out of what?" I asked. "This town? Your mom? *Me*?"

His silence said enough.

I turned away, staring out over the field, where the wind bent the grass and the clouds just kept moving like none of this mattered. I wanted to scream. I wanted to cry. I wanted to tell him not to go, that he was making a mistake—but I didn't. Because maybe it wasn't a mistake. Maybe him leaving meant there was nothing left holding me here either.

"When do you leave?" I asked again, quieter now.

"Bus picks me up at six," he said. "From the high school parking lot."

I nodded, more to myself than to him.

"You don't have to come say goodbye," he added, voice uncertain. "I'd understand if you didn't."

I laughed bitterly. "Yeah, well. You've been saying goodbye for the last six months, I just didn't know it."

I dug into the pocket of my jeans and pulled out a small, heart-shaped rock I'd found last week and wrapped in twine. His birthday was next week, and I was going to give it to him then. I'd wanted to turn it into a necklace, but we didn't have enough string, so I ended up tying it into a bracelet instead.

I had planned on finally telling him how I really felt, how I'd always felt but could never bring myself to admit. Maybe it was because everyone I ever loved always left.

"Here," I said, tossing it at him, not caring where it landed. "Happy fucking birthday."

Logan didn't say a word as he bent down to pick it up. And he didn't try to stop me when I turned and walked away through the tall grass, back toward the house that never felt full, even when it was. The clouds above shifted again, that willow-shaped one unraveling into nothing.

Just like us.

I didn't bother showing up to say goodbye, despite Gran's protests. If Logan hadn't cared enough to tell me when he made the decision to leave, then I didn't see why I should care enough to watch him go.

A few weeks after he was gone, letters started arriving—each one addressed to me in his familiar, messy handwriting. I never opened them. Why should I? What could he possibly say that would mend the raw, aching hole he'd left behind? The one he'd carved out of betrayal, then left abandoned to rot.

Still, I couldn't bring myself to throw them away.

Instead, I tucked them into an old hatbox inside my closet. Even in my anger, I couldn't let them go. They were all I had left of him—a fragile reminder of the friendship we once shared. Eventually, the letters stopped coming. I figured he'd finally given up, realizing I wasn't going to write back.

Then, on a dreary August afternoon, the phone rang.

By now, Logan had already graduated boot-camp. When Gran called up the stairs saying the call was for me, I paused—half hoping it was him on the other end.

"Emily?"

But it wasn't Logan's voice that bled through the phone. It was Katherine's.

"Hey," I said, swallowing my disappointment. "Is everything okay?"

It was a surprise to hear from her considering we hadn't heard a word in nearly five months. Ever since she left, it felt like we'd been shelved. Her calls always came out of nowhere, and they always left something bitter behind.

"Everything's great," she said brightly. "Perfect, actually."

Everything will be perfect. . .

"That's great," I said, forcing cheer into my voice. "How's Grant? How's the new baby?"

"Grant's. . . Grant," she replied. "And Bella is the most amazing little thing I've ever seen. I still can't believe I made something so beautiful."

"I can," I said with a smile. "I'm really happy for you, Kat. You got everything you ever wanted."

"Yeah. . ." Her voice dipped a little. "Almost everything."

I laughed lightly. "What? Living in California with a rich, handsome husband and a perfect baby isn't enough for you?"

Katherine laughed along with me. "It is—but it'd be better if I could share it with you."

I waited, expecting her to say more. When she didn't, the silence filled in the blanks for me.

"Are you asking me to come visit?"

"I'm asking you to come *stay*," she said. "But only if you want to."

My eyes glanced toward Gran, who was hunched over the kitchen sink, humming softly to herself. She hadn't spoken to Katherine since the night she left.

"What about Gran? I can't just leave her here alone," I whispered, pressing myself against the wall like it would muffle the conversation.

Katherine didn't hesitate. "Emily, you can't keep putting your life on hold for everyone else. She's had you for thirteen years. That's not nothing. You're not some keepsake she gets to keep tucked away on a shelf. You deserve to live your own life."

I stared at the floor, at the wide plank wood I'd scrubbed a thousand times.

"I don't know if I can," I admitted. "She wouldn't say it, but I think she needs me."

"Maybe she does," Katherine offered. "But maybe you need *you* more."

Her words landed like a stone in my chest.

"You've got to stop shouldering whatever misplaced guilt you're carrying," she continued. "Mom died. I left. And you. . . you stayed. You always stay. But Em, that doesn't mean you're supposed to."

My throat tightened. I didn't respond right away. I couldn't. The idea of leaving this place—of leaving Gran, it felt wrong. Disloyal, even. But the idea of staying, of living out the rest of my life in this small, miserable town that hated us, was suffocating.

"You wouldn't just be starting over," Katherine said, her voice hopeful. "You'd be starting something that's *yours*."

There was a long pause between us.

"Okay," I said at last. "I'll come."

Katherine's cheer erupted through the phone, loud enough that I had to cover the receiver with my hand. I shot a nervous glance toward Gran.

"I'll take care of everything," she said, her voice bubbling with excitement. "Flights, pickup—you just focus on packing."

After we hung up, I stayed rooted in the kitchen, the phone still warm in my hand.

Gran didn't turn around. She just kept scrubbing the same dish in slow, rhythmic circles, like she hadn't heard a thing.

"How's your sister?" she asked casually.

"She misses you," I said, testing the waters.

Gran finally placed the dish in the drying rack beside the sink and reached for another. "She made her choice," she said simply.

I swallowed hard, setting the phone down on the counter.

"She invited me out for a visit," I let out, carefully.

Gran didn't answer right away—just continued rinsing the plate in her hands, running it under the water like it might wash away whatever I wasn't saying.

Finally, she said, "You do what you need to do, Emily."

That should've felt like permission—but it didn't.

I left the kitchen and headed upstairs. In search of my suitcase, I dug through my closet, passing over the hatbox without looking at it. I didn't have the heart to open Logan's letters. I wasn't ready to unpack all that, but maybe me leaving would eventually help me get there.

As I started packing, I caught my reflection in the mirror. I looked like someone stepping into a new life, but I didn't feel like her yet. There was a strange pull in my chest—a gnawing guilt I couldn't quite shake. And I wasn't sure if it was because I was leaving. . . or because I was excited to go.

Forty Three

Now

May 31st, 2023

Dear James,

I've tried to start this letter so many times, always stopping to ask myself if any of this even makes sense. But then again, none of this has made sense. Maybe that's part of what makes it feel so real. Sometimes I catch myself saying your name out loud, just to hear how it sounds. You've become part of my days *now. Part of my quiet moments, my wandering thoughts. I see something beautiful, and I wonder if you'd find it beautiful too.*

The day I found your photo in the library, something changed. I told myself it was nothing. Maybe it was the lighting, or the way the quiet echoed throughout the library. Either way, I kept coming back to it and I started to wonder if choosing that book from all the others wasn't a coincidence. Honestly, I didn't want to admit it, but I felt something too.

My friend Danielle has this theory that maybe our souls already know each other. That we've done this before, in some other life. I'm not usually one to believe in fate or soulmates or anything like that, but. . . maybe she's right. Maybe time isn't as straight forward as we think. Maybe it folds, and in those strange overlapping places, people like us find each other again.

Since we're being honest with each other, there's something else I need to tell you. I wasn't sure if I should, but the guilt of not saying anything feels worse than telling the truth.

There's someone from my time. Or there was, I should say. Someone I thought I loved. I thought he loved me too. But it turns out, I was wrong and it's over between us now.

I wish I could reach through whatever invisible space lies between us. I wish I could stop you from going, or at least tell you to be careful. You said you didn't want to know what the future holds, and I'll respect that, but I've read enough about the Civil War to know what happens to the men in your situation, and the thought of never hearing from you again hurts more than I thought it would.

Still, I'm holding onto hope. I have to. Because if all of this. . . our letters, this weird connection, was just for you to vanish, then what would have been the point? Why would fate go through the trouble of bringing us back together, only to take you away again?

So write to me when you come back. Not if, but when. Because whatever this is, it matters. I feel that in my bones. I believe we've known each other before. And I believe we'll find each other again.

Yours always,
Emily

I spent three days in bed, tossing and turning between anger, heartbreak, and self loathing. For three days, I ignored Logan's calls. And I didn't move when he came pounding on the front door, pleading for a chance to explain.

Explain what, exactly?

Explain how he lied to me? How I unknowingly helped him cheat—with the one person who made my life just as miserable as Jackson ever did?

How do you explain that kind of betrayal to someone you claim to love?

That part cut the deepest.

I'd driven straight home from the hardware store that day, leaving Winston with Dani and the bags of dog food in her Jeep. So when someone knocked on my door a few hours later, I assumed it was Logan.

"Go away," I shouted through clenched teeth.

"I'd love to," came the reply, "but I kind of need my keys first."

My anger immediately gave way to shame.

"What's wrong? Are you okay?" she asked, concern washing over her face the moment I opened the door.

I collapsed into her arms, sobbing like a child as I told her everything.

"You want me to kick his ass?" she said, trying to be funny, but it didn't work. Another cry tore from my throat.

She offered to take Winston for a few days, to give me space, but I declined. He was all I had left.

As if I wasn't already drowning, the silence from James made it worse. Not a single letter arrived through the satchel. On the fourth day, hollowed out from crying, I finally dragged myself out of bed, got dressed, and managed to make myself something to eat.

I stood in the kitchen, staring blankly at nothing, when my eyes caught on Gran's urn. I'd moved it to the mantel, where it now sat untouched beside her photo.

That's when the guilt hit me.

I'd been back for nearly a month and still hadn't honored her final wish.

I wandered over to the kitchen window, my gaze landing on the garden. What had once been a peaceful refuge was now a wild, tangled mess. Weeds climbed through the broken fence, its white paint now cracked and flaking. Several boards leaned with rot, warped and ready to fall.

My chest tightened.

Gran's garden had once been her pride—a burst of life and color. Now, it was a graveyard of everything she loved.

How had it gotten this bad?

Was it my fault? Katherine's? Had our leaving felt like abandonment to her? Had she'd simply given up when we left, allowing the garden to mirror the emptiness she must have felt?

With a sudden urge of purpose I forced myself outside. This wasn't just about the garden anymore. It was about healing. About making something whole again.

The bags of soil and fertilizer Logan and I had bought days ago still sat on the porch, unopened. The potted plants we'd picked out together were beginning to wilt, now victims of my selfishness.

Not anymore.

I rolled up my sleeves and grabbed the first bag of soil, dragging it toward the garden beds at the back of the house. The earth was dry and cracked beneath my shoes, but there was still life underneath—I could feel it. The sun had finally broken through the clouds that had hung heavy the last few days, warming my shoulders as I worked.

With each weed I pulled, each thorn I clipped back, it was like I was cutting through the ache inside me. The grief didn't vanish—but for the first time, it had somewhere to go.

I dug my hands into the soil, bringing them away with dirt packed beneath my nails, and for the first time in days, I smiled. Gran used to say that dirt was good for the soul—and she was right.

I could almost picture her there, watching from the porch with a cup of tea in her hands, and a quiet smirk curling at the edge of her mouth. Not saying anything. Just nodding. Winston let out a soft bark beside me, tail wagging as if he could sense her too. Her unseen presence must have given him a jolt of energy, because moments later he took off running into the tall grass, chasing something only he could see.

The potted plants were struggling, but not gone. A little water, a little care, and they might make it. I planted them gently, giving each one a place in the beds that used to overflow with color. It wasn't much yet, but it was a start.

I turned to the fence and began tearing the boards loose with my hands. Some out of the lingering frustration still burning from Logan, others from a strength I hadn't felt in a long time.

The day slipped by in a blur, and before I knew it, the sun was melting into the horizon, casting a golden glow across the yard. Somewhere in the distance, Winston barked excitedly. Maybe he'd found something. Or maybe he just felt good running free.

I knelt to place the buddleia bush in the soil, my fingers gently pressing its roots into the earth, when a rough voice snuck up behind me.

"Hey, Emily. . ."

My blood turned to ice. A chill swept down my spine, causing the hairs on the back of my neck to stand on end. I turned slowly, hoping for a ghost. But what I saw frightened me more.

Standing there, hands in his pockets, wearing that same, self-assured grin. ... was Jackson.

Forty Four

Jackson's blonde hair was matted, darkened with dirt and grime. His navy button-down clung to him in wrinkles, and his gray slacks were torn at the knee. The bright blue of his eyes were dulled with exhaustion, and his once-flawless skin had been scorched by the sun. He looked like he'd been surviving in the wild for weeks.

"Jackson. . ." His name scratched the back of my throat, and I instinctively took a step back. "What the hell are you doing here?"

"What a strange question to ask your husband," he said, inching closer.

I raised the spade I'd been using in my hand, gripping it tight like a shield. "Stay the fuck away from me."

"Emily, really?" he tsked. "Don't you think you're being a little dramatic?"

My eyes darted across the field, scanning for Winston, but he was nowhere in sight.

"How did you know I was here?"

Jackson let out a short laugh. "You actually thought you could hide from me and I wouldn't find you?"

I thought of the rock—the flat tire, the word *SLUT* carved into my car. Of course he knew. He'd known all along while he lurked in the shadows. Watching. Waiting. Biding his time for the perfect moment to strike.

He stepped closer, and I immediately backed away—my foot catching on a root. I tumbled backward into a tangle of thistles, the thorns clawing at my skin. The sting barely registered. My heart thundered as I glared up at him, eyes fixed on his every move.

Jackson loomed above me, casting a long shadow in the fading light.

"You look scared," he said, crouching so we were eye-level. "That's not how I want you to feel, Emily."

I scrambled backward, the thorns biting deeper as I clawed through the bush. Blood warmed my skin in thin trails, but I didn't care. I just needed to put space between us.

"I'm not scared of you," I said, forcing calm into my voice and failing miserably. "Not anymore."

He paused, his smile twitching. "I'll admit, that night wasn't my finest hour," he said, straightening to his full height. "An unfortunate incident, to say the least."

"An unfortunate incident?" I echoed, disbelief tightening in my throat. "You tried to kill me!"

Jackson took a small step back, as if the accusation had struck him. "If I wanted to kill you, I would have." Like that somehow made it better—like beating your wife nearly to death was just a matter of miscommunication.

I scrambled to my feet, my heart crashing against my ribs. I gripped the spade tighter. "You need help," I said, voice shaking. "You're sick."

He tilted his head. "Maybe, but that doesn't erase our vows. And last I checked, you're still my wife." He swept a hand around us. "This little fantasy? It's over. It's time to come home."

A chill crawled up my spine.

"I am home," I bit out through clenched teeth. "And I'm not going anywhere with you."

Jackson's face darkened—causing his charming mask to slip. And for a brief, chilling moment, the monster underneath emerged.

"Don't make this harder than it has to be," he said, voice tight. "You knew this couldn't last. Hiding out here, playing house like some broken little bird. It isn't real, Emily. And no matter where you go, I will *always* find you."

I scanned the field, desperate for a glimpse of Winston—but all I saw were long shadows bleeding from the base of the mountains. The sun was almost gone, swallowed by dusk, and the moon was already rising like a warning. Hot panic surged through my veins.

"I'll just keep running," I said, my voice trembling with false bravery. I took another step back, my spine meeting the back of the house. I had nowhere left to go.

Jackson's jaw flexed. "You still don't get it, do you?" he said, advancing. "You're mine. You always have been."

"I was *never* yours," I spat. "You shattered everything the moment you laid a hand on me."

A flicker of rage ignited in his blue eyes. "You think anyone else would want you?" he snarled. "Your own parents abandoned you. Your sister left the second she could. I'm the only one who's ever stayed. The only one who's ever truly loved you."

"Your love is fucking poison," I snapped.

A low rustle sounded in the distance. My eyes flicked toward it—just for a second.

It was all he needed.

Jackson lunged, his breath hot as he grabbed my face with both hands, fingers digging into my skin.

"You've always been such an ungrateful bitch," he spat.

I struggled against him, the spade slipping from my grasp as his grip tightened. His thumbs pressed against my cheekbones, forcing my head back.

"Let go of me!" I thrashed, but he was stronger. Rage and desperation burned in my chest as I tried to fight back.

"I gave you everything," he growled. "You *belong* to me, Emily. You *owe* me."

"I don't owe you anything!" I screamed, twisting hard.

Jackson grabbed a fistful of my hair and yanked me forward. Pain exploded across my scalp as I hit the ground. I struggled for air as the breath knocked itself from my lungs.

"You never learn," he sneered, towering over me. "Maybe I need to teach you another lesson."

I curled onto my side, folding into myself as I braced for the inevitable blow.

But it never came.

A sudden, sharp yelp cut between us.

I lifted my head just in time to see Winston snarling, his teeth sunk deep into Jackson's ankle. Jackson reeled, trying to shake him off.

"Get the fuck off me!" he shouted, stumbling backward. But before he could break free, a shadow stretched across the lawn.

Logan.

He moved with an eerie calm—his face set in stone as he closed the distance. He didn't say anything as he slowly approached Jackson, raised his arm, and swung. Hard.

The crack of fist against bone echoed into the twilight.

Jackson's head snapped to the side, and he crumpled to the ground with a guttural grunt—Winston still growling at his feet.

Logan didn't stop.

He grabbed Jackson by the collar, yanking him up just enough to drive his knee into his gut. Jackson gasped, the wind knocked clean out of him, folding over with a strangled noise.

"Touch her again," Logan said, his voice lethal, "and I'll bury you myself."

Jackson coughed, choking on his breath. He tried to speak but Logan shoved him back down, hard—the impact sending up a puff of dirt.

Winston stood over him, teeth bared, body tense, ready to strike again. I sat up slowly, my entire body shaking from adrenaline and fear.

Logan turned to me then, concerned. He crossed the distance in two strides, dropping to his knees beside me.

"Are you hurt?"

I nodded, then shook my head. "I'm fine."

"You're safe now," he said, carefully brushing a strand of hair from my face. "I've got you."

Behind him, Jackson let out a raspy cough. Logan turned, the softness in his face vanishing as he stalked back toward him.

"People disappear in these mountains all the time," Logan said coldly, nodding toward the dark silhouette of the Appalachians. "No one's going to ask questions. Not even for someone like you."

Jackson pushed himself upright, fury still burning in his eyes. He opened his mouth to speak—but a low growl from

Winston quickly cut him off. He snapped it shut, his gaze flicking nervously to the dog.

"I'm going to count to five," Logan continued, voice like steel. "And if you're still standing here, Winston and I will personally drag your sorry ass into those woods. And I promise, once you're in there, you won't be coming back out."

Jackson glanced between the three of us. He dusted off his shirt, smirking. "Suit yourself. She's all used up anyway."

Logan didn't hesitate. His fist shot out, connecting with Jackson's nose with a sickening crack. Jackson reeled back with a cry, blood pouring down his face.

Logan shook out his hand. "Want to try for a third?"

Jackson stumbled, one hand clutching his face, the other groping for balance as he glared up at Logan. But he didn't step forward again.

He knew better now.

"This isn't over," he grunted through bloody fingers.

Logan stepped forward again, forcing Jackson to backpedal. "For you, it is. Now go. Before you bleed out right here."

Jackson hesitated—just enough to make me wonder if he was stupid enough to try something else. Then he turned and staggered down the drive, disappearing into the encroaching shadows.

The second he was out of sight, my knees gave out.

Logan caught me before I hit the ground, arms tight and steady around my shaking body. "Hey, hey—I've got you," he murmured, his voice low and soothing. "Everything's ok now. He's gone."

Winston circled us once, then sat by my side, pressing his weight gently against my hip.

But everything wasn't okay. Because while Jackson had hurt me physically, what Logan had done, left behind wounds that cut just as deep.

And now here he was, holding me like he hadn't torn me apart only days ago.

I pulled away from him, my body stiff. "You should go."

Logan flinched like I'd struck him. "Emily. . . please," he said, eyes begging.

But I didn't have the strength to argue, to hear whatever apology he thought would fix it.

"I can't do this right now," I sighed, too exhausted to carry the weight of my own voice.

He hesitated, his lips parting like he might say more. But then, slowly, he nodded.

I turned to Winston, resting a hand on his head as I walked toward the house. My legs felt heavy. My heart, heavier.

Before stepping inside, I paused, twilight pressing against my back.

"Thank you," I said, without turning around. "For saving me."

Then I closed the door behind me.

Forty Five

THE MORNING WAS STILL AND gentle, wrapped in a low fog that clung to the mountains. A fine mist floated in the air—a quiet warning of bad weather still to come.

My body ached. I was bruised, sore, and trembling in places I hadn't even realized could hurt. All things considered, it could've been worse. I was exhausted, but I hadn't really slept. I'd spent most of the night listening—holding my breath, terrified Jackson might come back, and that this time, nobody would be there to save me.

Logan showed up shortly before noon the next day. Raindrops clung to his jacket, sliding down his shoulders in slow rivulets as I opened the door. In one hand, he held a drink carrier with two cups of coffee. In the other, a rolled-up sheet of plastic.

"A peace offering," he said, lifting the cups. "And if you'll let me, I'd like to fix that window. There's a strong system moving in, and I. . ." his voice trailed off as he took me in.

I stepped back and let the door fall open wider.

He set the coffees on the table, and almost immediately, Winston came trotting down the stairs. The dog gave a soft, delighted bark when he spotted Logan.

"I'll admit, I had my doubts about you," Logan said, kneeling to scratch behind Winston's ears. "But you've won me over, buddy."

Winston's tail thumped against the floor as if he'd never known a reason to doubt Logan. I envied his trust.

Logan stood and peeled off his damp jacket, draping it over the back of a chair. He didn't say much as he unrolled the plastic sheet and set to work. I watched him for a moment, unsure what to do with myself. The silence between us was uncomfortable. Both of us had things we weren't ready to say yet.

When he was finished, the wind picked up outside, whistling faintly through the cracks. He glanced toward the window.

"This'll hold through the storm," he said. "Might not be pretty, but it'll keep the rain out."

I nodded, finally giving in and wrapping my hands around the warm coffee cup. "Thank you."

He looked up at me then, eyes searching mine. "You okay?"

The question hung between us longer than it should have. I wasn't. Not really. But over the years, I'd gotten good at pretending.

"I'm fine," I lied, adding another stone to the fragile wall I'd built around myself.

Logan didn't move. "Don't do that," he begged. "Don't shut me out like I don't know the difference."

I looked away, jaw tight. "I'm not shutting you out."

"Yeah, you are," he pressed. "And I get it—you don't owe me anything. But at least give me the chance to explain. After that, if you want me gone, I'll go."

"I wanted to believe you, you know," I said, my gaze fixed on everything but him. "When you said you loved me? God, I *really* wanted to believe it."

"I meant it, Emily," he said quickly. "I wasn't lying."

"No?" I scoffed, the words catching in my throat. "You just forgot to mention that you're married, right? Or that your wife happened to be Madeline? Was that a lie too, or did it just *conveniently* slip your mind?"

Anger rose in my chest. I took another sip of coffee, trying to force it back down.

Logan's eyes fell to the floor. "Madeline and I are separated. We split three months ago. She's a psychiatrist up in Boston and wanted me to move there, to follow her. But I couldn't. I thought she understood. She *said* she did. We'd been living apart when she suddenly showed up here—right after you did, claiming she wanted to give it one last try."

He rubbed the back of his neck, waiting for me to reply. When I didn't, he continued. "I'll be honest, I thought about it. I felt like I owed her... out of habit maybe, or guilt. But the truth is, our marriage had been over for a long time."

Part of me wanted to believe him. The same part that had clung to every kind thing he'd ever said, every time he made me feel seen, safe. But there was another part that reminded me I'd been here before—that trusting the wrong man had already cost me too much.

"Where were you when you disappeared that week?" I stared at him, trying to make sense of what he was saying, and what was the truth. "Were you with her?"

Logan hesitated. Then, slowly, shamefully, he nodded.

"I can't fucking believe this," I breathed, setting the cup down a little too hard.

"Please, Emily," he begged. "It's over between us. I swear. My lawyer's already drawn up the papers—"

"Is that what Clarksburg was?" I cut in, suddenly queasy. "Did you drag me out there unknowingly so that you could divorce your wife?"

His eyes dropped to the floor again.

"Are you serious, Logan? What the fuck?"

The room tilted slightly, narrowing at the edges. I grabbed the back of the kitchen chair and sat, afraid my knees might give out. There was too much happening inside me—grief, rage betrayal.

Heartbreak.

How could I have been so fucking blind? How could I have been so stupid?

"And Abernathy's?" I managed. "The way she looked at you, the way she cozied up to you. . . it didn't look like you two were on the brink of divorce." I flinched at the image of them together, her arm curled around him like some prized possession. "If you two are supposedly over, then why were you there with her in the first place?"

Logan ran a hand through his hair. "I told her I'd fix a few things around the house before we listed it. That's it."

"Before or after you went to lunch with her family?" I asked. "Was that just your way of saying goodbye, or were you letting her down gently over sandwiches and sweet tea?"

He looked up at me then, tired. "Her mom works in real estate now. She's helping us sell the house."

I laughed. "How convenient."

I didn't know what to believe anymore. Too many things had happened. Too many things had changed, and I was still too broken to allow myself to risk being shattered again.

I stared at the table, willing myself not to cry. Not in front of him. Not when everything I'd felt for him was now tangled in doubt.

"You should've told me," I said, my voice quieter now, not out of forgiveness but fatigue. "You should've told me from the start, Logan. You had so many chances."

Logan took a small step forward, then thought better of it. "I know."

"Then why didn't you?" I hated the way my voice sounded—hurt, not angry. "Why let me fall for something you knew was already tainted with lies?"

He didn't answer right away. He just stood there, motionless, like he wasn't sure if reaching for me would make things better or worse.

"I was scared," he said at last. "Scared of screwing it up—of ruining the second chance I'd begged for. You have no idea how much I wanted this with you. How many promises I made to whoever might be listening, swearing I'd give up everything if I could just have one more shot. I kept waiting for the right moment to tell you. But then the rock, the car. . . everything you went through with that bastard. I didn't want to risk hurting you more."

His words pierced something in me I didn't want touched. Because I knew that feeling—that desperate grip on something good, even when it's built on shaky ground.

And still, it wasn't enough.

"You don't get to use my feelings as a reason for lying," I said. "You don't get to say it was about protecting *me* when it was really about protecting *you*."

He winced. Good.

"Do you love her?"

Logan didn't hesitate. He shook his head. "No. Not now. Not then. Not ever."

"Then why?" My voice shook despite me. "Why *her*?"

He exhaled sharply. Then he sank into the chair across from me, elbows on his knees, hands laced together forcing them to stay steady.

Outside, the wind howled, rattling the window he'd just repaired. I wondered, vaguely, if it would hold.

"I told you," he said after a long pause. "I wasn't myself when I got back. I was barely anything at all. The Army stripped pieces of me I didn't even know I had, and then losing you—" He stopped, jaw tightening. "I was a wreck. Madeline was like fucking duct tape. She didn't ask questions. She didn't look too closely. She just wanted to fix me. And I was so tired of being broken."

"So she was convenient?" I pressed, bitterly.

Logan shrugged. "I think some part of her always knew I wasn't really in it. That my heart was never fully there because it still belonged to you."

I swallowed hard, but didn't look away.

"She wanted me to move to Boston because she knew, eventually, you'd come back," he added. "And she was right." For a moment, I saw the truth in his eyes—raw and unguarded. But it didn't dull the sting.

"Love doesn't mean much if it's built on half-truths," I said. Hot tears filled my eyes, and this time, I didn't stop them. They slipped down silently, one after another. "I let you in. I told you the truth, even when it hurt. And you. . . you only gave me half of yours, dressed up like a whole."

Logan looked like he wanted to close the space between us, to reach for me. But he didn't. Maybe he finally understood that whatever stood between us now couldn't be patched up with apologies or promises.

"You have every right to be angry," he insisted. "I messed this up—completely. But what I felt for you, what I *feel*. . . that's real. It's the only thing that's ever made any sense to me."

I didn't speak. Not right away.

Because what could I say to that? That I was flattered? That it somehow made this easier? It didn't. It only made everything murkier, like stepping into water you thought was shallow only to find yourself sinking.

"I'm not some echo, Logan," I said, my voice thin and trembling. "You don't get to keep circling back to me every time something else doesn't work out for you."

He flinched, like the words had struck a nerve, but he didn't argue. Maybe he knew better than to try.

"I don't know if I can come back from this," I admitted, staring down at my hands. "You keep saying I was the one thing that felt real. . . but if that's true, why wasn't it enough to tell me the truth?"

Silence settled between us, thick and uncomfortable. He looked like he wanted to answer, like he had a thousand things on the tip of his tongue. But none of them made it past his lips.

"I need time," I said, standing slowly. "I don't know what this is anymore. What *we* are. Or if we were even anything at all."

He nodded, his jaw flexing. "I'll give you whatever you need."

I patted my eyes with my shirt. "Right now, I think I need you to leave."

"Emily—"

"Don't," I said, holding up a hand. "Just. . . don't."

Logan stood, brushing his palms against his jeans like he needed something to do with his hands. "Ok," he relented. "You need space. And I. . ." He glanced toward the door, then back at me. "I've done enough damage for one day."

I didn't know what he wanted me to say. That I forgave him? That I understood? Because I didn't. Not yet.

So instead, I said nothing.

He walked to the door, pausing with his hand on the knob. "For what it's worth, I meant it. All of it. Even if I said it too late."

The door shut behind him, and I was alone.

I looked toward the window, the one he'd patched up with quiet hands and good intentions, and wondered, not for the first time, if some things were meant to be fixed. . . or if they were always meant to stay broken.

Forty Six

February 12th, 1864
West Virginia

Dearest Miss Hart,

My name is Finnigan Walker, and I write to you on behalf of my brother, Captain James Walker. As I'm sure you already must know, he entrusted me with the unfortunate duty of contacting you under grim circumstances.

It is with great sorrow and a heavy heart that I must inform you of his presumed death. Nearly a fortnight has passed since his company was dispatched to engage Confederate forces approximately seven miles west of our present position. While the remains of several of his comrades have since been recovered, Captain Walker is, as of now, still unaccounted for.

With limited provisions, we plan to take brief refuge at a nearby farmstead, less than two days' ride from where we are now. Should the enemy retreat in due course, we may be able to dispatch scouts to recover him. Until then, our numbers have grown thin, and our commanding officer cannot justify further endangering the men who remain.

I am truly sorry to write to you under such grievous matters. Though I do not know the precise nature of your connection to my brother, it is clear he held you in high regard.

Please accept my deepest condolences, though I know they can offer little comfort. Whatever bond you shared with James, I trust it will be enough to carry his memory with you as life continues its course.

May God bless and guide you,
Lieutenant Finnigan S. Walker
2nd Regiment, Union Army

I crushed the letter in my fist, as if destroying the paper might erase his words. James was dead. He'd always been dead. So why did it hurt so much?

I reached for a pen and paper, but my hand froze. What was the point? My connection had never been with Finn—it was with James. And as shocking as it was to find his letter tucked inside the satchel, I doubted anything I wrote would even reach him anyway.

It rained for days, a fitting soundtrack to close out the week. Dani dropped by at one point, and I filled her in on what happened with Jackson, explaining how Logan and Winston teamed up to send him packing, bloodied and bruised.

"Winston attacked him?" she asked, eyebrows raised. I could tell she was surprised, but also impressed.

"Yeah," I said, still a little stunned myself. "Went straight for the leg. Clamped down hard, too."

Dani let out a low whistle, shaking her head with a half-smile. "I didn't think he had it in him."

"Me neither," I admitted.

"Why do I always miss the good shit?" she teased.

I let out a short laugh. "I'm glad my personal disasters are keeping you entertained."

"I live at the shelter," Dani said with a sigh. "The most exciting thing that ever happens there is when one of the dogs figures out how to open the latch and leads a jailbreak through the kennels."

I grinned. "That's actually kind of amazing."

"It is, until you're chasing half a dozen of them through the halls, trying to talk them back into their kennels like some kind of hostage negotiator," she said, shaking her head with a tired laugh.

"How's everything else going over there, by the way?" I asked.

She'd been overwhelmed lately, overrun with intakes. Each kennel was now holding two, sometimes three dogs, and she'd had to stop accepting cats altogether.

Danielle's smile faded. "I tried. I really did. But it looks like I'm going to have to start euthanizing again."

My eyes drifted to Winston, whose ears perked. He was one of the lucky ones. My chest tightened at the thought of Ruger and Brutus—their lives cut short through no fault of their own.

"I hate it," Danielle sighed. "Every time I have to make that call, it feels like I'm betraying them."

"You did everything you could," I reassured her.

She rubbed at her eyes with the heel of her hand. "I tell myself it's mercy. That at least they're not dying cold and alone on the streets. But it doesn't make it easier."

"No," I said. "It doesn't."

Winston let out a soft huff and rested his head on my foot, as if he understood. Maybe he did.

"I wish there was more I could do," I added, feeling helpless.

Danielle managed a small, sad smile. "Talking about it helps. Most people don't want to hear it. They love the happy endings, the adoptions. But not the ones we lose."

"They deserve to be remembered too," I said.

"Yeah," she whispered. "They do."

We sat in silence for a moment, the soft patter of rain against the windows filling the space between us. Outside, the world looked washed clean, but everything inside me still felt muddied and tangled.

Dani glanced at me. "You okay?"

I nodded slowly. "I think so. It's just. . . a lot."

"Yeah," she said, leaning back. "It usually is."

I crossed the living room into the kitchen, pulled two mugs from the cabinet, and set the kettle on to boil. Dani didn't drink coffee, and honestly, between the weather and the weight of our conversation, tea just felt right.

"How are things with your soldier?" she asked, taking the Earl Grey from my hands a few minutes later.

"James is dead," I said, sinking into the armchair across from her. "His brother sent me a letter."

"Wasn't he always?" she asked, raising the mug to her lips. She took a careful sip, winced at the heat, and set it gently on the coffee table. "I mean, technically he lived almost two hundred years ago."

"Yeah," I said, running a hand through my hair. "But if what you said about us being soulmates is true. . . then what was the point of all this? Why bring him back into my life just to take him away again?" I shook my head. Between James, Logan, and Jackson, I was about ready to swear off men—past, present, and probably future.

Danielle gave a small shrug. She picked up her mug again, exhaled gently over the top, the steam bending over the rim at her breath. "That's the thing about the universe. It's not really meant to be understood."

I followed with my own, hesitant sip. "You sound like my Gran."

Both our eyes drifted toward the mantel where her urn sat quietly, watching over the room.

"I'll take that as a compliment," she grinned.

I smiled, the warmth of it tinged with grief. She truly did remind me of her, and that thought filled me with a bittersweet mix of sorrow and joy.

"Can I see it?" Dani asked abruptly.

I blinked. "My Gran?"

"No," she laughed. "The satchel, or bag, or whatever it is. And the letters. Can I see them?"

I paused for a moment, then gave a quiet nod and disappeared upstairs. When I returned, I carried the leather satchel over my shoulder, placing it gently on the coffee table between us.

Carefully, I pulled out the stack of letters—some addressed to me, others to James's wife, Charlotte.

Dani reached out, her fingertips gliding over the delicate paper like it might crumble beneath her touch.

"These are from James?" she asked, a hint of awe in her voice.

I nodded quietly.

I watched her as she read, her bright green eyes flicking over the words with quiet reverence.

"That's wild," she finally breathed, setting the letters down with care before leaning back against the couch. "I still think there's a soulmate connection here. But I can't wrap my head around why the universe would separate you two by centuries."

"What about his wife?" I asked, motioning to the letter that had started it all. "It's obvious he loved her deeply. He told me that himself."

Danielle rubbed her jaw thoughtfully. "Maybe she died before she was supposed to. And instead of bringing her back to him, it brought you."

"You think the universe got it wrong?"

She shook her head. "The universe doesn't make mistakes. Its choices are rarely simple, but they're always purposeful. Maybe this wasn't about reuniting two people—it was about awakening something in you. Guiding you toward wherever you're meant to go next."

I stared down at the letters, my fingers absently tracing the edge of his words.

Dani's hand reached over to cover mine. "Maybe James was meant to show you a love that transcends time. Not to keep, but to remind you of what's possible. Of what you deserve."

She squeezed my fingers gently, like she knew I needed grounding more than comfort.

I stared down at our joined hands for a moment before whispering, "But what if I don't know how to want it anymore?"

She was quiet for a moment, then said softly, "Maybe it's not about wanting it right now. Maybe it's about believing you *could*... someday. Even if it doesn't feel real yet."

I didn't say anything else, and neither did she. There was nothing left to untangle, no answers hidden in the corners of the room or between the folds of the yellowed paper.

Outside, the rain had softened to a drizzle, as if even the storm was learning to let go.

Funny how love could live in the spaces between time—yet still die from the weight of so many unsaid things.

Forty Seven

A LOUD CRASH JOLTED ME awake. At the foot of the bed, Winston stirred, ears pricked, tail rigid. For a moment, I thought it was just the storm. Rain hammered the roof, and lightning flared behind the curtains, casting fleeting shadows across the room. A sharp roar of thunder rolled in after.

"It's just a thunderstorm," I grumbled to Winston. "Go back to sleep."

I was about to lie back down when I heard it again. The sharp, splintering sound of glass breaking.

Someone was in the house.

Winston sprang from the bed, a low growl rumbling in his throat. I snatched the candlestick from the nightstand and crept toward the door.

Another crash. Followed by the unmistakable sound of something being dragged.

I pictured Jackson downstairs, tearing the house apart, smashing memories with his bare hands—waiting for me in the dark.

My heart pounded in my chest, loud enough that I was sure whoever was downstairs could hear it. I paused at the door, straining to listen. Another thud echoed from below—closer this time. I tightened my grip on the candlestick.

I eased the door open, its hinges groaning. I froze, wincing. The storm outside covered some of the noise, but not enough.

Step by step, I crept down the hallway. Every floorboard felt like it screamed beneath my feet. The hallway ended at the landing, where the stairs curved down into the darkness.

A dim glow flickered faintly below, like candlelight or maybe the broken remains of a flashlight. I leaned over the banister, trying to get a glimpse of the intruder.

Then I caught movement as a shadow shifted across the wall.

"Jackson?" I called out before I could stop myself.

Silence.

Winston snarled, his hackles raised as he crept down the stairs, one careful step at a time. I followed, the candlestick still clutched in my hand like it would be enough to save me.

A low creak bled through the silence. Whoever was down here wasn't trying to be quiet anymore.

I paused at the base of the stairs. Books had been swept from the shelves. Picture frames lay face down or shattered. The armchair had been knocked over, one leg snapped clean off. The glow I'd seen from upstairs came from the lamp in the corner, now lying on its side, casting warped shadows across the room.

Next to it, the coffee table lay overturned, its splintered legs jutting out like broken limbs. Below the mantle, Gran's urn was on its side, porcelain cracked, her ashes spilled like dark, fine sand across the faded rug.

Then I saw it. A single muddy footprint near the open door—too small to be Jackson's.

Someone else was here.

Winston lunged forward with a bark, and a figure stepped from the shadows.

"Call him off," came a soft, birdlike voice.

I froze, dropping the candlestick to the floor. "Madeline?"

She stepped into the low light and I blinked, unsure if my eyes were playing tricks on me. But it was her.

Madeline moved closer, and I sucked in a breath. In her right hand, was a gun. . . and it was leveled at Winston.

"Now, or I'll shoot!"

"Winston," I said, my voice trembling. "Go."

He glanced back at me, confused.

"Now!" I barked, jerking my head toward the stairs.

Startled by the sharpness in my voice, he turned and bolted, claws scraping the floor as he bounded up the steps. A moment later, the sound of his paws faded.

Madeline jerked the gun toward the couch. "Sit," she ordered.

I obeyed without argument.

"What the hell are you doing here?" I asked, panic threading through my voice.

But she didn't answer me, not right away.

A flash of lightning illuminated the room, and for a fleeting second, I saw her clearly. This wasn't the composed, polished woman I'd seen last week. That Madeline had perfect hair, flawless makeup, and a tight, practiced smile.

This one looked hollowed out. Dark circles bruised the skin beneath her crystal eyes, and a bone-deep restlessness clung to her shoulders.

She continued pacing in front of me, gun still raised. "You shouldn't have come back," she said, her voice brittle. "You should've stayed in California. None of this would've happened if you'd just stayed away." Finally, she stopped pacing, her wild eyes snapping to mine. "Why did you come back?"

My gaze drifted to Grans urn, my heart breaking at the sight of her ashes scattered like dust across the floor.

"My grandmother died," I whispered. "You know that."

Madeline let out a sharp laugh. "No, no, no," she said, shaking her head. "I did a little digging on you, Emily Hart. Or should I say. . . *Emily Bishop*."

It wasn't exactly a secret that I was married, but the way she said it sent a shot of panic through my chest.

"How's that husband of yours anyway?" she asked, her voice laced with venom. "Or do you even know? Since you've been so busy playing house with *mine*."

My eyes widened. Lightning flared again, followed by a crack of thunder that rattled the windows. In the flash, I saw her hands trembling, the gun wavering ever so slightly.

"You really thought I didn't know about you and Logan?" she said, tilting her head with a cold smile. "Sneaking around behind my back like a couple of cowards."

"I didn't know you two were married," I confessed. "I only found out when I saw you at the hardware store."

She took a step closer, jaw clenched. "Was that before or after you fucked him?"

"We didn't—" I started, but stopped. There was no point. She wasn't interested in the truth.

Madeline resumed pacing, more agitated now. "I didn't want it to come to this," she mumbled. "I thought if I scared you enough, you'd run back to California and leave everything alone. Leave *him* alone."

I stared at her, the pieces clicking into place. My breath caught. "Oh my god. . ." My voice trembled as realization crashed into me like a giant wave. "The door. . . the rock through the window. . . the car. All of it. That wasn't Jackson—it was *you*."

Madeline's lips curled into a cold, triumphant smile. "You're harder to scare off than I thought. So when the subtle warnings didn't work, I had to move on to plan B."

"Was this your plan B?" I asked, nodding at the barrel, only inches away.

"No silly," she replied with a satisfied smirk. "This was plan C."

I watched as she reached for the photo of Gran, still standing on the mantle. Her fingers curled around the frame, examining it. Then, without a word, she let it drop. It hit the floor with a dull crack, the glass splintering across Gran's face. A soft, involuntary whimper escaped my throat.

"I have to admit," she said, turning back to me, "your husband was a hard man to track down. But not impossible."

"*You* brought Jackson here?" I asked, forcing my voice to stay level.

"I thought it was the right thing to do." She adjusted her grip on the gun. "You *are* his wife, after all. He deserved to know you've been sneaking around with another man."

My pulse roared in my ears. I tried to stay still, to hide the rage boiling in my chest, but it was no use. Anger burned hot on my tongue.

"You bitch," I cursed. "Do you have any idea—"

"Ah, ah, ah," she cooed, waving the gun in my face. "One more outburst like that and it'll be your last."

My voice lowered, ripe with fury. "Do you have any idea what you've done? Jackson could've killed me."

"He could have," she said with a casual shrug. "But he didn't. Logan made sure of that. He really can't help himself when it comes to saving you." She paused, then tossed a phone onto the couch beside me. "Speaking of which. . . call him."

I stared at my phone like it had grown teeth. "Where did you get this?"

Madeline rolled her eyes. "You ought to be more careful about where you leave your things."

My stomach twisted.

"*Call him*," Madeline snapped.

My fingers shook as I unlocked the phone and dialed Logan's number.

It rang once. Twice.

"Emily?" His voice came through, groggy and thick with sleep. "Is everything okay?"

Madeline leaned in, her eyes sharp as knives. "Tell him Jackson's here," she whispered into my ear.

"Jackson's here," I repeated. "I need you to come. Now."

"I'm on my way," Logan answered, suddenly wide awake. "I'll be there in—"

The line cut out. Madeline had snatched the phone and ended the call without flinching. She flung it across the room, where it hit the wall with a loud *thud* before clattering to the floor.

"He was a wreck when you left. Did you know that?" Her voice steady. "Do you have any idea what it did to him, coming home to find his perfect little Emily gone? And after everything he did for you?" She shook her head, almost laughing. "I was the one who picked up the pieces. *Me*. I stitched him back together when you tore him apart."

She started pacing the room again, voice rising. "And what do I get for all of it? A lying, cheating husband and a messy divorce."

I could see her unraveling now. She wasn't holding it together anymore—just holding on.

"Madeline, I'm sorry. I never meant—"

"SHUT UP!" she screamed, the gun jerking up to meet me again. "Shut the fuck up! You're not sorry. You're just sorry you got caught." Her blue eyes narrowed, wild and wet. "You weren't supposed to come back. You weren't supposed to stay. And Logan—he was *never* supposed to choose you."

My voice barely found its way past the knot in my throat. "I didn't ask him to."

"No," she snapped, stepping closer. I could feel the coolness of the barrel against my skin. "But you didn't tell him no, either."

"You don't have to do this," I said carefully. "We can fix this."

She let out a sharp laugh. "There is no fixing this. Not anymore."

A deep roll of thunder rumbled overhead, followed by an engine. Seconds later, the front door crashed open, and Logan burst inside, eyes wide, adrenaline pumping.

When he saw Madeline, he stopped.

His gaze bounced from her to me, then froze on the gun between us. "What the fuck is this?"

Madeline kept the gun trained on me, her breath shallow and uneven.

"Don't come any closer," she warned, not glancing his way.

Logan raised his hands slowly, palms out. "Okay. I'm not. Just. . . let's talk, alright? This doesn't have to go any further."

Her lips curled, a bitter smile stretching across her face. "Now you want to talk? After everything?"

"I don't want anyone getting hurt," he said, eyes locked on the trembling weapon in her grip. "Put the gun down, Mads. Please."

"You don't get to call me that!" she spat. "You lost the right to call me anything the moment you started sneaking around with *her*."

I held my breath, afraid to speak, afraid to move. Logan took a slow step forward.

"You're right," he said softly. "I screwed things up. But this isn't the way, Maddie. You think this fixes anything? You think killing anyone makes any of this hurt less?"

"I don't care about fixing it anymore," she snapped. "I cared for so long. I bent over backwards trying to be what you needed. And then *she* shows back up, and suddenly, I'm not enough."

Her voice cracked, and for a split second, the rage in her eyes faltered—replaced by something raw and broken.

Logan took another slow step forward. "Mads, listen to yourself. This isn't you."

She laughed, but it was hollow. "You don't know me at all."

"But I do," Logan said, pleading. "And I know this isn't what you really want."

Madeline turned slightly, her eyes wounded. "I wanted *you*," she said. "I've wanted you since we were kids. But you never wanted me back, did you?"

"Mads. . ."

"*DID YOU?*" she screamed, snapping the gun toward him. "She's what you really wanted. It was always her."

Another flash of lightning lit the room. With her attention shifted, I slowly eased off the couch, one eye on the phone still lying on the floor.

Logan exhaled. "I'm sorry. I *tried* to love you that way, I really did. But I couldn't force something that wasn't there."

Madeline's face crumpled as tears poured down her cheeks. Even now, as messed up as it was, part of me still ached for her. Heartbreak that deep doesn't just wound you—it reshapes you, hollowing out the person you used to be.

I inched sideways, careful to stay behind the couch, my focus split between her and the glint of my phone.

Just a few more steps. . .

But the floor betrayed me. A loud creak snapped her head in my direction.

"Well then," she said, her voice now eerily calm as she wiped her tear-streaked face with one hand. "Since you broke my heart. . . it's only fair I break yours."

The flash that followed wasn't lightning.

It was the flash of the muzzle.

The shot stole my breath entirely, searing through flesh and bone like fire. I cried out, staggering back—when a second blast rang out.

This time, Logan jumped in front of me.

His eyes widened, body locking in place. For a breathless second, an eternity pressed into a heartbeat. Our eyes met. Then the light in his gaze dimmed. His body jolted once, then collapsed against mine, heavy and terrifyingly still.

Madeline stumbled back, eyes wide in disbelief, the gun clattering to the floor. She backed away slowly, her expression blank now, the adrenaline draining as she sank where she stood.

I lay helpless as the world tilted and spun around me, the air thick with eerie silence. Blood pooled beneath me, dark and spreading, swallowing the floor where Logan and I lay.

I reached for him, but my fingers were numb. My vision tunneled as I tried to hold on.

"What have I done?" Madeline whispered. Her hands hung useless in her lap as she stared blankly ahead. "Oh my God. . . what did I do?"

I tried to scream, but nothing came out. I couldn't tell if Logan was breathing. I couldn't feel anything anymore. My vision dimmed as everything softened, floating somewhere between pain and silence as I drifted.

Inches away, my phone lay where it had landed. I bit down hard, pushing through the white-hot pain that tore through me with every shallow breath. Using the slick trail of mine and Logan's blood, I dragged myself across the floor, inch by inch, stretching my arm as far as it would go—until finally, my fingers closed around it.

My hand shook as I brought the phone closer, smearing blood across the screen. It slipped once, nearly falling from my grip, but I caught it.

I punched in the numbers, my eyes flicking to Madeline. She sat frozen in place, staring down at her hands in stunned silence, like she didn't recognize them anymore.

Then a voice crackled through the speaker. "911, what's your emergency?"

I tried to speak, but nothing came out—just a strained gasp.

"Hello? Can you hear me?"

I swallowed the blood in my mouth and forced the words out, hoarse and broken. "Shot. Two of us. Bleeding. . . 981 Crescent Hill Road. . . please. . ."

"Emergency units are on the way. Stay with me on the line, okay?"

But the phone was heavy now. Everything was. The voice on the other end faded, drowned by the rush of blood in my ears and the rasp of my own slowing breath.

I turned my head toward Logan, my fingers brushing his.

"Just. . . hold on," I breathed, unsure who I was saying it to.

"Ma'am, are you still with me? Talk to me please, let me know you're okay," the dispatcher pleaded. But her voice was little more than an echo now, following me into the dark.

Forty Eight

Golden light slipped between the canopy of leaves, casting fractured beams across the magnolia trees. Their petals floated to the ground around me, but they didn't wilt as I stepped over them. The gravel driveway was bone dry—despite the storm that had passed. And the air was no longer sticky with humidity but crisp and light.

In the distance, the old farmhouse stood peaceful and still against the rise of the mountains. But something was off. As I walked closer, I saw fresh paint on the siding, a newly stained porch gleaming in the sun, and the barn that had been crumbling for years, now stood tall and sturdy.

Where the hell was everyone?

I closed my eyes and saw a snapshot of Maddie, her face twisted with rage. And Logan. . . Oh God, Logan. Where was he? Was he ok? He had to be.

A breeze stirred, carrying with it the faint sound of someone singing. I froze, fearing it was Madeline, back to finish what she'd started. Moving cautiously, I crept around to the back of the house.

But what I saw stopped me—not from fear, but from disbelief.

Bent over a bush of blooming violet hydrangeas, was Gran. Her back was facing me as she pruned, her white hair braided neatly beneath a wide brimmed hat.

"Gran?"

She turned, and I staggered back. Her face was younger, her eyes clear, and radiant. She looked like the Gran I remembered from when she first brought Katherine and me here, not the old, weary woman she had become when we left.

"Well don't just stand there, Emily," she said with a warm smile. "Grab a shovel and dig in."

I couldn't believe it. Tears stung my eyes as I rushed to her, arms flinging wide as I wrapped myself around her.

"Oh my God, Gran. . . you're alive."

I breathed her in—basking in the comforting and familiar scent of patchouli and sage.

But she gently pulled me back, her gaze soft. "No, my darling girl. I'm not."

I searched her face. "Does that mean. . ." I looked down at myself, my hands gliding over my body, but I was whole, and unbroken. No blood. No pain.

Gran smiled. "You're alive. You're just. . . wandering."

"Wandering?" I echoed, confused.

She eased herself down onto a bare patch of earth and patted the ground beside her. I followed, still unsettled.

"Your body's still in the world," she said, "but your soul is lingering. You're not quite here. Not quite there. But somehow. . . here we are."

I blinked. "How is that possible?"

Gran tilted her head, her gold eyes twinkling like they always did when she was about to say something that sounded like nonsense. "There are places in between. Cracks in the world where time and reason don't exist. And sometimes, your soul manages to slip through."

I thought of the storm. The way Logan's body jolted, then crumpled to the floor. The crack of the gun.

Then nothing.

"Where's Logan?" I asked, bracing myself.

Gran leaned over and plucked a blossom from the hydrangea bush, tucking it behind my ear. "I can't tell you that, even if I wanted to," she said softly. "It's not for me to say."

"But I need to know," I insisted, my voice rising.

She looked at me with quiet patience. "Some truths don't come all at once. They arrive when you're ready—when your heart can bear the weight of them."

I hesitated, torn by a longing I couldn't explain. "I miss you Gran. I miss you so much." Heartbreak lodged itself in my throat, too big to swallow. "I'm sorry I left. I shouldn't have abandoned you. But I'm here now."

She cupped my face in her hands. "Oh, my sweet girl. Life is too short to carry the weight of regret on your shoulders. You had to live your life. You were never meant to spend it tethered to mine."

Tears slid freely down my cheeks. "I want to stay here with you—in this garden, in this peace." I glanced at the open field beyond us, the tall grass swaying like a sea beneath the breeze. "I won't leave you again. I promise."

Gran gently took my hand in hers. "If you stay too long. . ." she whispered, "you might forget the way back."

I wavered. I didn't want to leave her again—but deep down, I knew what it meant if I stayed.

"What would you do?" I asked.

She rose slowly to her feet, her silhouette glowing in the gilded light. "I've already made my choice," she said, reaching out her hand to me. "And one day, you'll make yours. But not today."

I stood beside her, reluctant but understanding. "Where do I go?" I asked, my voice trembling.

Gran turned her gaze toward the farmhouse. "There," she said, nodding toward it.

I followed her eyes, confused. "I don't understand—"

But when I turned to question her, she was gone.

No sound, no footsteps—just the lingering scent of patchouli and the shimmer of light dancing where she'd stood, like the moment itself had folded in on its own secret.

Carefully, I stepped onto the porch, the railing smooth beneath my palms. The porch swing, once broken, now hung sturdy and brand new.

The oak door creaked open easily. But the moment I crossed the threshold, everything changed.

I wasn't in Gran's farmhouse anymore.

I was standing in the old rental house on Wildwood Loop.

The same faded recliner sagged in the corner, and the familiar sound of Montel Williams drifted from the television.

"Hello?" I called out, shutting the door behind me.

"In here," a voice answered.

A voice I hadn't heard in years.

I rounded the corner into the kitchen, stumbling over my own feet as I struggled to take in the sight of my mother.

"Hey kiddo," she gleamed.

Her auburn hair cascaded down her back in soft waves as she stood at the stove, flipping pancakes.

I sank into a chair at the counter, unable to take my eyes off her as she slid a purple Barney plate in front of me.

"Mom?" I managed, barely able to get the word out.

She didn't answer me—just smiled softly and turned back to the stove.

I caught a glimpse of my reflection in the microwave door. My cheeks were round, my hair an unbrushed mess. Even the familiar gap where my tooth hadn't yet grown back, stood out.

I was six years old again.

"What's wrong, Emmie?" she asked, glancing over her shoulder. "I thought blueberry was your favorite?"

I gazed down at the stack of steaming pancakes, syrup slowly trickling down the sides, butter melting gently on top.

"They are," I said quietly, still trying to understand how she could be here, alive and whole.

I picked up the fork, my hands small and clumsy, just like they used to be. I pierced a corner of pancake and lifted it to my mouth. The light, fluffy texture melted over my tongue. I took another bite, and this time, a burst of tangy-sweet blueberry exploded across my taste buds.

Mom turned off the stove and sat across from me, chin resting in her hand as she watched me eat.

"Slow down, honey," she chuckled. "It's not a race."

I nodded, trying to swallow both the food and the lump forming in my throat.

"How are you here?" My voice didn't sound like mine. It sounded like that six-year-old version of me—higher and unsteady.

She shrugged, as if it were the simplest thing in the world. "Same way you are."

"But you've been gone for years. You. . ." my voice trailed off.

Mom leaned in a little closer, her expression warm. "Sweetheart, love doesn't vanish just because a person does."

Tears welled up again, spilling over before I could stop them. "I didn't get to say goodbye."

She reached across the counter, wiping a tear from my cheek with her thumb. "You didn't need to. I always knew."

"I was so mad at you," I admitted, shame burning in my chest. "When Katherine told me what you did, I didn't understand. I still don't."

"Not everything is meant to be understood," she said softly. "No matter how much we wish it were."

I dropped my gaze. "Would you have still done it if you'd known how much Katherine and I still needed you?"

She smiled, that same quiet, knowing smile she'd given me when I'd skinned my knee or told her I wanted to live on the moon.

"Emmie," she said gently, "I never stopped being with you. Even when you couldn't see me."

A peaceful silence settled between us. Then she stood and moved around the counter, kneeling beside my chair so we were eye to eye.

"You have a choice to make, baby," she said. "You're not meant to stay here."

I shook my head stubbornly. "But you're here. And Gran. I feel. . . whole."

She tucked a strand of hair behind my ear, the way she used to when I was little. "You feel safe. That's different."

I looked around at the familiar comfort I'd lost so many years ago. But something inside me shifted as a quiet understanding began to take root.

"If I go," I said, "will I lose this?"

Mom's eyes shimmered. "Not all of it. The love always stays. But the rest. . ." Her voice caught. "Is meant to live in your heart, not your footsteps."

I didn't want to go. But somewhere beyond this space, someone was waiting.

I pushed my plate away, slipping my small hand into hers as we stood. Her grip was soft and warm—just like I remembered, as she led me down the familiar hallway.

At the end stood the bathroom door, closed and waiting.

"In there?" I asked, my voice heavy with fear.

She nodded.

The last time I'd passed through that door, I lost her. The thought of stepping through it again made my legs feel like lead.

Mom knelt beside me, her hands resting gently on my shoulders. Then she kissed my forehead. "Be brave," she whispered.

I drew in a shaky breath and turned to face the door. My hand hovered over the knob, but before I could bring myself to open it, I looked back one last time.

"I love you," I said, more steady now.

Her smile was radiant. "I love you too, Emily. Tell Katherine thank you. . . for everything."

"I will," I promised. Then I closed my eyes and walked through the door.

Forty Nine

THE THUNDER OF BATTLE CRY shattered the silence. I stepped forward into the tent, the air thick with smoke and the scent of wet earth. The ground beneath my feet squelched with mud and god only knows what else.

The interior was dim, but a single candle flickered on a writing desk at the far end, casting soft light across the canvas walls.

In the distance, a horse whinnied, followed by the deafening boom of a cannon.

I looked down, startled to see a floor-length wine colored gown soaked at the hem with dirt and rain.

I knew *exactly* where I was.

Still, I moved toward the desk, needing confirmation. Letters lay scattered in messy piles across the surface, and an overturned ink bottle had spilled its contents, dark liquid bleeding over the edge.

Her name was scrawled across every envelope, the ink looping in a hand I recognized too well. As I sifted through the letters, paper whispering beneath my fingers, the sudden rip of the tent flaps startled me.

"Charlotte?"

I turned, my breath catching.

James stood in the entrance, framed by the chaos behind him. The gold buttons of his dark blue uniform glinted in the candlelight, his coat soaked through and streaked with mud. Blood clung to his trousers in thick smears, the crimson echoing the sash knotted at his waist.

"God's teeth," he breathed, his voice ragged. "It's really you."

In two strides, he was in front of me.

I didn't hesitate. I fell into him, the past collapsing between us.

"James," I whispered, my voice trembling against his shoulder. "I thought you were dead," I said, breathless. "Finnigan told me—" I stopped short, pulling back just enough to see his face. "Wait. . . what did you call me?"

James brushed a gloved hand over my hair, the leather rough against my skin. "Charlotte," he said affectionately. "That is your name, is it not?"

"No. . ." My heart stuttered. "James, it's me. It's Emily."

His smile wavered for a heartbeat, then widened again—broadening the dimples peeking out beneath a week's worth of stubble.

"Of course it is," he said. "You must think me mad not to recognize my own wife."

Wife?

He reached into his coat and pulled out a small, tarnished mirror. "Here," he said, offering it to me. "See for yourself."

I stared at it, suddenly afraid.

But my fingers moved on their own, unclasping the tiny metal latch on the copper lid. It creaked open, and I tilted the mirror toward the candlelight.

The face staring back wasn't mine.

Her features were familiar, but barely—like seeing yourself in a dream. Auburn hair pinned neatly under a lace cap, cheeks smudged with soot and war fatigue. Her eyes were the same coppery brown as mine, but older somehow. She wore my bones like a memory—close, but not quite mine.

I blinked, but the reflection didn't change.

"What is this?" I whispered, my voice barely audible over the distant rumble of cannon fire. "Why do I look like her?"

James placed his hand over mine. "You know why. Deep down, you've always known."

"I don't understand," I said, still staring into the mirror. "I'm not Charlotte. I'm Emily. I was—" I paused, the images fracturing in my head. Flashes of long-forgotten memories flickered between us. The two of us on our wedding night, wrapped in the warmth of each other as the shadow of war crept closer.

Our final goodbye—James holding me tight until he no longer could. His rich chocolate hair swept over his eyes as the sound of his horse faded into the distance beside Finn's.

Then suddenly, I was bedridden, frail, weak, and coughing up blood. Until, finally, there was nothing.

My stomach flipped.

"Oh my God. I'm... her," I breathed. "Or I was. Once."

I snapped the mirror shut and turned away, heart pounding. It all made sense now—the letters, the satchel, that quiet, persistent ache in my chest. The feeling that we'd done this before.

"What are we now?" I asked.

Pain and wonder etched across his face. "I think we're what happens when love doesn't end the way it was supposed to."

I looked at James, and knew with bone-deep certainty that I had been his wife, Charlotte. That we had loved each other fiercely in some forgotten time.

But that would mean...

"Logan," I said, his name ripping from my mouth like a gasp. "Where is he? If I was once Charlotte, and we were meant to be... what does that make me now, as Emily, to Logan?"

James leaned in, his lips brushing mine as he whispered, "Whatever life you're living, Charlotte or Emily... I will find you in every one."

Then he kissed me. It was hard and desperate, like time itself was collapsing around us. Like he had waited lifetimes for this moment and couldn't afford to waste it.

My arms curled around his neck, pulling him closer as the sound of death echoed around us. I didn't want to let go. I held him like he was the last real thing in a world unraveling.

Outside, the wind howled, rising into a storm as the canvas tent flapped violently around us. I wanted to scream at the world to stop. Just for a second. To give us one more minute before everything came undone. But time didn't pause for love. It never had.

I pulled back to tell him all the things I never had the chance to say. That I loved him. That I was here. That I remembered. But James was no longer James.

He was Logan.

The ground beneath us shifted, and the walls of the tent melted away, revealing wisps of clouds drifting lazily overhead. Around us, tall grass swayed in rhythm with the breeze, and somewhere nearby, bees hummed over wildflowers.

We were lying on our backs in the field behind the farm-house, the sun warming my face. Logan's hand was laced with mine, our fingers threaded together like we'd done a thousand times before.

"You found me," I said, tears slipping quietly into my hair. "Across time. Across death. You found me."

He squeezed my hand. "I always will."

"I remember now." My voice wavered, not from uncertainty but awe. "You were James, just like I was Charlotte. Different names. Different lives. But the same us."

He looked over at me, his tawny eyes warm and bright. "Crazy huh?"

A gentle breeze drifted between us, rustling the tall grass as we lay side by side. I knew what him being here meant, and I wasn't ready to face it. Not yet.

"I think I liked being James," he said. "There was something about galloping across open fields with the wind at my back, riding a horse that didn't want to be tamed."

I rolled my eyes. "You just miss the uniform."

"Can you blame me?" He laughed. "Those coats were kind of badass."

I nudged him gently. "You only liked them because they made your shoulders look heroic."

Logan grinned. "They did look heroic. And don't even get me started on the boots. I had a whole strut going on."

"Oh, I remember," I said, laughing now. "God you were so dramatic, you still are."

"I was committed," he said proudly. "James was a man of principle—and flair."

We lay there for a moment longer, catching our breath from the laughter. And for a fleeting second, it was easy to pretend none of this was temporary. That this moment, this fragile joy, could last.

He turned his head toward me, eyes soft. "You know, if we get another life, I hope I meet you somewhere crazy. Like ancient Greece, or maybe a pirate ship."

"Oh, definitely a pirate ship," I said, laughing. "You'd make a terrible pirate."

"I'd be amazing," he insisted. "I'd have a sword, and a tragic backstory. You wouldn't stand a chance."

I smiled, my voice soft. "I never do."

He leaned forward, brushing his knuckles along my cheek, the touch both real and not. "I wish we had more time. Real time. Not this space between."

The ache in my chest returned. "We never get enough, do we?"

"No," he said, sadly. "But we make it count."

I sat up beside him, brushing the grass from my palms, blinking hard. "What happens when I wake up?"

"You live," he said. "You keep living. For both of us."

"But how?" My voice fractured, the weight of it all finally breaking through. "How do I walk back into the world knowing you're not in it—knowing I have to go on living somewhere without you?"

Logan reached for my hand, grounding me. "You'll find me again. We always do."

I leaned into him, resting my head on his shoulder. "It's always been you."

"And it always will be," he promised.

The wind stirred again, whispering through the field like a final breath, and I knew, deep down, that the moment was ending.

"It's time to go, Em."

I turned my face back to the sky, the clouds now shifting into something new. And for the first time in what felt like centuries, I wasn't torn between lives. I wasn't Charlotte or Emily. I was both. And he was mine.

Then. Now. Always.

Fifty

A FAINT BEEPING TUGGED AT me, like a rope dragging slowly through water. Voices drifted everywhere—soft and distant, but I couldn't make out the words. I tried to open my eyes, to speak, but nothing happened.

No. I left. I let go.

Didn't I?

Panicking, I strained to move, to scream, to anchor myself to something real, but my body still felt far away.

Was I stuck?

The voices grew louder, but I still couldn't tell who they belonged to. Did someone say my name?

My eyelids slowly fluttered open, and through a haze of grey, a shadow hovered above me. Light poured in around it, too bright at first, and then softening, like the world remembered how to make sense.

A face.

I knew that face. Even through the fog, I'd know it any-where.

"Nurse? Can we get a nurse in here?" Katherine called out.

Footsteps approached, followed by a flurry of voices. A deep, burning ache flared through me when I tried to sit up.

Her fingers brushed softly across my forehead. "Try to relax. Everything's going to be okay."

"Mom says hi," I bit out, but my voice didn't work right, just a dry rasp in the back of my throat.

Her eyes filled with tears.

And just like that, the space between slipped away.

I was here. I was real.

I was home.

Monitors beeped steadily beside me, each tone anchoring me a little more in the now.

I turned my head slightly, wincing at the pull of something. Tape? Tubes? My throat burned like I'd swallowed sand.

"How long. . ." I croaked, unsure if I even said it aloud.

My sister leaned in, her tear-lined face managing a small smile. "Three days. You've been out since the surgery."

Surgery.

The word rang through me like an echo in an empty hall. Bits and pieces started stitching themselves together—Grans house, Madeline with a gun, Logan, the deafening silence that followed.

My fingers curled slightly, as if reaching for a memory I hadn't fully caught.

"You're safe now," she said. "You made it."

My gaze drifted to the window. The sun was rising, or maybe setting. It painted the room in shades of gold and lavender, colors too tender for pain. I let myself breathe it in. The moment. The light. The safety.

But beneath the surface, beneath the pain, the drugs, the sterile white noise of the hospital—a single thought began to stir. One I didn't want to let in.

"Logan?" I rasped, searching the room. But he wasn't there.

Katherine didn't move. She just looked at me, her usually warm, sun-kissed complexion drained of all color. Her mouth opened, then closed again. What could she say?

Finally, she shook her head. "I'm so sorry."

I already knew. I'd known the moment I saw him in that field. But knowing didn't soften the blow. My heart splintered under the weight of it, the shards lodging deep in my chest as a guttural sob ripped loose. The kind that didn't feel like it came from my lungs but from somewhere deeper, somewhere that had only ever belonged to him.

The pain in my chest didn't compare to this. I bit down on it, welcomed it, let it blaze through me like fire as the truth of losing him soaked into my skin and settled in my bones.

Logan was gone.

And I didn't know who I was without him.

Time passed in vague waves over the next few days. My body ached less now, but the heaviness hadn't left. It clung to me like a second skin, thick with questions I hadn't found the nerve to ask.

The bullet had torn through my chest, grazing my lung and missing my heart by a fraction. The doctors said I was lucky. Everyone said that. They used the word like it meant something. But luck didn't explain the shadow that still lingered at the edge of my thoughts, or the way I'd felt before I woke up, wandering in the space between. Truthfully, I didn't want to come back.

Not without him.

A light knock sounded against the door.

"Come in," I called, my voice a little stronger now, but still raw.

Katherine stepped into the room carrying a Starbucks cup like she stole it.

"I had to sneak past two orderlies and the nurses' station," she said with a wink.

I'd been at CAMC General for almost a week now, surviving on nothing but watery broth and bitter hospital coffee. Once in a while, if the night nurse was feeling generous, she'd sneak me a muffin or a cafeteria cookie. But this? This was nectar from the gods. I savored the first sip like it might disappear if I wasn't careful.

"Thank you," I smiled, setting the cup gently on the tray beside me. "How's Winston?"

"Missing you," Katherine scooted her chair closer. "Danielle's. . . unique. She wants to sage the house."

I forced a pained laugh. "Gran would've loved her."

Katherine's gaze dropped to her cup. "Yeah, you're probably right."

We sat in silence, the soft shuffle of nurses and doctors outside filling the quiet. I didn't tell Katherine about what I saw while I was out. And she didn't ask. Part of me wanted to keep it to myself, to hold onto it. She probably wouldn't have believed me anyway.

"Emily," my sister's voice trembled. "I'm sorry I haven't been there for you like I should've. The truth is, I didn't know how to be. I let things that weren't worth my anger take over, and I. . ." Her shoulders slumped. "I ran away. From Gran. From you. From myself."

I didn't know what to say. The words were stuck in my throat, tangled with the weight of everything that had been left unsaid for so long.

"I was angry too," I admitted finally. "I didn't know how to deal with it either. And maybe that's why I pushed everyone away."

Katherine's eyes lifted, her expression raw. "I know, but it doesn't make it any easier. I should've been here. I should've been the one helping you pick up the pieces."

I shook my head. "We were both lost, Kat. I can't blame you for that. I *don't* blame you for that."

There was a long pause, the kind that stretched between us like a thin thread. Finally, Katherine reached across the bed, her hand shaking slightly as it rested on mine.

"I'm here now," she whispered, her voice thick with regret. "And I'm not going anywhere."

I curled my fingers in hers, the memory of what our mother had said while I was wandering, echoed in my mind.

You're not meant to stay here.

"Gran might have raised us, but you were always the one who kept us together," I said. "You had to grow up too soon, long before you were ready. Now you're a mother, a wife, and you've built a beautiful life, a beautiful family. You'll always be my sister, Katherine, but I grew up too. It's not your responsibility to take care of me anymore."

Katherine's eyes softened, a hint of vulnerability flashing across her face. She opened her mouth, then paused, as if weighing her words carefully.

"I never wanted to stop taking care of you," she said, struggling to keep her composure. "It's just. . . I didn't know how to help without making everything worse."

My thumb brushed gently over her knuckles. "You didn't make anything worse. We both have our own paths now. But

I need you to know I'm okay. I'm stronger than I was before, and I can stand on my own now."

She let out a shaky breath, nodding slowly. "I don't think I'll ever stop wanting to protect you. But I get it, Em. You're not the same girl I left behind. Maybe I'm not the same either."

"Good," I said with a soft smile, my heart lifting a little. "We're both finding our way."

A gentle knock at the door broke the silence, pulling our attention toward it. A petite nurse in pale blue scrubs stepped inside, her eyes immediately zeroing in on the Starbucks cup.

"I'm going to pretend I didn't see that," she said with a playful smirk, making her way between me and Katherine. "How are we feeling today?"

"Fantastic," I said, wincing as I tried to sit up straighter. "Never better."

She glanced at the monitor beside my bed. "Vitals look good," she said, scrolling through the data. "Your doctor will be in to see you at some point today. If he likes what he sees, you should be cleared to go home in a few days."

A silence settled between us, broken only by the rapid tapping of her fingers against the keyboard.

After a moment, she glanced up again. "There are two detectives here to speak with you. They've been lingering at the nurse's desk all morning. It's up to you. If you want to meet with them, I can let them in. Otherwise, I can tell them to come back later."

I hesitated. "What do you think?" I asked, looking to Katherine for guidance.

She gave a small shrug. "It's your choice. You don't need me to help you make it."

I gave a brief nod to the nurse, who was still standing nearby.

Katherine flashed me a reassuring smile as she made her way to the door. "I'll be right here," she promised—then quietly stepped away, not because she needed to, but because she knew I was finally ready to stand on my own.

Fifty One

As promised, the discharge papers came through early Thursday morning. I'd need to see a regular doctor weekly for the next month along with physical therapy. But overall, I was recovering well.

The door eased open and Dani poked her head inside, hesitant but hopeful.

"Ready to bust out of here?" she asked with a small smile.

"Just about," I said, waving her in.

She stepped inside, wearing ripped jeans and an oversized, threadbare t-shirt that hit mid-thigh. Her raven hair was a mess, like she hadn't bothered with a brush in days, and the dark circles under her eyes told me she hadn't slept much either.

"Thanks for taking care of Winston," I said, easing myself off the bed.

Dani hurried forward, offering her hand for support. "Of course," she said, helping me settle into the waiting wheelchair. "That's what friends do."

Friends. A month ago, that word was foreign to me—almost taboo.

Over the past month, so much had changed. I had been a stranger to myself, trapped in the remnants of a life I thought I could never escape. I had built walls so high, I didn't think I'd ever let them come down. But somewhere along the way, those walls slowly cracked. And in doing so, I'd found a strength I didn't know I had.

Once seated, I glanced up at Dani. "Listen," I said, my voice quiet but serious. "I'm probably going to need some help getting back on my feet. Winston's a great dog and all, but unfortunately, he hasn't exactly mastered cooking or making coffee."

Dani laughed. "Don't sell him short just yet. He's really grown into his own, hasn't he?"

I smiled, thinking back to the day I adopted him. His little head resting on his paws, curled in the corner, trying so hard to blend in and not be noticed. Not like the others.

"He has," I admitted. "But that's not what I need right now."

Dani shot me a curious look.

"I was thinking. . . maybe you could move in with me," I said, the words tumbling out before she could argue with me. "There's plenty of room. And I think we could both use a fresh start."

She blinked, taken aback for a moment. "You sure about that?"

I nodded, feeling the weight of the offer settle between us. "More than I ever have about anything."

Danielle looked at me for a long moment, her eyes searching mine. Then, slowly, a smile began to form on her lips. "Can I bring Henry?"

I laughed, pushing past the sharp ache in my chest. "I'd be disappointed if you didn't."

The Jeep rumbled down the familiar drive, as Gran's house slowly came into view—paint peeling, porch sagging, but still standing like it had been waiting for me to come home.

We came to a stop next to the Focus, its tire still slashed, the word *SLUT* still carved into the side. The sleek black Mercedes Katherine had rented looked out of place beside it.

My sister stepped out onto the porch, Winston darting out behind her. As soon as I opened the door, he bounded over to me, his tail thumping wildly, his whole body wiggling with excitement.

"Whoa, whoa, Winston!" Dani called, rushing to the passenger side. "You've gotta be gentle, buddy! She's still healing!"

But I didn't care. The second I saw his goofy face and felt his warm, frantic licks on my hand, I laughed—really laughed, for the first time in days. I buried my face in his fur, letting his excited whimpers chase the heaviness from my chest.

"I missed you too," I breathed, fighting the ache pressing against my ribs.

"Thanks for picking her up," my sister said, walking over to greet us.

Danielle handed her my bag, offering a small smile. "Of course. Anytime."

Katherine gave me a look, her eyes softening. "I'm glad you're home."

I nodded, feeling a lump rise in my throat. "It's good to be back," I said, the weight of the past few days settling over me.

Danielle lingered for a moment, her gaze flickering between the two of us. "I should probably get going. Looks like I've got some packing to do." She gave me a tight squeeze. "Call me if you need anything."

Once Danielle left, I stood there for a moment, staring at the house, hesitant to take that next step. Katherine, sensing my hesitation, placed a hand on my shoulder. "You ready?"

Truthfully, I'd never be ready. But I couldn't let fear hold me back any longer. Logan was gone. As much as I hated it, as much as I longed to undo the past, I couldn't. All I could do was keep moving forward. For me. For us. And when the time was right, we'd find each other again. Just like we always had. Just like we always would.

"Almost," I replied, walking to the edge of the porch. I bent down slowly, feeling the blood rush to my head as I sifted through the rocks, carefully picking out a few that called to me. When I stood again, I took a deep breath. "Now I'm ready."

Inside, I slowly braced myself for what I might find. Katherine had worked tirelessly to clean everything, replacing the broken furniture with new, more modern pieces. I appreciated the effort, but it left me with a strange emptiness. My eyes fell to the floor, landing on the spot where Logan had taken his last breath, right beside me.

"Emily. . ." Katherine's voice curled over my shoulder, soft and tentative. But I waved her off.

"I'm fine," I said, folding my legs and sitting down beside the spot. The floor was stained, a dark mix of mine and Logan's blood, a reminder of the night that would forever haunt me.

"I tried to get it out," Katherine said, her voice tinged with guilt. "I was going to call someone to redo the floors—"

"No," I cut in firmly, despite the rawness inside me. "I want to leave it."

One by one, I placed the stones on the floor, arranging them into a circle. An infinite loop. A never-ending cycle.

I pushed myself to my feet, my fingers gripping the back of the new couch for support. My attention wandered to the mantel, where a new urn sat, quietly waiting.

Katherine followed my stare, and I saw the sadness flicker across her face. "I figured we'd do it together," she said, crossing the room. "Whenever you're ready."

I took a deep breath, my eyes never leaving the urn. "It's been long enough," I whispered. "We shouldn't make her wait any longer."

Katherine nodded as she lifted the urn with a tenderness that broke something inside me. Together, we stepped back outside, the weight of the moment pressing heavily on my chest.

The garden was quiet, bathed in the soft glow of the early afternoon creeping over us. The air held the faint scent of blooming jasmine and freshly turned earth, a gentle reminder that life moves forward even after loss.

"You fixed the fence?" I asked, my eyes tracing the freshly painted boards and the new gate standing firm and bright against the yard.

Katherine carefully lifted the lid. "I only finished what you started."

Together, we tipped the urn gently, letting the fine, pale ash catch the breeze and scatter over the soil. Winston sat close, his eyes calm but watchful, as if understanding the gravity of the moment.

I closed my eyes, imagining Gran's laughter being carried away on the wind, her spirit blending with the life around us.

When I opened them again, Katherine set the urn down and folded her hand in mine.

The garden seemed to breathe with us, alive with memories and new beginnings. For the first time in a long while, I felt a quiet peace settle inside me—a promise that while grief never truly leaves, love keeps us rooted, growing stronger.

I paused for a moment, breathing in the warm, fragrant air. Glancing at Katherine, her hand still holding mine, I knew that whatever came next, I wouldn't have to face it alone.

Winston let out a soft bark, pulling me gently from my thoughts. I smiled, feeling the warmth of the moment settle deep inside me.

Sometimes, letting go isn't the end—it's the start of something new.

Fifty Two

Later

"THAT'S THE LAST BOX," DANI said, setting it on the floor before flopping onto the couch.

"It's the only box," I replied, raising a brow.

She smiled, stroking Henry's fur as he settled into her lap. "Perks of traveling light."

Outside, Winston barked from somewhere off in the field, sending off a symphony of other barks as several more dogs joined in.

The Harrison County Animal Shelter lost its funding, but thankfully, none of the animals had to be euthanized. Thanks to Katherine and Grant's generous donation, we were able to rebuild the barn, allowing Dani and I to open up our own shelter, here at the Magnolia House.

We named it: **The Hart Meadows Rescue Garden**.

Between referrals from local and out-of-state shelters, and help from privately funded donors, our numbers were manageable—usually fewer than twenty dogs and just a couple of cats at any given time.

As for Jackson, I hadn't seen or heard from him since that night in the garden. Turns out, the merger he'd been chasing with Max wasn't something he wanted—it was something he desperately needed.

Bishop Enterprises was broke. So was Jackson. And when the deal collapsed, so did his company. He filed for bankruptcy, and shortly after, he lost everything—the house, the cars, and whatever else he wrapped his ego in.

His downfall opened the floodgates, as several women he dated before me finally came forward with allegations of abuse—claims too heavy for him to outrun.

With the law closing in, and a mounting stack of lawsuits tied to his shady dealings through Bishop Enterprises, Jackson did what cowards do best. He fled the country.

No one has seen him since.

Rita found a new family to work for—a couple named Lydia and Benjamin Edwards. They worked in television, owning and running several network stations along the California coast. As for Mia, she followed her aunt, taking on the role of caretaker for the couple's young children.

I told them they were always welcome to visit, though I wasn't sure if they ever would. Still, I meant it. Some people carve out a place in your life whether they stay or not.

Madeline McBride's trial was scheduled for October. The night of the shooting, she was taken into custody without incident. She entered a not guilty plea, citing temporary insanity, but the prosecution wasn't buying it and was determined to secure a first-degree murder charge.

I went to visit her in jail, at the resistance of both Dani and my sister. They thought I was crazy, and maybe I was, but I needed to see it through—not for myself, but for Logan. She refused my visits, and after several more failed attempts, I finally gave up. I didn't know what I had expected. At the time I had wanted—no, *needed* answers. Still, something shifted in me after that. I let go of the anger I'd been carrying—not because she deserved forgiveness, but because I did. Forgiving her meant I could breathe again. And in doing so, I realized I could forgive Jackson, too—not for his sake, but for mine. Life was too short to keep bleeding from wounds I refused to let heal.

The grief didn't come in waves like people said it would. It sat with me, quiet and constant, like a second shadow. I carried it through the routines of my day, tucked beneath smiles and polite conversation, pretending I was healing—until the wounds left behind finally started to scab over.

I started spending long afternoons in the garden. It gave me something to do with my hands, something to care for.

Danielle helped at first, but eventually, I preferred doing it alone. It felt more honest that way, more like a conversation between me and the silence left behind.

Another chorus of barks erupted as the rumble of an engine echoed down the drive. A small sedan I didn't recognize pulled up beside my new white Impala, another gift from Grant and Katherine.

Danielle turned to look, and Henry hopped out of her lap.

"You expecting someone?" I asked, heading for the door.

"Not that I know of," Danielle replied, following close behind.

Both the driver's side and passenger doors swung open, and out stepped Georgia and Alabama Baker.

I paused, my hand on the doorknob, as they stepped into the sun, their presence as unexpected as it was unsettling.

"Well, this is a surprise," I said, trying to mask my confusion. "What brings you two here?"

"We brought you a gift," Alabama said, holding out a large fruit basket. "From the church."

Danielle shot me a cautious look. "I'm gonna go check on the dogs," she said, sidestepping the twins as they made their way over to us.

"Actually," Georgia drawled, a mischievous glint in her eye. "The fruit basket is just a formality. Daddy promised Allie here a dog, and she was very eager to see what your. . ." She let her eyes sweep over the barn, "facility has to offer."

Alabama, her steps light and eager, glanced at Danielle. "Are they friendly?"

"Most of them," Danielle smiled. "They're more bark than bite."

As the three of them headed over to the barn, Georgia paused, glancing over her shoulder. "I'm glad to see you're doing okay," she said, a hint of softness in her voice. "Alabama and I. . . we've been praying for you."

I smiled, lifting the fruit basket slightly. "Thanks, Georgia. That means a lot."

Back inside, I set the basket down on the table. Danielle's box of stuff was still sitting in the middle of the living room. I picked it up and carried it upstairs to mine and Katherine's old room.

I had cleared out most of my things, but a few random items were still tucked away in the closet. I set the box down on the floor and wandered over to it. The door creaked open with the familiar stick it always had. I reached up and began sorting through the clutter. There wasn't much, just old toys from when Katherine and I were kids and a cracked snow globe from a thrift store we used to frequent. Then came a few yellowing photos, edges curled, of me and Katherine when we first arrived at Gran's—wide-eyed and awkward, trying to look braver than we really were.

But behind all of that, tucked in the very back, beneath a worn flannel blanket and a shoebox full of costume jewelry. . . was an old hatbox.

A lump formed in my throat.

I hadn't seen it in years—but there it was, right where I'd hidden it, with Logan's letters still inside. The ones I never read.

I sat back on my heels, heart thudding. Dust coated the lid, and for a moment, I just stared at it—frozen between dread and curiosity. Then, without really thinking, I scooped everything up, crossed the hallway, and set everything next to the bed.

Sitting on the edge, I rested the box in my lap. My fingers hesitated on the lid, trembling slightly as I opened it.

The letters were exactly as I remembered—neatly folded, each one with my name written across the front in Logan's familiar handwriting. I picked one at random and unfolded it slowly, as if giving it too much air might make it disappear.

The first few lines hit like a punch to the gut.

He wrote about missing me, about the ache of silence between us, about the things he hadn't known how to say before he left. His words were raw and tender, a mixture of regret and love. I felt like I was holding pieces of him that had been frozen in time, and now they were thawing, melting right into my hands.

Tears blurred the ink as I read.

Some letters were short, just a few lines. Others went on for pages. He wrote about the future he imagined for us. About forgiveness. About how he'd always felt like he was running out of time but never knew how to stop long enough to say what mattered.

By the seventh letter, I was curled on my side, the box beside me, the letters scattered across the bed like fallen leaves. Each one cracked something open in me that I didn't even realize was still locked away.

I hadn't expected to feel peace. But somewhere between the pain and the words he left behind, I did.

When I finished, I gathered the letters and placed them gently back inside, arranging everything just as it had been. Easing off the bed, I lowered myself to the floor, coughing as a swirl of dust bunnies scattered from underneath.

I carefully slid the hatbox to the far corner under the bed, nestling it beside the old satchel I'd tucked away weeks earlier.

From downstairs, I heard Danielle call my name.

I was about to push myself up when something caught my eye—a thin strip of paper peeking out from the folds of the satchel. Confused, I reached for it, my fingers tingling as they brushed the familiar leather strap.

Winston had been hiding under here the night Madeline broke in. He must've knocked something loose. Maybe one of the letters had slipped free.

Slowly, I pulled the satchel forward, careful not to disturb anything else inside. The envelope slipped further out, and my breath caught.

It wasn't an old letter.

At first, I thought it must be a mistake. Maybe it had been wedged deep in the lining all along, only now working its way free. But even as I opened it, some part of me knew better.

My pulse quickened, and my hands shook violently as I fought to steady myself. But the moment my eyes met the spidery script, so unmistakably his, I felt the world tilt beneath me.

My Dearest Emily...

Authors Note

This book is for anyone who's had the courage to step out of the shadows and create a life on their own terms. It's a reminder that we all carry a spark, even when it feels like the world is doing its best to snuff it out. Like Emily, we all have the capacity to heal, to grow, and to find beauty in the places we once thought were broken.

As you read through these pages, I hope you found a piece of yourself reflected in her journey—whether it's the courage to confront your past, the hope to embrace the future, or the strength to keep going, even when the road feels long. May it remind you that, just like Emily, you too can rise, rebuild, and thrive. No matter where you are, or how lost you might feel, the light you seek is always within reach. Keep going. Your journey is far from over. It's only the beginning.

Acknowledgements

I have to start by thanking my husband. After all, this book is loosely based on our own love story. His support and encouragement mean everything to me—I honestly couldn't do any of this without him. On the nights when I doubt myself, when I feel stuck, he's always there, reminding me that I can do this, that I am enough. I've always considered myself a spiritual person, and I'll proudly say without hesitation that my husband is my soulmate. I knew from the moment we met, I felt it in my bones. And every day with him, the universe finds new ways to remind us of that. I don't know what life we've shared before, but I imagine it was something adventurous and wild. Maybe we were wanderers, maybe we were dreamers, but I know we've always been connected in ways that go beyond this lifetime. He's not just my partner, he's my home, my safe place in a world that can often feel uncertain. Through every high and every low, he's been the constant that keeps me grounded, reminding me that love isn't just something we find—it's something we build, together. And for that, I will be forever grateful.

To my children—who ground me, who challenge me, who create a constant whirlwind of chaos in my life, thank you. You are the reason my imagination continues to bloom, the reason I keep dreaming even on the hardest days. Your laughter, your questions, your endless curiosity, fuel the stories I tell. And in the midst of all the mess and noise, you remind me daily of the beauty in life's simplest moments.

To my friends and family, who continuously champion my wins and stand by me through every challenge—thank you. Your unwavering belief in me, even when I falter, has been my strength. You celebrate my successes like your own and lift me up when I feel like giving up. I am beyond lucky to have you in my corner, reminding me that no achievement is too small to celebrate and no setback too big to overcome. Your support means more to me than words can express, and I carry that love and encouragement with me every day.

To Danielle Moore—without her entry in my *Name My Next Novel* contest, this book might've ended up with a ridiculous title. . . or none at all. Funny how over 70,000 words can pour out with ease, yet finding the right few for a title nearly broke me. Thank you, Danielle, for giving this story the name it didn't know it was waiting for.

And lastly, but certainly not least, I want to thank you, the reader. For believing in me, for reading my books, for allowing my stories to take root in your heart. Your support means the world, and I am deeply honored that you've chosen to spend your time with my words. Every page turned, every review shared, every message of encouragement has kept me going. Writing can be a solitary journey, but knowing that my stories reach you, that they resonate in some way, makes it all worth it. Thank you for being a part of this adventure with me. Without you, none of this would be possible.

Also by

Read on for an extract from
What Lies Beneath the Tide

"The open sea is a dangerous creature, unpredictable and heartless. It will swallow you whole and dissolve your bones into foam. It is a lawless, wretched thing and yet it is equally seductive, alluring, and elusive. I cannot think of a better thing for a monster to be."

Maeve Anderson is just like everyone else in Saltridge. She's lived here her entire life, works a dead-end job, and for the most part, keeps to herself. Between waiting tables at the Captain's Quarters, taking care of her trainwreck mother, and keeping her disgruntled cat fed, Maeve doesn't have much time for a social life. Not that she wants one anyway, given the small number of options she has in this town.

Still, nothing prepares her for the sudden arrival of Alex Hayworth, whose presence in town has not gone unnoticed. And it's not just his peculiar interest in her that makes Maeve unsettled. It's that he seems to have an uncanny knack for showing up in the most unexpected places—although the same could be said for her if you asked him.

Alex Hayworth is no stranger to tragedy. After all, his entire career as a detective is centered around it. However, when his life suddenly becomes upended by his own personal trauma, Alex soon finds himself in the middle of a mystery even he can't seem to solve. Desperate for a distraction, he travels to Saltridge, where he unwittingly begins to unearth a sinister secret this quiet little town has been harboring beneath the tide for far too long.

Extract:

What Lies Beneath the Tide

Chapter One

Alex

THE THIN LINE BENEATH the strap of her cardinal dress was barely a faint marker against her khaki-colored skin. She'd worn it on purpose. Not just for the comfort but for the ease with which it might be slipped off her later.

Too bad it was a wasted effort.

She was attractive. Her honeysuckle hair was curled loosely at the ends, settling just below her peaked breasts—the plummeting neckline forcing them together. It was meant to be an inviting distraction that hopefully persuaded Alex to take her home later.

Another wasted attempt.

He wasn't opposed to a nice dinner with a beautiful woman. After all, he'd agreed to it, though more out of obligation than for personal desire.

When Diego asked him for a favor, Alex thought it was a joke.

"You want me to go out with your ex?"

"She's not my ex," Diego insisted. "She's just some woman I used to go out with."

"That's an ex," Alex countered, his voice laced with humor.

Diego didn't find it funny. "I just need you to get her off my back."

Reluctantly, Alex agreed. And now, as he sat across from the slender woman, whose crystal eyes glazed over him in hunger, he understood *exactly* why his friend called in this favor.

A badge bunny.

He didn't judge him for it—couldn't have even if he wanted to, considering they'd all taken one home at one point or another. Even Alex wasn't innocent. It was a rite of passage, a statement throughout the force with some guys competing on how many they could tally by the end of a quarter.

Usually, they were a one-and-done deal, but some were harder to shake than others. Judging by the woman sitting across from him now, Alex realized that Diego had dug himself a hole he couldn't escape alone.

She was bouncing in her chair all night—one hop away from slipping out of her dress entirely, and Alex had no intention of being treated to a show.

"You seem a little tense," she purred. Her blue eyes, glossy from the bottle of wine she'd insisted on having. Leaning over, she twisted a strand of hair between her fingers. "What's wrong Alex? Am I making you nervous?"

He tried not to roll his eyes. Sure, it would be easy to take her home and bury himself between her legs, but then what? By morning, he would have forgotten her name—*what was it again?*

"Oh my god, Jessica! Is that you?" A woman yelped behind him, sending Jessica flying out of her seat.

Great, he thought, turning slightly in his chair and typing a quick message into his phone.

"Prick."

"You can thank me later," Diego replied quickly.

"Don't worry, I plan to."

Three dots appeared on the screen, lingering for a moment before disappearing. After a few minutes without a reply, Alex assumed the conversation was over—*for now.*

At the sound of his name, he turned to find both women staring at him.

"I was just telling her how we met," Jessica said as if they were in some whirlwind relationship.

He plastered a smile on his face and reached out to shake her friend's hand. "It's nice to meet you."

The woman blushed—her delicate fingers lingering around his a little too long before finally pulling away.

"I think it's so romantic. You know her father was a cop?"

That explained it.

"Alex is a detective," Jessica corrected, taking a step towards him. She lifted her hand, wrapping it around his arm and tightening her grip.

Internally, Alex groaned.

In a matter of minutes, he'd somehow become an unwilling participant in whatever pissing match these two were having over him. Not that it mattered since he wasn't interested in either of them anyway.

When his phone rang and Diego's name scrolled across the screen, Alex was relieved.

"I'm sorry, I've got to take this," he said, peeling himself away from Jessica's side.

Official detective business, she mouthed to her friend—who nodded as he slipped away.

Once he was out of earshot, Alex answered. "Are you calling to apologize?" He asked triumphantly.

Diego's voice came in, short and firm. Alex recognized that voice—it was his cop voice. The one he used when something terrible happened.

"Alex—" he said, his voice cracking through the phone. "There's been an accident."

Alex silently thanked whatever poor bastard had done something stupid enough that he would need to be called in—despite knowing there'd be a victim, and for that, he felt selfish. But as he looked over his shoulder at the two women, still vying for his attention, Alex promised he'd make up the hail Mary's for it later.

"Send me the location," he grunted into the phone, but there was a pause. "What is it Diego? Spit it out."

A deep breath. One so heavy it sucked the air from Alex's lungs, followed by hollow words. *"I'm so sorry. . ."*

Alex stared at his phone, confused. "What the hell are you talking about? Sorry for what?"

There was a tightness in his chest, like something heavy was sitting on it, making it hard for him to breathe. He tried to swallow it, to clear his lungs by clearing his throat, but it was useless. Alex knew *exactly* what would cause his best friend of twenty years to be so elusive.

Still, the impact of it, the sudden blow that loosened the tightness in his chest, was a massive one, and it caused him to crack, right down to his core.

Tears swelled in his eyes. "Just say it!" He shouted.

His sudden outburst caused the entire restaurant to go still, but he didn't care. From their table, both Jessica and her friend gaped at him.

Finally, Diego said softly, "They're gone."

***

The dark, moonless night made the strobing lights of blue and red seem more haunting as he approached. They blocked the road, forcing Alex to drive alongside the narrow shoulder.

It was because of those lights, he could see menacing streaks of black on the asphalt. Evidence of where tires attempted to stop but couldn't—not in time at least. They curled down the road a few feet before disappearing.

That's where their car came to rest, on its side—both windows blown out. The entire front end was smashed in.

Alex didn't see the other vehicle right away. Instead, his attention was drawn to the yellow sheet covering the passenger side window, where the outline of a body could be seen through the shattered glass.

The driver was sprawled onto the hood, their feet dangling over the mangled steering wheel, and Alex's heart twisted in on itself. It was hard to tell them apart from here, although he could wager a guess. His mother hated driving, so that left his father behind the wheel—*slumped* over the wheel.

Alex had been to hundreds of crime scenes—had stood amongst carnage and calamity but not like this, never like this. Never had he seen it through the eyes of the families whose loved ones were covered under the same yellow blanket.

They were victims too.

Now, as he stood there, his breathing shallow and his body rigid—unsure of what to do, unsure if there was anything he *could do,* Alex found himself a victim too.

He'd never given it much thought, other than the usual empathy he felt whenever a call came in. In law enforcement, things don't get easier—you just learn how to become more numb.

You know that at the end of every call, there's a life involved—a family who lost a loved one, someone whose life was severely impacted. But by the time Alex gets involved, they're considered cases, not people.

You can't fit someone into a file. Who they are, what they like, and the people they might have influenced. Those are the variables that make a person who they are. And yet, those are the exact details that are stripped away once they become a victim.

It's how men like Alex stop themselves from making it personal. They have to, otherwise they'd never solve anything.

Staring at the husk of twisted metal and broken glass wrapped around his parent's lifeless bodies—broken inside, it was nothing *but personal.*

He didn't realize he'd walked up to the scene—wasn't in control of his body until he was face to face with Diego.

"You can't go up there," Diego insisted, pressing his large hands against Alex's chest as if that would stop him.

"Like hell I can't," Alex argued. Diego was right in front of him, and yet Alex couldn't see him at all. All he could focus on were those bright yellow sheets.

"Alex, it's an active scene, and you even being here goes against every protocol we have set in place. I can't let you go any further."

Drinking in the world around him, Alex steadied himself against his best friend. He knew Diego was right, and he hated him for it.

Even as he stared at the crumpled metal that was once their car, now unrecognizable, part of him was still convinced there was something he could do.

"You don't want to see them like that," Diego said, his voice softening.

Again, he was right, and again, Alex hated him for it.

"Where's the other driver?" It was more of a demand than a question as Alex scanned the hellish view, his eyes tracing over the red BMW a few yards away from where the impact occurred. It was dented and beat up, but nothing compared to the pretzel his parents were in.

Diego surveyed him cautiously, no doubt assessing his mental state. Alex knew he was trying to determine what he could tell him as an officer and what he wanted to say to him as his friend.

"Paramedics just loaded him up. He's in rough shape, but he'll live."

"Good," Alex bristled, and Diego knew what he meant.

"Assaulting him won't bring them back."

"You're right, it won't, but it will make me feel a hell of a lot better. Besides, it's only assault if I leave him alive." Alex realized what he said was foolish, but he didn't care.

Diego leveled a warning look at him.

"I want the results of his blood test as soon as the lab has them," Alex conceded.

Diego nodded but didn't move, not until Alex finally took a step back. "I know this isn't easy, but I need you to walk away right now and let me do my job," he said.

Alex flinched as those words clanged through him. They were the exact words he'd found himself saying countless times to others who'd been insistent on staying. Hearing them from this side, they sounded hollow—light and weightless.

Alex turned on his heels and stalked back to his truck—midnight black and outlined against the night. His colleagues had nicknamed it "The Reaper."

The title tasted sour in his mouth now.

The short walk seemed like an eternity, yet he kept his head up and his back straight so nobody could see how heavy he felt. He didn't wait for them to move his parents into the black nylon bags, where they would be taken from the scene directly to the medical examiner. Alex knew witnessing that would be his undoing, and he wasn't ready to give in.

He drove back to his apartment in silence, ignoring the calls and texts slowly trickling in. Walking into the dark and unwelcoming quiet, he didn't turn on the light or take off his boots. Instead, he stood there, enveloped in the shadows and eerie silence that seemed so loud now, before allowing his knees to buckle.

In the moment, Alex thought he felt something. The smoothness of a hand pressed against his back as he shook and shuddered into the shadows blanketing him. But he knew better than to believe it was anything other than grief announcing its arrival.

Amongst the despair, the whirlwind of emotions he was free falling through, he turned to it and whispered, "I guess it's just you and me now."

Extract:

WHAT LIES BENEATH THE TIDE

Chapter Two

Maeve

I HATED THE WAY she said my name. I hated the way it pulled off her tongue and slithered into my ears, dripping down into my bones and echoing deep into my spine.

"Maeve—"

I don't know why I hated it so much. Maybe it was because I never felt like her—*like a Maeve*. Or maybe it was because whenever I looked at myself in the mirror, I saw pieces of her staring back at me.

"For the love of god, Maeve, HELLO?!"

"What?!" I demanded.

My mother has this way of looking at me, like I've done something wrong—like I'm always doing something wrong. Her eyes, sea green and bright, were defined in the corners as she glared at me from across the room.

"Have you been listening to a single word I've said?" she asked, her face pinched together like she'd eaten something sour.

"Yes," I lied.

Clicking her tongue, she returned to her vanity, where several lipstick tubes rolled off the table. Then, with a heavy sigh, she continued talking about things I didn't care to listen to.

That's how she's always been. My mother has this insatiable thirst to stand out, to do things differently, to be a little *extra*.

We are the complete opposites.

Where she enjoys vibrant colors spilled onto the low-cut shirts and skintight pants she adores, I prefer comfort over beauty—wearing more casual clothes rather than high-end, uncomfortable style.

Where she paints glitter and lipstick the color of rose petals onto her lips, I barely wear Chapstick on my own pouted smile. To some, these are minor differences that hardly run skin deep, but to me, they're part of a much bigger picture.

Her bright, bleached hair rested in tight curls around her face and shoulders. Her tan—the one she continuously pays for at the local salon—stained her skin a rusty color, several shades darker than it should be.

I rested my elbows on the counter and leaned over as I watched her apply an eclectic array of soft blues and white hues across her eyelids. I stared at her while she swiped thick mascara over her long, full lashes—her mouth hung open as if in shock, eyes wide and hand steady so she wouldn't poke herself with the wand.

"You should let me curl your hair," she suggested—my gawking at her an open invitation.

I reached up and twisted my ponytail inside my fist, where strands of charcoal hair loosened from its bind.

"We've talked about this," I said, trying not to sound bored. "I like it this way."

"I know, but you would look so beautiful if you did something other than that," she insisted—gesturing at me with her perfectly manicured hand.

Here we go again.

It's as if I'm not beautiful without blush and lipstick. As if I desperately needed some heavy foundation to cover up my already flawless skin.

In reality, it's not about makeup at all—it's about envy.

It's about *control.*

If she can paint me into something else and cover up my natural beauty the way she hides hers, we will finally be the same. Men will drift their eyes to her instead of lingering only on me, and she will no longer see me as competition in a game I don't even want to be a part of.

When I was little, random strangers constantly praised her for what a beautiful child I was. As I got older, blossoming from adolescence into womanhood, those innocent compliments became bold comments—mostly made by men.

It's why my mother puts so much effort into her appearance. Maybe it's jealousy, perhaps it's competition. Either way, it's not speculation.

I've seen the way her crisp green eyes cut sideways glances at me every time a man's gaze lingers too long on my porcelain skin. Or the way her face drops—just minimally at the mention of my own eyes, a shade so blue, they might as well be teal. I'm a walking contrast, sticking out when I desperately want to blend in.

"You know, it wouldn't kill you to come out with me tonight," she insisted as she slipped into a pair of six-inch heels. They're gold and gaudy, and they hurt my feet just by looking at them.

"Thanks, but no thanks," I said—peeling myself away from the table. "I have plans anyway."

We go through this every week, and every week, I find myself re-explaining to her why I don't want to hang out at the local bar alongside her.

"With your cat?" She asked, raising an eyebrow.

I flinched because she wasn't wrong. Still, I didn't want to openly admit that I'd much rather trade in a night filled with cheap booze and shitty music to hang out with Charles Lickens.

Instead, I rolled my eyes and laughed. A poor attempt at convincing her—*at convincing myself* that my life was not as pathetic as it outwardly seemed.

For a moment, things were quiet, with the uncomfortable weight of our relationship stripped bare between us. It was brief—mere seconds even, but it was long enough to irritate an already infected wound—one that's been festering for years.

I'd waited well into adulthood for that moment when things would change. When our relationship would inevitably shift from that of a parent and their child to one of a mother and her daughter. The kind that carries a bond. I thought it would happen instantly. I stupidly believed that when I became an adult, I would understand her more.

Now I understand her less.

***

Twilight cut across the sky as I walked along the sidewalk, winding through the neighborhood on the south side of the shore.

It was warm but still barely June, and the night air still held on to a leftover chill from the wet spring season.

By now, vacationers and summer residents have already started returning to Saltridge, and at the end of the month, our quiet little town would be roaring with life again.

I decided not to head straight home but instead, headed for the beach.

The moon hung heavy and full, casting a shimmering glow onto the water as the tide swept in. The view was stunning. The reflection cast off the waves looked like it's own galaxy, spilled across the sea.

I've lived here my entire life, yet I've always been an outsider—a stranger in my own home, in my own skin, someone who openly doesn't belong, like a puzzle piece that doesn't quite fit. Yet here, where the edge of the world is stitched together on a fine seam—constantly on the brink of unraveling—I feel most at peace.

There was a spot just out of reach of the hungry water, where the sand was left dry and untouched. Sitting down, I dug my toes deep into the sift, inhaling a breath of salty air. The slight sting of it tickled the back of my throat, but I didn't mind because it left behind a familiar aftertaste—one I could never seem to hold onto for very long.

For a while, I watched as the waves rolled onto the shore, crashing and pulling away slowly, dragging pieces of the world back as they retreated. It was a beautiful and well-rehearsed dance, and I wondered how long it would take before the earth had no more of itself to give. How often would the water kiss the sand before stealing every grain, leaving nothing but disappointment and emptiness upon its return?

I've always been fascinated by the ocean—its vastness, its hunger. And although I've never been in it, I can't stay away from it either.

The open sea is a dangerous creature, unpredictable and heartless. It will swallow you whole and dissolve your bones into foam. It is a lawless, wretched thing, yet equally seductive, alluring, and elusive. I cannot think of a better thing for a monster to be.

Sitting here, I craved it. Every part of my body vibrated as I stared into the dark horizon, my skin becoming covered in gooseflesh. It happens every time I come here, and I can't tell if it's from excitement, or fear.

I've tried countless times to walk into the water but can never seem to reach it because I falter every time. All the confidence I've mustered, all the courage and self-assurance I've managed to build up, somehow spills out of me and onto the shore, where I remain rooted in apprehension.

And yet, every night, it calls to me.

Every night, I lie in bed, listening to it sing. There's this part of me, a dark and wicked thing coiled beneath my skin that rattles itself awake when I listen to it cry. As if the ocean's songs were meant for it—beckoning it home.

Maybe it's not the dark and menacing water that scares me, but this ache inside my bones, the one that wants to drive me far out into the horizon until my head is underwater and my lungs give out.

Shuddering, I drew my knees to my chest, catching a glimpse of my mark in the moonlight. It was a blended shadow of purple and crimson, and like smoke, it snarled its way from one leg onto the other. A nearly perfect line, creating an almost perfect imperfection.

It is the only blemish I own, the only stain that brandishes my skin. There are no moles or wrinkles, no sun-weathered dark spots. I've never had a pimple nor found a single freckle stamped along my skin. This is all I have—this single linear signature that cuts across my legs like some faded and forgotten path.

They say birthmarks are an imprint of a past life—evidence of how you once left the world before you came back into it as someone else. But mine are tied to a life I was supposed to live—to a life I was *doomed to survive*. Now, I didn't know where I belonged.

About the author

When not lost in the labyrinth of her own creations, you can find Daphne exploring alternate dimensions (also known as the local coffee shop) or engaged in intense debates with her children on why they can't have cake for breakfast—okay, why they *sometimes* can't have cake for breakfast.

A Michigan native, she lives with her husband, their tiny minions, their menace of a cat, and one lazy dog. *The Black Hat Society*, previously released and currently pulled for republishing, was her first publication, followed by *What Lies Beneath the Tide*, available now! Please visit her website or follow her on social media for more information on upcoming releases and updates.